A HOUSE
FULL OF
WINDSOR

KRISTIN CONTINO

Wyatt-MacKenzie Publishing
DEADWOOD, OREGON

A House Full of Windsor

Kristin Contino

ISBN: 978-1-948018-99-9

Library of Congress Control Number: 2021936477

Wyatt-MacKenzie Publishing
DEADWOOD, OREGON

Wyatt-MacKenzie Publishing, Inc.
Deadwood, Oregon
www.WyattMacKenzie.com

✿ Dedication ✿

For Mom Mom, because I promised I'd write more books.
I wish you were here to read this.

And Diana, Princess of Wales, whose inspiration lives on.

A thorough cleaning of your home is important before company comes, but don't forget to take time for yourself. You should be dressed and party-ready before you fluff the pillows, light the candles and hang those colorful hand towels. What's worse: your guests walking in on you pushing a Hoover, or having no one there to answer the door because you're still showering?

DIRTY SECRETS ARE BEST SWEPT under the rug, and when it comes to my family, I'm akin to a professional housekeeper. Just hand me a broom, and I'll brush away anything unseemly, leaving a perfectly normal and color-coordinated scene behind. The problem is, dirt builds up under that rug.

Eventually, it starts to show.

From the exterior, I'm sure my mother's house looked like a typical colonial in her tree-lined suburban Philadelphia neighborhood. But I knew better. And it was time to actually do something about it.

"So..." I gestured to the tidy fraud of a house as Will and I got out of our sister's SUV. "Can you promise not to freak out this time?"

My brother let out a small huff. "When have I ever freaked out about anything?"

I raised an eyebrow. "The last time you and Anne showed up, Mum had to pop a Xanax. And if I recall, so did you."

"Way ahead of you there. Want one? Or is there a *Sarah Says* tip against self-medicating?"

I shook my head and turned to look for Anne. She leaned

against the driver's side of her Audi Q7 (no minivan for this soccer mom), texting with gritted teeth. Probably something to do with the kids. Not that she'd tell me, anyway.

"Twin! You in or you out?" Will said, and finally Anne dropped the phone into her oversized leather tote.

"Fine. Let's get this over with."

Leaves crunched under my Hunter wellies as we headed toward the side door, and soon enough Anne's riding boots clacking against the driveway drowned the sound out. Will trudged along a step behind in his signature Chuck Taylors, ever the Brooklyn hipster.

"Should we knock?" He tapped me on the shoulder as I stared at the rusted old storm door. The awkwardness of this question wasn't lost on me; it was our mother's house, for God's sake. But the situation wasn't exactly normal.

I shrugged. "Anne? Do you know if the side door is still blocked?"

"How would I know? I haven't been inside since the last time the two of you decided to make an appearance." She might as well have said, *since you guys moved to New York and left me.*

I swallowed the guilt trip and rang the doorbell, giving the belt of my red pea coat a quick tug, as if tightening it would somehow prepare me for the battle ahead.

We waited outside for a good three or four minutes, chatting about the weather and Anne's kids, and my anxiety heightened with every passing second. I knew it could easily be another five minutes before Mum reached the door. And how would she react when we broke the news about the cleanup? We were there under the pretense of a belated Thanksgiving lunch, but I knew she probably saw through our intentions.

"Should we try again? Or go to the front?" Will plopped down on the little wood bench in the carport and soon his thumbs were flying across the keyboard of his iPad. "Fourteen emails since we got off the train. If I wasn't leaving this job soon I might just sprawl out in the middle of Times Square and wait for the tourists to trample me to death."

"God, don't be so dramatic," Anne said, not looking up from her cell. "And wait? What's going on with your job?" Her voice dipped just slightly, enough for me to register her annoyance. I guess twin intuition didn't extend across the Hudson.

"That's part of why I suggested we come here. I mean, other than the Thanksgiving thing ..." he gritted his teeth and wrinkled his nose in a "sorry for bringing it up" type of face.

"Unfortunately, the news doesn't stop for holidays." I kept my tone light, but inside my stomach twisted. If I'd put an ounce of focus on something other than my career, I'd probably be married with one or two curly-headed munchkins instead of spending Saturday nights alphabetizing my bookshelves and Googling dumpster rentals for Mum.

Anne finally looked up from the phone. "It's okay to put your career first sometimes. But you can't be such a robot. I mean, we've all got baggage because of this." She whirled a slender finger around in a circle, gesturing to the house. "It's called compromise. You could've taken the train down after your show."

"You know what? I hardly think ..." I closed my eyes for a second. My sister, of all people, should have understood what Mum's "baggage" had cost me. Boyfriends, the friends I'd kept at arm's length, a parade of therapists ... but arguing with Anne was just as pointless as trying to convince my niece, Ruby, that her little brother's name actually wasn't Charlie Poop Pants. Why bother?

Instead, I told them I was going to call Mum before we got into Will's job news. I whipped out the same forced, cheerful tone I used with my *Good Morning New York* audience. "Mum! We've been waiting outside for a while now, so I just wanted to make sure you heard—"

"Patience, my dear!" was my greeting. "Do you expect me to *run* to the bloody door?"

"Of course not. Just wanted to make sure everything's all right."

I could sense her irritation before the words even came out.

3

"You know I've got that pesky arthritis; I'm not as young as I used to be. Give me a minute. Or would you rather just bin the whole idea and I'll meet you at lunch? Spare us all the trouble of ... well, you know."

"No, no. Don't worry," I said, trying to rescue the day before her mood turned sour. "I'll see you soon."

I sighed and slumped down on the bench next to Will, resting my head on his shoulder. "How the bloody hell did we end up in this situation?"

I could hear a bit of Essex slip back into my accent, as it sometimes did around my family ... despite twenty-plus years of living in America, thousands of dollars in elocution lessons, and the countless "how to sound posh" YouTube videos I'd watched and pronunciation books I'd read since we'd moved to the States. It must've been the stress.

"This is partially my fault," Will said. "I should come more often. I had no idea how bad she'd let it get." He tapped his foot so fast that Anne, ever so gently, stomped on it with her boot.

"You know I hate it when you do that. It reminds me of—"

Will shot her a look. "Point taken."

You'd think the two of them were married, but maybe sharing the same uterus for nine months counted as much.

I glanced over at the little Union Jack sign still hanging next to the door after all these years. It said "The Windsors" in red letters above the flag, and decades later it still riled me up that Mum somehow thought it was fine to conveniently ignore that her children had a different last name. I guess "The Windsors and Percys" didn't have the same ring to it.

"Don't get me started on the sign," Will said, noticing me staring.

Anne rolled her eyes and the three of us said at once, "No relation to the royals, but you never know!"

"Okay, new topic," I said. "What's going on with this job?" Just as Will was about to respond, the door creaked open.

"Ah, hello, hello darlings," Mum said with an ear-to-ear grin.

I hadn't seen her that happy since her favorite online shop, Chee-rio, had a seventy-five percent-off sale. Her wild gray curls had been tamed down more than usual, and she was wearing a crystal poppy brooch on her sweater, her secret good luck charm. "Come on in then, but watch your step."

I took a deep breath, counting backward from five as I let it out. It obviously meant a lot to Mum that we were willing to come inside, so I knew I had to push back the feelings of shame and disgust I connected with my teenage home. But like most things having to do with my mother, it was easier said than done. At least the mess couldn't have gotten too much worse since I'd visited in September. Or so I hoped.

The way Anne's mouth dropped open as she stepped into the kitchen told me everything. That, and the choice expletives she muttered under her breath.

"Welcome to the House of Windsor, my dears! Mind your step."

I was glad Mum's back was turned as she said this so she couldn't see our expressions, which ranged from shocked (mine) to disgusted (Anne's) to slightly bewildered mixed with morbid curiosity (Will's).

The strawberry wallpapered, stuck-in-the-1990s kitchen, although cluttered, had never been the problem. The mess started with the dining room, where boxes, plastic storage bins, and bags that hadn't even been emptied of their purchases cov-ered every conceivable surface. The disaster grew progressively worse through the rest of the house, or at least it had the last time I stepped inside. Despite Mum telling me she'd done a big cleanup, I was still stepping over boxes of Golden Jubilee china and *Hello!* magazines in plastic sleeves, so I figured it was business as usual.

"I thought you said she straightened up," Will whispered. Then I lost my footing and crashed into his back.

"She did."

Will reached for my hand as we attempted to squeeze through

5

the narrow passageway leading to the living room, and I turned to grab Anne's behind me. Plastic storage bins stacked at least five high flanked us on both sides, and I gasped as a large container marked "Diana fashions: 1985" wobbled precariously when my shoulder hit it. I'd been to the ER enough times in my life thanks to Mum's collecting, but having to explain a cast or bruise to my colleagues would feel a thousand times worse than another sprain or concussion.

My only consolation was the house smelled, as usual, like fresh English lavender (albeit mixed with dust). It wasn't like those hoarding documentaries when the people have to wear gas masks to deal with the smell of rotting cats.

"Did you say something, kids?" Mum asked. She expertly sidled through the boxes despite her arthritis, her pleated khakis and turtleneck sweater still pristine.

"Nothing. I just said we shouldn't stay terribly long if we want to make lunch at a decent time." The lie came out automatically, but I'd had years of practice.

We carried on in silence, stepping over boxes, old history books about the monarchy, and piles of tea towels. Claustrophobia had overtaken Will. I could tell by the sweat on his palms and lack of snappy remarks; my brother didn't even like taking the subway. And though I'd had years of practice, even I felt the room closing in on me. I kept my focus on the bay window with its stained-glass Union Jack sun catchers, the literal light at the end of the tunnel. *Keep calm, Sarah.*

I kept picturing the look on my ex-boyfriend's face when he found out I was a hoarder's daughter, and not the posh English girl from a fine country estate he (and everyone in my viewing audience) had in his mind. Both versions of the story were true, but sometimes I wondered if the part of me I'd left in England was still worth mentioning.

Finally, we reached the clearing in the living room, and by "clearing" I mean the small area you could at least walk through without potentially killing yourself. Anne let out a massive sigh and smoothed her Keratin-straightened brunette hair back into place. "Wow. Okay, we need to do something about this."

Mum plopped on the sofa, the corners of her mouth turned down. "I know my house isn't as fancy as you three are probably used to now, but it's home."

"A home that's unfit for anyone to live in."

"Anne, calm down." I sat next to Mum, bracing myself for the backlash.

"No, no, it's fine. Let your sister get it off her chest." She folded her arms and shot Anne a go-ahead-and-try-me glare.

"I'm only saying this out of concern for you. But you've got to see this isn't a safe place. You can barely walk through the house. What if there was a fire?"

"Not to worry about that, dear. I do regular drills to test myself, just in the event of an emergency. Actually, I had my best time ever last week. That notebook should be around here some-where ...."

She lifted the blanket draped across the back of the sofa, looked under the bed pillow behind her, then moved on to search-ing on top of the end table. *She must've filled the bedroom with stuff again*, I thought, eyeing up the pillow and blanket, which upon closer inspection was the pink paisley comforter from her room.

"Ah, here it is," she said, triumphant. "And have a seat, Anne. You're making me nervous standing there like that."

"I'm fine, thanks," she said, shifting her weight from one foot to the other and biting her lip. I could see the wheels turning in Anne's head, analyzing the sofa for stains, hoping she wouldn't have reason to change into her emergency leggings in the car. Ruby was so used to—and influenced by—her mother's behavior that she started undressing the second she got in the door from school, stripping out of her "bus clothes."

Mum didn't seem to process any of this, and flipped through a spiral-bound book with a photo of Will, Kate, and newborn Prince George on the cover. "Six minutes, two seconds to get out last time."

I reached out and touched Mum's shoulder. "I'm glad you've improved. But ideally it should take less than a minute. This is still a really dangerous situation."

A ghost of a frown crossed her face, but she gave me a dismissive wave. "I'm fine, love."

I closed my eyes for a second and sighed. I should've told her how much it pained me to imagine the house crumbling down around her, or the fact she needed to set a timer to try and climb out of the house as fast as possible in the first place. On those shows where they have interventions with addicts, they always have families list the ways that the person's addiction has affected them. But with Mum, where the hell would I even start? Her hoarding had impacted everything from the way I dressed to my career choice to where I lived ... it was a bit difficult to pick a highlight reel.

But at the end of the day, it wasn't about how screwed up I was, or my siblings (and believe me, they had their share of issues). This was about Mum's wellbeing and quality of life, so I decided to try a more empathetic approach first.

"I know you think all of this isn't bad, but you've hurt yourself before," I said. "Remember how upset Ruby was when you broke your leg?"

"That was my own fault for moving too fast through the kitchen. And I relocated that pile so it wouldn't happen again."

"But there's a wall of boxes there now instead," I said.

Will raised his hand as if he expected a teacher to call on him for the right answer. "What if we got some outside help? I think—"

"Exactly. How about we have Sarah ask around, and she'll call some cleaners in to help. Just clear a few things out so you can get some space to breathe." Anne said this with a helpful smile and tilt of her head, as if she were the first person on earth to think up such an idea. Or that I hadn't suggested it three months prior. And the year before that. And why was I the one who had to call around and figure this out?

"We've been down that road before," Mum said, and I sat on my hands to keep myself from adding how she'd caused such a fuss the guys quit after the first afternoon. She refused to throw away even one thing, and made us vow never to spring an intervention on her like that again. Meanwhile, Will had nominated her for that hoarding reality show, *Stuff*, at least twice since then, but unfortunately (or thankfully) they never called.

"I appreciate the concern, but I'm fine. End of story." Mum's jaw set, and she gripped the arm of the sofa. I locked eyes with Will, hoping he'd slip into his typical role as peacemaker.

"Well, all things considered, I have to say you've got quite a ... collection here," he said. I watched Will turn in a slow circle, taking in the rest of the room. It must've been four years since the last time Will had stepped into the house, long enough for her to amass even more stuff than he was used to growing up. Glass curio cabinets filled every available space, brimming with porcelain dolls, figurines, china, souvenir bells and every other sort of knickknack on earth. Unfortunately, most of the curios were at least partially blocked by plastic bins, so the whole display purpose had become moot.

Will pulled a cream-and-white polka dot dress off the top of a bin behind him and eyed the price tag.

"Kate wore that when she was pregnant with George, but unfortunately I could only snap one up in a size twelve."

Anne, always queen of tact, looked at the frock, then back at Mum. "So you bought a dress that's way too small just because Kate Middleton wore it?"

I sat up straighter, suddenly defensive. As ridiculous as Mum's collecting habits were, her recent weight gain was a sore subject. But at the same time, I saw my sister's point.

I looked back and forth between Anne and Mum. I wasn't sure whose side to take, so I chose the one who I thought needed the most coddling.

"She thought I might want to take the dress and get it sized down, but I didn't, so ...."

"That's all right, Sarah," Mum said. "It will be worth money someday. Even if you don't like it."

She'd used my all-time least favorite excuse for the hoarding, and just like that, the defensive feelings were replaced with annoyance. It's funny how parents can turn us into complete teenagers the second we walk in the front door.

"It's Topshop. It probably only cost fifty dollars to begin with," I said. "And I wish you wouldn't blame it on me that you've got this sitting here with no one to wear it. Ask first if you think I might want something."

"I know you don't approve, but shopping is what I do for fun. It brightens my dull little suburban world. We can't all be lifestyle experts in the Big Apple, now can we?" Mum made air quotes as she said "lifestyle experts." Her comment bit, but I ignored the sting and took my phone out.

I opened my notes app and typed: "*Sarah Says*: Air quotes are a don't—blog post idea??" then threw the phone into my black Longchamp bag. "Just like the ones Kate and Pippa have!" Mum said when she gave it to me for my birthday.

"Well, you look nice today," I said, using one of my favorite *Sarah Says* tips: Giving people sincere compliments always lifts their mood. "The shade of that top brings out the blue in your eyes."

Mum did look lovely, but she always made an effort with her appearance. That was what would shock people the most, I think, if they found out about the house. Despite her wiry, long gray hair that looked more like it belonged on a hippie, she was always dressed like she could head off to the office or a nice restaurant at a moment's notice. And while she'd put on a few extra pounds, I suspected that had more to do with lack of access to the kitchen and eating out versus getting older.

"Thank you, I saw this sweater on Princess Sofia and had to buy it," Mum said. "Or was it Crown Princess Victoria? One or the other. I love how they always wear H&M and Zara, it's so affordable and I can just pop online, then bam! It's at my door."

"Oh great, she's branched out to the Swedes now," Anne said.

"You really should brush up on the European royals," Mum said. "They do such great work with—"

"Speaking of work," I said, desperate for a subject change, "how is *your* job going?" Maybe it was better to wait until we went out to lunch to bring up the subject of a cleanup again. She wouldn't dare freak out at us in public. What would the neighbors think?

"Oh, the usual. Sissy Winthrop's kid is in detention again."

Mum had worked as a receptionist at the local elementary school for almost as long as we'd lived in the States, and she adored bringing home gossip about all of the families in town. But unfortunately, our neighbor's detention was the most interesting story she had, and we sat in awkward silence for a good twenty seconds or so.

Will looked at his oversized black watch, then at me, mouthing "need to speak to you." Mum ignored the hint and turned to us with a tea tin from the Queen's 90th birthday in hand. She must've kept the thing right next to the sofa, but I suppose when you live like that, everything needs to be at hand or else it disappears.

"Excuse my manners for not asking sooner. Lady Grey for you, Sarah? Anne, Will, I've got a few new herbal infusions from Whittard of Chelsea if you want to have a look. Used one of those lovely voucher codes."

"We just had a cup of coffee on the way here. But thank you." Anne pointed at Will, speaking for both of them as usual.

"No worries." Mum to normal person translation: *You've committed a massive social faux pas in my book, clearly indicative of some sort of mental imbalance.*

As she got up and busied herself with making my tea, a process I knew would take a while, considering the trip back and forth to the kitchen, I waved my siblings over to the sofa. "It's gotten a bit worse since the last time I was here."

Will sat down and raked a hand through his floppy hair.

"I think 'a bit worse' is the understatement of the year. But it's okay, because I've got a plan."

"I'd *love* to hear this," Anne said, hovering over me, then sighing deeply before taking her quilted barn jacket off. She spread it across the cushion next to me and took a seat on top.

"Me, too," I said. "With Will and me in New York, it could take months, if not a year of us coming back and forth to clear out." I might've given tips on TV about how to make homemade spray cleaner or the best way to label your clothing storage bins, but this was even out of *my* league.

"So, what I was talking about earlier ..." Will leaned in closer, speaking in a loud whisper. "I didn't want to tell you guys until I was sure, but I interviewed for an associate producer position on *Stuff*, and I got the job."

Typically, the phrase "I got the job" would be reason for high fives, celebratory drinks, or an expensive dinner where you're stuck splitting the check even though you only got a salad. But my eyes widened. *Oh no he didn't.*

"Just to clarify, you mean the compulsive hoarding show?" Anne asked, digging her nails into the arm of the sofa. I wondered if she had a manicure set hidden in her bag, or if this situation was so dire she didn't even care.

He nodded. "What other show called *Stuff* is there? And aren't you excited for me?"

"Isn't that a bit, I don't know, close to home?" I asked.

Will snapped a few pictures of the living room with his phone, turning to look toward Mum's path from the kitchen every so often. "That's the whole point. They like me because I've got experience in that milieu."

Only Will could use the word *milieu* without a hint of irony.

I could see what was coming next, but Anne said it before I got the words out. "I hope you didn't tell them about Mum's *condition*."

"Once I mentioned her, I couldn't really back out of it. She's got quite a unique angle, you know. But when I mentioned Sarah

Percy was my sister, I think that sealed the deal."

I could feel my cardigan getting damp under the arms and undid a few of the top buttons. "Excuse me?"

"Yeah. It'll be like an intervention, but you know, with hoarding. And some DIY stuff thrown in. Totally your thing. You'd help clean up the house and then if her episode goes well, they might bring you in as a consultant for more episodes."

"Whoa. Back up a second. What about GMNY? You know I can't do another show without getting approval from the higher ups, and even if I could, what would my viewers think? It would hurt my credibility if everyone found out I grew up in a hoarding house."

Will shot me a look of restrained annoyance. "You could work around your schedule. It's only filming a few episodes here and there. Plus, wouldn't it make you seem more sympathetic? 'Girl comes from hoarding background and turns into domestic superstar' and whatnot? Just because our mum collects Princess Di china doesn't mean your experience is suddenly invalid."

When he put it that way, it made sense ... which scared the hell out of me. That was the kind of stuff my producers would eat up. They'd probably *insist* I do it for the ratings boost, which frankly, we needed.

"Well, you can't volunteer Mum without her consent, for God's sake," I added, hoping that would put the final nail in the *Stuff* coffin. Even if I wanted to be on the show—and I definitely didn't—there was no way we'd be able to convince our mother it was a great idea to let not just our entire town, but the entire *country* see her carefully orchestrated appearance was a sham.

"I'm confident we can get Mum to do it," Will said. "That's why I wanted us all here together."

Anne shook her head. "Do you want to humiliate our entire family on national TV? I mean, what the actual fuck, Will. I thought we were trying to get her to hire a cleaner or let us help her organize. Not this."

"I can't believe I'm actually agreeing with Anne, but she's

right. And while I appreciate the chance to work on a national show, being a television host who happens to be good around the house doesn't make me qualified to handle this situation. I'm not a professional therapist."

If Will was thrown off kilter, he didn't show it. "You don't need to be, because we've already got one on the show. Don't overthink this. Pierce is really excited to talk to you. And Mum of course. That's why I've got to take these pictures." He zoomed in on the Prince George section of the curio cabinet in front of the window, snapping shots of the teacup, the pill box, and the doll … that ridiculous china doll. I felt a full-body cringe thinking about people sprawled out on their sofas, laughing over her collection.

"So you're on a first-name basis with Pierce Thompson, then?" A picture of the show's host, a tan, spiky-haired Southern charmer, flashed in my mind, the one I'd seen on the cover of last week's issue of *People* next to the headline "REALITY STARS GIVE BACK TO TORNADO VICTIMS."

"He's my boss, so yes. And most women would be dying to meet him. Doesn't Kareena have a picture of Pierce in her cube?"

I shook my head, picturing my best friend at the station and her Home Channel obsession. "Yes, but meeting a C-list celebrity isn't a great reason to splash my family's business on TV."

I could've thought of a million more reasons to say no, but then I heard Mum's footsteps, and the bins lining the living room started to wobble.

"Quit it with the pictures," Anne said, "and let's speak about this later."

"Speak about what?" Mum asked, coming into view a few seconds later.

Will cleared his throat. "Hey Mum, remember that show you saw about compulsive hoarding?"

She handed me my cup of tea, set hers on the coffee table, and then arranged herself on the sofa before answering. "Darling, don't trouble your old Mum now. I hope you haven't been trying to concoct some sort of intervention again."

"Not precisely. But, well ... you see—"

"Will's got himself a job on a hoarding show," Anne said, spitting out the words, then turning to Will. "Sorry! But you would have sat there dithering around it all day."

At first, Mum didn't say anything. She pursed her lips, and then her shoulders drooped and her entire body seemed to deflate by fifty percent, much like a balloon the day after a party. "I see."

"I thought it would be best to tell you in person," Will said, twisting the stupid Topshop dress between his fingers. Mum just sat there staring into space, so Will went into babble mode. "It's an amazing opportunity. And my boss, well, you've probably heard of Pierce Thompson, but he really does care about everyone on the show. Keeps up an email correspondence with most of them, actually."

The more Will talked about *Stuff*, the more animated he became, and I realized how much he actually cared about this new job, and how good he'd be on their team. Not that it changed my mind about me participating.

"Pierce sounds lovely, and you know my affinity for accents, but I'm afraid the answer is no." Mum took a sip of tea and smiled at us, as if we were sitting around having a casual discussion about the weather and not discussing bringing a camera crew in to throw out her collection of replica Princess Eugenie fascinators. "And I can't imagine it would be terribly interesting to film a house full of organized and labeled boxes. You kids are making a fuss over nothing."

Denial was her usual MO, but this was ridiculous.

"Could you at least think about it?" Will asked. Beads of sweat formed on his forehead.

Anne's Twindar must have kicked in. "You didn't actually promise them we'd be on an episode, did you?"

"I *might* have said something along those lines."

"William David Percy! How could you?" Mum said, covering

her face with her hands. "Think about the family's reputation, if nothing else. What would your cousins at the court of Henry VIII think?"

"Here we go with Henry the sodding Eighth again," Anne said, forming a pretend gun with her fingers and aiming at the side of her head. "And they'd roll over in their graves. If one can do that without a head."

I slapped Anne's knee. Mum *loved* to bring up the famous Percy cousins, no matter how massively far removed they were from our father's line. Ironic, considering she never wanted to bring up the only reason we were connected to them at all.

"It wasn't Will's fault, Mum," I said. "I'm sure he thought it would help him get the job if he mentioned your house. And then they found out I'm his sister ... not that I'm thrilled about the situation, but can you see where he's coming from?"

Some nonsensical sputtering noises that may or may not have been words came out of Mum's mouth, and she got up and paced around the room as much as one could without crashing into something, stopping to shake a London Eye snowglobe. We all fell silent, watching the glitter flutter down on the ferris wheel, and I envied how peaceful and sparkly it looked inside that little bubble. Maybe that was how Mum felt surrounded by all her stuff.

"Well, one thing we can agree on is that the house needs help," Will said. "And this won't cost you anything. If we did it ourselves, you'd have to consider the price of a cleaning team, and a dumpster, and—"

"Sure, it won't cost anything. Just my dignity."

Anne threw her hands in the air. "I don't know why you even bothered, Will. Our mother doesn't want our help. She wants to die alone in a house full of royal crap." Anne yanked her jacket off the sofa and marched away, not hesitating for a second before she climbed through the maze of boxes leading to the side door.

"Anne, wait," Will called. He glanced back at me, an unsaid apology in his eyes, but I shooed him ahead. I would have to deal with Mum alone.

She was crouched on the floor, gathering a pile of books. "I can't let them take all of my things, Sarah. I just can't."

"I know it's tough for you, I really do. But you can't live like this anymore."

She stood, clutching the books to her chest as if someone was about to yank them away. "Well I'm sorry I'm such an embarrassment. But everything's not always my fault."

"What's that supposed to mean?"

"If your father hadn't ...."

"Enough about Dad! He didn't force you to buy all of this. And you can't blame the divorce on your stuff forever."

I'd crossed the line, and I knew it. But I was sick of her putting everything on my father, as if she had no control over her own actions. I turned to the passageway and lifted my right foot, then paused and put it down. Part of me felt guilty for snapping at Mum; the other part was wary about traversing the shoddy path to the door.

"Bottom line is we're worried about you and your health. If this show can help, maybe the risk will be worth the reward."

Mum stared at the floor for a second and then met my gaze. "How about we have lunch another time? This place ..." She turned and looked at the passageway. "I think it's best that you leave."

This time, I didn't hesitate before heading for the door.

⊶ Debbie ⊷

THE AIR HUNG STILL and heavy around me after Sarah slammed the door, and I stood there staring at the empty pathway for a few moments, willing myself not to chase after her.

I knew it. I bloody well knew it, but I still let them come. It's my own fault, really. Maybe I thought the kids had grown up enough to separate what I did in my house from their own lives. Or maybe I wanted all three of them back home again, even for a couple of hours. Was that too much to ask?

My hands shook as I made my way back to the sofa. You'd think they'd never seen a few boxes lying about. To be fair, I suppose it must have been overwhelming to someone like Will, who lives in such a sparse environment. Sarah called it "sleek, modern style" but I call it cold and boring. Would it kill him to put out a few picture frames or a nice Waterford vase? Maybe my house was cluttered, but it looked like no one lived in Will's apartment at all, and Sarah was no better with her color-coded, alphabetized, sanitized little bubble of a place. And Anne? Don't even get me started.

But brooding wasn't going to convince them to come back, and it certainly wouldn't change that Will had gone and nominated his own mother for a hoarding program. Part of me (and a very tiny part, I might add) wanted to watch an episode or two, to see what I was up against. It had been at least a year since that time Will "accidentally" flipped past *Stuff* at his apartment and suggested we have a look. But the overruling part of my brain switched the TV on to BBC America (poor substitute for the real thing, but it had to do) and as usual, a "Top Gear" marathon was on. No need to make myself more upset by watching those sad, filthy people with their piles of 1990s cereal and mildewed scrapbooking supplies.

Is that really what my kids thought I'd turn into?

Since I needed a bit of cheering up, I pulled an opened cardboard shipping box from under the coffee table and set about unwrapping my latest Royal Collection purchases, four lovely little pink, white and purple plates from the Queen Victoria range. I ran my finger along the cursive "V" in the center and the tiny crown above it and smiled. Sarah didn't know what she was talking about. These would be worth money someday, and in the meantime, they'd be quite useful. I imagined arranging some lovely scones on them in the morning for breakfast—well, first I'd have to find what I did with that scone mix—and maybe even enjoying a little snack before bed. How much nicer would it look to eat your biscuits off a beautiful little saucer than straight out of the plastic package?

After I stacked the plates on the counter, scooting some unopened mail out of the way, I put the kettle on and wondered what to do for the rest of the night. Busy work would be the only thing to keep my mind off the mess with the kids. As they say, idle hands ....

I could've continued cataloguing the rest of my magazines; I'd finally finished the eighties, and the nineties were in various locations throughout the house; a task that could take days, if not weeks. But at least it would make my children happy, and if I showed them some sort of progress, maybe they'd get off my back for once.

I stepped over a few empty Rubbermaid bins (I'm always ordering more because you never know when you need to store something new) and headed for the pantry to get the tea, but my foot caught on a bag, and the next thing I knew my hands were breaking my fall. Not the first or last time it would happen, but pain shot through my wrist.

Oof. I fought back tears, but then thought *why bother?* Who exactly was I saving face for? No one. And it was my own fault.

It's funny when you watch TV and see these people and think, *God, how did they get to this point? Surely, they must realize they've got a problem.* Well yes, I did realize I had a slight problem, realized it for years in fact. But it starts out small, like the first raindrops of a storm. Then a few more drops show up, and the winds start, and suddenly it's a full-blown hurricane and you're powerless to stop it. There are the people who leave at the first sign of distress, or the old ladies who hunker down and ride it out with their fifteen cats in the house they've always lived in. Somehow, I'd become that cat lady, minus the cats.

The problem was, every time I wanted to clean up, I'd find something new to read, or watch, or reminisce about. And how could I throw any of it away? The kids got so angry when I told them I had to save duplicates of all my important books and magazines, but if one of them got destroyed, I'd have nothing left. How would I remember the happy times? Everything was in order by date and occasion at least. But that wasn't enough for them.

"When you die, do you really want Will and Sarah and me to have to deal with all of this stuff?" Anne said the last time she tried to "help," which was at least four years ago. It was one of their favorite lines, and if I had a dollar for every time I'd heard it, I could've paid Martha bloody Stewart to come fix my house years ago. Anne then picked up a magazine with a newborn Princess Beatrice on the cover and tossed it across the room. "We left England two decades ago. Cut the cord!"

That's when I told her to get out.

It was bad enough when my kids tried to clean up, but if I let them bring in some kind of organizing team, they'd just toss everything into a dumpster and I'd simply die letting all of my memories be taken away in front of millions of viewers. It wasn't worth the stress. The answer would have to be no.

It would get tidied up one day, but these things take time. I told Sarah when I retired, I'd have all the time in the world, but she'd said "and years ago, you said when all of us moved out, you'd have the time to clean. And then it was after Ruby was out of diapers, you'd have time to clean, because you were too busy helping Anne with a baby. It's always something."

To be fair, she had a point. But everyone's lives were busy, and there really always *was* something. Why spend all my time organizing when I could be enjoying my life?

I took a second to wipe my face and regain my composure, and when I sat up, shaking out my wrist, the worn edge of a Charles and Diana postcard caught my eye. My heart felt like it had dropped into my stomach. I knew Alan's stuff would turn up eventually, but still, a part of me hoped all of it would stay lost in the shuffle.

Diana smiled shyly back at me, looking so uncertain in her engagement photo, while Charles's image was hidden by a wicker basket filled with Lord knows how many other postcards, letters and photos. I stared at her picture as if I'd never seen it before, wishing I could go back in time and tell her—tell both of us—*it's not worth it.*

Finally I sighed, sliding the card out from under the basket with the precision of a surgeon. Even after everything, I couldn't let it tear.

A mixture of relief, dread and nostalgia washed over me once the yellowing postcard was in my hand, and no matter how much I wanted to block them, the memories flooded back.

London, May 1981

No one goes to England for the weather, but the second the sun comes out, life feels like a holiday. It was eight o'clock on a Thursday evening and inside The Volunteer, ale flowed, Blondie blasted, ties were loosened, and it felt like no one had the heart to return home after the gloriousness of the spring day.

Carol and I had blown off classes for the afternoon, sunbathing and taking an only semi-disastrous paddle around the Boating Lake in Regent's Park, and a quick check of my pink digital watch confirmed we'd been at the pub for the better part of five (!) hours.

We stood shoulder-to-shoulder, sweating in the abnormal seventy-degree "heat" and singing along to "The Tide is High" when a sandy-haired guy in a baggy white blazer locked eyes with me.

"You all right?" he asked.

I took in his expensive-looking chinos, striped t-shirt and strong jaw before responding, "Yeah, you?"

"I haven't got a proper chat-up line, sorry." He said this with a twinkle in his eye that inferred he actually had many lines, and they usually worked. His two friends could barely contain their laughter, and I heard the word "wanker" hidden by a well-timed cough from one of them.

"Well, hello then," I said, ignoring the guys and extending a sunburnt hand. "I'm Debbie. This is my roommate, Carol."

Carol jumped at the sound of her name and stopped mid-sing, making it sound like she was saying "Nuuumberrrr WHAT?"

His grin grew broader. "Americans! I didn't suspect it."

Carol preened. She *loved* being mistaken for a local. Hell, so did I, but I'd never admit that to her.

"Alan," he said, touching his chest. "George," he pointed to the tall one, "and Reg, who's thick as two short planks," he said, gesturing toward the skinny guy who'd called him a wanker.

George's eyes lit up, probably thinking we were loose Yanks up for holiday shags or something. *Been there, done that, buddy.*

"Fantastic weather, right?" he said. "Bet you probably thought it just rained all the time here."

"Not really," Carol said, tossing a dark curl over her shoulder and swaying to the tropical-sounding beat. "My parents have been bringing me here since I was a kid. I know there's more to England than rain. Not like *some* Americans."

Alan and I exchanged smirky glances. Luckily he didn't know

how many umbrellas and pairs of rain boots I'd brought to the dorm my first year. "Well, enjoy the first—and probably only—taste of summer," Alan said. "Back to the usual 12 degrees tomorrow, I'm sure."

I leaned in closer, breathing in his scent of Drakkar Noir ... my ex-boyfriend's favorite. Strike one, but I'd give him the benefit of the doubt.

"I've never seen it this busy," I said, taking in the well-dressed crowd around us. A girl in a black, poofy strapless dress, no doubt trying to copy the soon-to-be princess, waved her arms wildly to the music, nearly whacking us in the process.

"You come here often then?" Alan asked. I'd come to learn Brits don't typically ask you straight out what you do, or where you live, and instead start an elaborate guessing game involving a series of questions. He was obviously trying to figure out if this was my local. I decided to keep the game short.

"Often enough. I'm through the park, at Bedford College."

Alan nodded. "Lovely campus. My cousin is there, she's a first year. You might know her—Sally Kerr?"

"Sorry, doesn't ring a bell. But you know, you could just ask me what year I am," I said with a laugh.

"But what fun would that be?"

"Touché," I said. "But for the record, I'm graduating. I fly home in a month to Philadelphia." The mood suddenly shifted, and I looked down at my scuffed white pumps.

"God, don't be such a downer, Debbie," Carol said, shaking her head and squeezing past us to talk to the friend I'd later refer to as "Wanker Guy," having immediately forgotten his name after Alan told us.

Alan turned to me, tilting his head. "You'll miss it here?" he said, although it was more like a statement than a question.

"I'll even miss Carol." Our heads turned to see her arm draped around Wanker Guy, swaying drunkenly and belting out the chorus to "Don't Stand So Close to Me," at which we both burst into laughter.

"And," I said, "and keep in mind that's a massive AND—I'll be missing the wedding, which sucks most of all."

Alan rolled his eyes. "I assume you mean Diana and bloody Charles?"

"Obviously. Is there any other wedding to think about these days?"

"What is it with women and their royal wedding obsession?" He set his glass of Guinness on the bar, folding his arms as he leaned against the dark wood. "To be fair, I'm looking forward to a bank holiday, but I could leave the rest of it."

I shrugged. *How did you even respond to that?* "It's just so ... romantic. Gives us girls hope that if Diana could snag a prince, we could, too."

Alan winked and lifted his pint glass in my direction. "To romance."

"To romance," I said with a surprised smile, clinking my glass with his.

A few beats of silence passed as I watched Carol and Wanker Guy dance, and remembered how many times this same scene had played out in different pubs and clubs across my beloved city. A chat, a dance, a sneaky kiss, a walk home. What would I do in the middle of suburbia with my parents?

"God, this is so depressing," I said out of nowhere.

Alan's head turned abruptly. "Pardon?"

"Leaving this," I said, gesturing around the room, "is unbelievably depressing. Like, what's the point? I might as well just go home now. Why delay the inevitable?"

He laughed, touching my shoulder in the process. "Come now, it can't be that bad at home?"

I thought of my parents, the rusted porch swing, the dog. A normal house, a normal family. No, it wasn't bad. It was worse. It was boring.

"I don't know. I suppose the first time I saw London, I felt like I was home."

Whether Alan was humoring me or not seemed unclear, but

he listened intently anyway. "Straight away? Just like that?"

"Maybe not at first, I guess. To be honest, at first when we left Heathrow it looked kind of like New Jersey."

"New Jersey??" he said, eyes growing to the size of saucers and nearly spitting out his Guinness. "Home of Bruce Springsteen?"

I'd never seen a guy, let alone an English guy, get so excited about anything, and I raised an eyebrow, curious. Once he regained his composure he said, "Love the Boss. Brilliant. Me and George got tickets to his show at Wembley in June."

I groaned. "Lucky. I'd kill for tickets."

"Come then," he said, as if it were as simple as that.

"I wish."

"No, I'm serious. We've got an extra ticket. My brother can't make it. My treat, in fact."

I looked at him like he was nuts. "Um, I've got a flight home and everything, and—"

"So change it."

This guy had to be kidding. Or at the very least, wealthy or naïve enough to be unaware of the cost of changing an airline ticket.

"It's not exactly that easy," I said, but before I could continue, my throat burned and my stomach rumbled. The contents of my lunch, or lack thereof, threatened to come back up after our day-long drinking binge.

"Excuse me for a minute? Loo break!" I pushed my way through the crowd as best as I could, breathing in and out to try and distract myself from the fact that I was surely going to puke all over my new denim skirt. The one with the price tag hidden inside the waistband. I couldn't afford to keep it, and I doubted Topshop would look kindly upon me returning a vomit-covered garment.

Safely in the bathroom stall, I leaned my head against the cool black-and-white wall tile for a second and wondered if Alan would be waiting for me. Maybe he'd slipped into conversation with the next girl who passed when I left the room. Bruce

Springsteen and my royal obsession were hardly earth-shattering conversation topics. But still, I liked his cheekiness and bright green eyes and wanted the night to continue. If I could only stand up....

I straightened my floral blouse in the mirror, popped a breath mint in my mouth and gave my satisfyingly shaggy, bottle-blonde hair a quick inspection. No puke. Good enough.

My spirits lifted as I spotted Alan leaning against the wall by the bathroom when I came out, a look of actual concern crossing his features. "Christ," he said, most likely noting my green complexion. "I think you could use a good lie-down."

Great. Just when I thought a semi-decent guy came into the picture....

"No offense, but I'm trying not to—"

Alan's face dropped. "No, no, I meant you seem like you need to get to bed, you know, not in the erm, rude sense."

"Oh!" I said, relief washing over me. "I'm sorry, I've obviously had way too much to drink. I don't really want to go home yet, though." I took a step forward, but stumbled enough for Alan to have to catch me.

He draped an arm around my shoulder. "Me either, but how about I walk you back, and we do this another time instead?"

My stomach flip-flopped again, but in an excited versus drunk manner, and I nodded. "I'd like that. But since I'm on borrowed time here, it'll have to be soon."

He held up one finger and guided me over to the wall, then disappeared to the bar, returning with both a pen and two cocktail napkins. His number was scrawled on one of them, and he handed me the other so I could write mine. I took the napkin and pen and leaned against his back, copying my phone number and "Debbie Windsor" in neat script, drawing a heart over each "i."

"No relation to the actual Windsors, obviously," I said, handing him the napkin.

Alan took a moment to read it, then smirked. "Well, you never know. Maybe a long-lost cousin or something?"

"I wish. But alas, just boring old American me."

Alan studied me for a second before saying, "I don't think you're boring at all." It was a matter-of-fact statement from someone I hadn't even known for an hour, but he delivered it with such confidence that even I believed him. But then a group of girls chose that moment to shove past us, and the spell was broken.

"Let's get you home, Miss Windsor," Alan said, placing a protective hand on the small of my back as he guided me toward the exit.

Carol was still deep in the flirt zone with Wanker Guy, so I pointed toward the door and mouthed "see you at home." She laughed, giving me the thumbs up and a crude gesture over Wanker Guy's shoulder.

Outside, the crowd had spilled onto the sidewalk, the air filled with a mixture of smoke and excitement that sobered me up a few notches.

"I'm going to catch the Tube home," I said, silently cursing that while the college was a stone's throw from the pub, our tiny student flat was much too far for Alan to walk me back. Baker Street station was only a minute or so walk at best; borrowed time indeed.

"You sure? I'll hail you a cab instead."

I shook my head. Cab fare wasn't in the cards that week.

"Well, at least let me come with you," he said, offering me an arm as we crossed Baker Street.

We walked in comfortable silence, my heels clacking on the concrete, and I tried to remember every detail about the night, about him. But the journey was a short one, and soon we were standing in front of the brightly lit station. He walked inside the lobby with me, and I grinned as I noticed we'd stopped right in front of the souvenir stall ... with a huge display of cheap Charles and Diana souvenirs.

Before I could say anything, he plucked a postcard with their engagement picture from the rack, along with a plastic pen with a giant Big Ben suspended from the top.

"What the hell?" I asked, laughing as he paid the cashier, then scribbled something on the back of the postcard.

"For you, my lady," he said, handing it to me with a flourish. On the back it said:

Dinner. Tomorrow night, 8:00. I'll meet you outside the station. Let's make Di and Charles jealous.

-A

My cheeks flushed, and not just from a day in the sun. "It's a date."

He smiled. "Brilliant."

"Well, the Bakerloo line is calling my name, I'm afraid." I shifted from one foot to the other. *Was he going to kiss me? Should I kiss him? Ugh, I had to pee.*

He leaned forward and kissed my cheek, lingering a second before saying, "Right. Off we go, then."

"See you tomorrow," I managed to squeak out, squeezing his hand goodbye.

"Did you think I was going to let you take the Tube home at night alone and completely pissed? I'm not, as my friends might think, a wanker."

"Oh," I said, taking a step back in surprise. "Very well then. But no funny business."

Alan crossed his heart across his stupid blazer. "Let me get a ticket."

I clutched my postcard as we walked through the turnstiles, wondering how early I could call the airline in the morning.

Sarah Says

Let's Do Lunch

During meals, it's time to sit up
straight, mind your manners, and forget
about your problems. Conversation should
be light and entertaining—leave the
politics, religion and family squabbles
behind closed doors. The next table over
doesn't need to know the details of
your breakup, right?

"SO, *THAT* WENT WELL."

The three of us had gathered around the island in Anne's
kitchen, abandoning the lunch reservation in favor of Indian
takeout and wine. Lots of wine. Which was probably poor planning on our part, considering my stomach felt as twisted up as a
Philly pretzel.

"What did you expect to happen? Mum jump up and down
and insist you get the producers on the phone straight away?"
Anne asked.

Will rolled his eyes and refilled his glass. "I figured she'd
react like that, of course. But we needed to get it out there, and
now that she knows, we'll let the information sink in a bit. Maybe
she'll even watch an episode now that it's on her mind."

"Are you mad?" I said. "She'll probably just stress-buy a bunch
of Princess Diana collector plates or something."

"True," Anne said. "But either way, I really don't want to get
involved in this. I mean, even if she does agree—and I'll eat your
Louboutins if she does—I don't want to be on TV. And I doubt
Rob would be fond of the idea either."

I looked around her gleaming, Tuscan-themed kitchen with
its Sub-Zero fridge, carved columns, and intricate marble tile-

work. No, my brother-in-law wouldn't be fond of tainting his spotless reputation, but neither would Anne.

I could almost hear Nanny's clipped, upper-class accent saying, "No paper plates for a Percy" as I watched my sister scoop another portion of butter chicken onto a pink china plate, then grab a wet wipe to make sure a tiny drop of sauce didn't sully her counters. Despite Anne's attempts at distancing herself from Dad's side of the family, she still followed most of our grandmother's directives to a T.

"So, what do we do next?" I asked.

"Give it a few days," Will said. "Then I'll call her. If she thinks my job is on the line, surely she'll consider it."

"So you're going to guilt trip her into being on TV so you don't lose your job? Sarah, guess you should remind her your last boyfriend dumped you because he was embarrassed to be associated with our family. I'll send her a copy of my latest bill from the cleaning service and personal organizer."

Anne was on a roll, and I picked at the corner of my napkin, trying to think of an applicable *Sarah Says* tip for the situation. But I'd never tackled "sibling rivalries over damage caused by parental hoarding" as an etiquette quandary.

"Can we please change the subject for a bit? I don't want to hear the word hoarding for at least ten minutes if that's at all possible," I said.

"Fine. What's the latest at GMNY? Us suburbanites have to live vicariously through you." Of course Anne had to throw in a side dish of "remember, you guys left me," even when she was trying to be nice.

I could've told her I was going to meet the new cast-off from *Dancing with the Stars* or how Gordon Ramsay was even better looking in person. That's what she probably wanted me to say. But why bother keeping up pretenses?

"Stressful. You know how I told you we got a new station manager? She's been on this rampage wanting to revamp all of our shows for no reason. I feel like she's just trying to prove to everyone she's in control."

"Ah," Will said. "Classic case of new boss syndrome."

"Yup. On one hand, I absolutely get it. And we're under all of this pressure to take over the top spot. Who wants to be number two?" I looked around to make sure the kids were still in the playroom. "But it's not fun anymore. I feel like all I think about is ratings. I have *nightmares* about freaking ratings."

"But that's not news, no pun intended," Anne said. "I mean, all the pair of you talk about are your ratings. Even I know that."

"Yeah, but this ... it feels different. It's like I have to prove myself all over again with her. With our old boss, I never had to worry. He basically gave me free reign with my segments. And now with Leslie ..." I stabbed a piece of chicken with a bit more force than necessary. "I can't do anything right."

"It's an adjustment period," Will said. "You'll make it through."

"Easy for you to say."

Anne sighed. "At least you've got some sort of purpose other than changing diapers, acting like a chauffeur and watching the same episodes of *Sesame Street* over and over."

It never occurred to me that Anne, purveyor of organic snacks and developmentally-appropriate fair-trade toys, actually resented her situation. But maybe the swimming pool is always larger on the other side of the fence. It wasn't a topic I felt comfortable wading into at that moment.

"Anyway, back to Mum," I said. "Maybe we should have your BFF Pierce speak to her, too."

"That's actually a brilliant idea," Will said. "He could charm the pants off a nun, that one."

I tried to push out the image of a nun throwing off her pants at a reality television host and nodded. "Great. Arrange it and let me know what I can do."

"Wait, so is that a yes from you?" Will asked, hopping off his barstool.

"It's a 'we'll see if I can manage taping two shows without

getting fired.' So, basically a yes. I just have to figure out how to explain this at the station."

I eyed up the platter of chocolate-covered strawberries on the counter. Normally, I'd abstain: who wants a few extra pounds on camera? But stress got the best of me, and I grabbed a plate and plopped two strawberries on it, arranging them just so. *This would look really nice on Instagram.*

I refreshed the screen over and over until I got a response from one of my 112,012 followers.

@SarahSaysNYC you're so perfect! wish I could have lunch with you!

I smiled, satisfied, and slipped the phone into my pocket.

"Hello? Earth to Sarah." Anne waved a hand in front of my face. "I know tweeting or whatever you're doing is of vital importance, but we were asking if Andrew would help you talk to the new lady."

"Normally I'd say yes, but he's been pretty overwhelmed with the changes at the station." My shoulders tensed at the memory of Friday's meeting with my producer, when he broke the news about our dismal ratings. Now I was going to drop the bomb about *Stuff* on him. Fantastic timing.

I picked at the chocolate shell on my strawberry, methodically removing it until there was a satisfying pile of light brown shavings on the plate.

"Anyway," I said. "The only problem is I'm worried they'd think this cuts down on my credibility."

"You mean, you're this domestic superstar and suddenly you'd be admitting to everyone you grew up in a house you can't even walk through?" Anne said. "Yeah, that crossed my mind as well."

"True, but I hope they can see the benefit in—" Will stopped midsentence and grabbed a strawberry from the platter, popping it into his mouth all at once, letting out a loud "Mmm." Typical Will, going for what he wanted without finding fifteen different reasons to talk himself out of it ... or picking it apart until the end product barely resembled what you saw in the first place.

It was the fundamental difference between us, and I envied him for it.

"Sorry," he said. "These are fantastic. But yeah, you've got a point. Your mother's behavior doesn't determine who you are. Maybe the viewers will like you even more if they learn about your background?"

"Hmm," Anne said. She stared at me like she was at one of her Young Friends parties at the Philadelphia Museum of Art, debating the meaning of a painting.

"What?"

"Nothing. This is all just really ... interesting. You're about to risk your dream job, and Mum hasn't even agreed to be on the show."

I rubbed my temple. "I really can't afford to get sacked. You know how hard I've worked to get where I am."

"And so has Will," Anne said. I don't know why she was defending him, considering how against the show she was, but I chalked it up to a twin thing. "So, what can we do to make sure no one loses their job, and Mum gets some help?"

"I've got an idea." Will shook his head in the way people do when they can't believe what they're about to say next.

"Mum's house. It's not hers, you know. So if she talks to Pierce, and still says she won't be on *Stuff*, we do have one last bit of ammunition ...."

Anne's mouth dropped open. "Seriously? We couldn't."

I looked at Will with a fair bit of shock, and to be honest, admiration. For him to bring our father into it, the situation had to be dire indeed.

"It might be the only way," I said. "She signs up for *Stuff*, or Dad takes back the house."

✑ Debbie ✑

I WOKE UP THE MONDAY after the kids' visit with a splitting headache and a tinge of regret. I'd spent most of Sunday slightly tipsy and listening to Blondie CDs after finding that Charles and Di postcard.

I stared at the card for a second, still lying on the floor next to the sofa (picture side up, because I obviously wasn't going to read that little note again). I'd been fine, *really fine*, for a while, and suddenly one silly little postcard and the threat of humiliation on national TV set me back twenty years.

Even worse, the rest of the stuff was sitting there in the basket, taunting me. I couldn't look. Not yet, at least.

Why had I let Alan get to me like that? He was off in Essex, living his carefree life with his new family, and what had happened to us was a million years ago. He surely didn't care a whit about what I was doing, and I was certain he hadn't saved any mementos of our courtship. Gemma would've seen to that, even if he had.

But if I got rid of the postcard, or anything else, it was like those happy times and that untroubled part of me never existed. And what would my kids and the grandkids have to remember their parents by? Once I was gone, no one would know about my tiny flat in Soho with the wonky toilet, or the way Alan used to wear those ridiculous Miami Vice blazers. We all had to leave some sort of legacy behind, and this was the only way I knew how.

I trudged into the bathroom through the new path I'd created after the white wine spritzer fiasco from Sunday, ran a hot bath with some of my Woods of Windsor rose soap and took fifteen minutes to try and relax. Relaxation, sadly ... not my strong point. And I wondered where Sarah got it from.

I'd be babysitting Ruby and Charlie on Tuesday so Anne could go to her mother's club meeting; knitting group Thursday night; brunch with some of my school friends on Sunday. That left loads of hours in between to think about the kids' betrayal, and thinking was my worst enemy. *Should I come up with some other things to fill the week?* I could do with a visit to the bookstore ... or perhaps scour the shops on Lancaster Avenue and pop in to see my friend Rich. He *had* asked me out for dinner again; maybe it wouldn't hurt to give it a go.

But a real date felt much scarier than the casual coffee meet-ups we'd been having, and anyway, my heart had closed off long before I left the UK.

I pushed that nonsense out of my mind and focused on ironing my trousers and choosing a scarf to match my sweater instead. Even though the scarf organizer Sarah bought me hung from the back of my bedroom door, I still couldn't find the silk floral style I wanted. Eventually I gave up, wrapped a plain black pashmina around my neck and moved the mountain of clothes piled on the ironing board to the floor. It was hard to tell if they were clean or dirty, and after a few seconds of debate, I moved all of it to the hamper. I'd deal with it later.

As I stood there in my underwear, ironing my standard winter business casual look of crisp black trousers and a wool sweater, I burst out laughing. What would Pierce Thompson and his minions think if they showed up with me ironing sans pants in a room where I couldn't even sleep?

By the time I got into the car, I was so out of breath I had to take a few minutes to compose myself before pulling the lint roller out of my glove compartment. I gave myself a full once-over with the roller and was finishing up the trousers when an unfamiliar number flashed on my phone.

"Hi there, may I please speak to Debbie?" a man with a deep Southern drawl asked.

"Speaking," I said, although what I wanted to say was, "Please tell me my credit card bill isn't late again."

"This is actually Pierce Thompson, ma'am. How are you doing today?"

It came out like "huhyalldoointoday," and it actually took me a second to process what he was saying, and who he was. When I realized, the lint roller dropped out of my hand. Maybe Pierce was used to people being stunned into silence by him, because the man just kept on yammering away.

"Your son asked me to give you a call. Can we chat for a minute or two if that's all right?"

"Chat about what? That I refuse to have cameras come in my house and humiliate me in front of the entire country?" My jaw tensed. *That little bugger, getting his boss to try and sweet talk me into it.*

"Now I know it was probably a shock for you, what with Will and the girls busting in and laying that news out there. But Will thought I might have some ideas to help with your house, and I hope you'll hear me out."

I slumped back in my seat and closed my eyes. I knew my son wanted to help, but he was way out of line. The only outsider I'd ever talked to about the house was that shrink Alan forced me to see back in Essex, and look how much that helped.

"Hello? You still there, ma'am?"

I exhaled deeply. "Yes, and I wish you'd stop calling me ma'am."

He laughed, a deep, musical chuckle that actually gave me goose bumps. "All right, Debbie. It's a deal." He must've been able to charm someone into doing nearly anything with that laugh. Well, except sign up for that exploitive show of his.

"Look, I appreciate you taking the time to call, Mr. Thompson. Really, I do. But I'm not interested." *Not interested* being an extremely diplomatic way of saying, *sod off.* "Have a nice—"

"Wait, Debbie. Can you hear me out for a minute? Please." Something in his voice kept me from pressing the "end" button, and it wasn't only the charming accent. Authority? Compassion? Whatever it was, I didn't hang up.

"I know it's difficult to imagine changing the way you live, and it's a touchy subject, but I've had a tremendous success rate with helping people. You don't have to do anything you don't want to do. Everything would be on your terms."

"No offense, dear, but I don't think you can help me. And my house isn't nearly as bad as Will probably made it out to be. All of this fuss over some collectibles."

"Well, I've heard you've got some pretty awesome stuff in there, and that's exactly why everyone's making a fuss. You've spent years gathering all of these beautiful things, am I right?"

"Since the eighties, yes."

"Now do you want all of those collectibles to be hidden away for no one to enjoy?"

I pictured all of the gorgeous tea towels, and china, and books I hadn't read in years, sitting in boxes. My shoulders slumped. "No. Of course not. But—"

"So why don't we show it off? I'd love to build you some real nice shelving units, maybe one of those big entertainment centers with bookshelves on either side. Give us a week, and you won't believe how good that house will look."

His tone sounded genuine, but maybe that was a Southern thing. "I'll think about it," I said, hoping that would be enough to get him off my back.

"That's all I can ask. And the approach isn't nearly as scary as it probably looks on TV. It's all about managing what you've got, and finding new ways to organize what's useful."

"And who determines what's 'useful' and what isn't?" An image of strangers tossing my bins into a dumpster flashed in front of me. Suddenly my breathing became shallow, and the interior of the car felt like it was closing around me. I rolled down all the windows and whipped out the little Victorian fan I kept in my purse from the hot flash days.

"Contrary to popular belief, I'm not the guy who's out to

throw away all of your things," Pierce said. "Nothing would get donated or tossed without your approval."

"Then what's the point of you coming? Because I don't want to get rid of my stuff."

"Would you mind if I visited the house one day with Will just to talk, and get a lay of the land? Is that something you'd consider?"

I'll give it to the guy—he was persistent. I said again I'd think about it, but really, I was trying to get off the phone.

My hands shook as I drove to school, but what could I do? Both Will and Sarah would be on set, so I couldn't call, and I knew Ruby had a dentist appointment that morning. And it's not like I could vent to my coworkers; that would mean telling them about the house.

Normally, work proved a welcome distraction from my worries, but even the gossip about our principal's hair transplant gone wrong couldn't keep my mind off the call. Soon enough it was time to lock my desk drawer and tackle the lengthy five-minute commute back home. The second I got in the door and made it to the living room, I picked up the phone.

Will didn't answer, so Sarah was next. Voicemail. Might as well call Anne, then.

"Mum, I only have a minute before Charlie wakes up. You all right?"

"I've been better, dear. I'm guessing you know something about the phone call I received from Pierce Thompson this morning."

"Oh. Yes, about that ... I know you're probably not happy, but we just thought—"

"You just thought wrong, then." A few beats of silence passed before she spoke again.

"Please, try and see this from our perspective. Will's concerned. We're all concerned. And this job, well that makes everything a bit more tricky."

I snorted. "Tricky isn't the word I'd use, but all right then."

"You know I'm not thrilled about the idea of our family's business being thrown all over television, and frankly I can't say I'd agree to take part myself. But Will's never had an opportunity like this before, Mum. And he might never get one again. *Stuff* is huge right now, and from what I've heard, Will's old show is basically on the chopping block at the Food Channel."

"So you're saying it's my fault if he winds up unemployed."

"You're putting words in my mouth."

"Hardly. But no matter. Look, I talked to Pierce. He seems like a lovely person, and I'm sure he means well. But I don't know about any of this."

I looked around at all my cherished things, patting the worn cover of the *Princess Elizabeth Gift Book* next to me. The person whom I felt bad for was Pierce, making judgments about other people's mothers and other people's lives. But that wasn't my place to say. "Well, if you talk to your brother, tell him I appreciate the thought but I'm doing just fine. No assistance required."

"You can't see even a *little* bit of logic in the idea?" I could tell Anne was gritting her teeth, a bad habit years of etiquette lessons still couldn't shake.

"Would it be nice to get someone to redecorate my house and give me some new furniture for free? Sure! But that's about the only thing that appeals to me about this fiasco."

"Do us a favor and hear the guy out, all right? However, if you don't like how this meeting goes, then I really think ...."

"You think what?"

"Nothing." She said it in a quick, dismissive tone, as if she'd lost the courage to spit out what she really meant.

"I'll think about it," I said for the hundredth time that day.

Anne sighed. "Fine. Listen, I've got to—"

"It's all right, dear. You have important things to do. We'll chat later."

After we hung up, I flopped back on the sofa and stared at the boxes around me. Anne asked me to try and see it from their point of view, and to a degree, I could. Of course it would be nice to be able to walk from the front door to the living room without wondering if I'd be crushed to death by commemorative mugs. And yes, I could've stood to dust more often, but who had the energy to move everything around? I wasn't getting any younger, no thanks to the pricey eye cream the lady at the La Mer counter convinced me to get last month.

If my collecting seemed horrible to them, I actually could take it as sort of a compliment. I had a passion. Something interesting to show, years of memories and stories to tell. Maybe this wasn't the most organized way of showing off my beautiful things, and I knew I needed to do something about it. But the kids couldn't see the progress I'd made. When you start unpacking, the mess does sort of spiral out of control, but if I left everything in the bins forever, I'd never get to look at them, and what's the sense in that?

My gaze stopped on the basket I'd dug into the day before. I hadn't planned on pulling anything else out so soon; the memories from that one postcard had already slapped me in the face. If I rooted through more, I could either savor the good times and accept the bad ... or all of the stuff would throw me down like a TKO.

Open me, Debbie.

I browsed the Royal Collection website, I tried to watch "Dr. Who," but eventually curiosity got the best of me and I threw my arms up in the air in defeat.

Oh sod it. Just one more look.

I climbed over a few bins, moving plastic shopping bags of stuff and letting them fall to the carpet as I went along. It was all second nature to me, but the feeling of normalcy was probably the worst part. I knew it certainly was *not* normal to have to create a game plan to walk through your own home; I wasn't that far gone. I wouldn't have a hoarding documentary courting me otherwise. But as the saying goes, people can get used to anything if they're around it long enough.

Knees creaking, I sidled over one last box, finally landing

with a thud directly in front of the troublesome basket.

And there it was, sitting right on top. Faded, slightly bent, but mostly intact ... a Bruce Springsteen ticket.

∾

London, June 1981

"So," Alan said, leaning across the tiny, wobbly table. "What was your favorite part?"

We'd left Wembley Stadium on an unbelievable high (both emotionally, and to be honest, chemically) and finally decided to unwind at my local, The Dog & Duck. I turned down another pint in favor of a room-temperature glass of water and sipped it as I considered the show. The music, obviously, was awesome, but spending the night with Alan (even if his friend George was in tow) made the experience a hundred times more exciting. We'd ducked George and finally, blissfully, were alone ... with at least a hundred other Londoners at the pub.

I grabbed his hand. "It's so hard to choose. I can't believe he played for so many hours."

"Fucking fantastic," he agreed.

The phrase could've summed up the past few weeks of my life, but I'd never tell that to Alan. Our relationship, fan-fuck-ing-tastic or not, was temporary, and our time was running out. No need to complicate things.

My parents hadn't been thrilled about the change in plans, but really—after two years, what was the difference if I flew home a few weeks late? I made the hard sell; it didn't make sense for me to miss out on one of British history's biggest moments, and finally they agreed. The royal wedding was one thing, but being able to spend more time with Alan was an added bonus they didn't have to know about.

The opening notes of "Hungry Heart" played, and we exchanged grins.

"So," Alan said. "Tomorrow's the first of July. A month left for your last hurrah in London. What's left to tick off your list?"

As often happened, I turned melancholy at the thought of leaving, and the pot didn't help any. I remembered why I usually just said no; smoking made me feel like Eeyore, walking around slowly with my head down whilst a rain cloud followed overhead. I couldn't quite drum up my usual enthusiasm for the capital, and sighed.

"Other than the wedding celebrations, I've got a few things here and there. Might be hard to cram it all in, especially on a limited budget, but we'll see."

The words "limited budget" never applied to Alan, so I didn't expect him to understand. He folded his arms and rested his head back against the burgundy leather banquette. "Let's not worry about that. Show me this list of yours and we'll get a plan sorted. My treat. Might as well enjoy the time while you've got it, right?"

"Thanks. And you don't have to treat."

He shrugged. "Well, I am, so that's that."

While "my treat" was probably the most often used phrase in his vocabulary when we were out, it still made me a bit uncomfortable.

"I haven't got a proper list written down, but I suppose I'll make it official then." I dug into my purse and pulled out the tacky souvenir pen he'd bought at Baker Street station and a receipt from Boots, smoothing out the wrinkled slip of paper and flipping it over.

I scribbled:

Stand on the Greenwich Meridian Line

Day trip to Bath

See the Anne Boleyn portrait (was being restored last time at gallery)

Kensington Palace (again)

One last trip to Selfridges

Gifts for the family from Harrods

Portobello Market – vintagey souvenirs?

Go to a posh afternoon tea

I slid the paper across the table and chewed the end of the pen as Alan read it. "Hmm. I'm sure I'm missing something."

"How about 'fantastic sex at Alan's flat at least three times per week'?" he said, flashing a sly grin.

I laughed, feeling my cheeks flush. "I mean proper tourist type of things." We hadn't slept together yet, but his comment made me wonder why I was hesitating. Not like I'd ever see him again, so what was the big deal?

Unlike mine, Alan's buzz didn't appear to have worn off, and he smiled lazily. "I've got it ... MEET DIANA SPENCER."

I coughed, almost choking on my water. "That's not the most realistic goal, but 'A' for effort."

"I respectfully disagree."

I shook my head, impressed as usual at his glass-half-full attitude. When your parents funded your entire lifestyle, it probably wasn't too hard to sip from a full glass, though.

"Well, if we run into her on the street, consider it a bonus goal," I said, and scooted my chair to the left as a woman in a smart red skirt and ruffly blouse slipped into a seat at the table next to us. Earlier in the evening, I'd been pretty pleased with my outfit for the night (American flag t-shirt tucked into pleated paper bag waist pants with a tie belt) but suddenly I felt frumpy and childish.

The woman's Tom Selleck-esque husband took the seat closest to Alan, not taking his eyes off the lady in red for a second. Since our tables were close enough that I could reach out and touch them, it wasn't hard to overhear that they were American, newly married and just moved here for work. *What must it be like to never have to leave?*

I tried to reel the broodiness in, but failed. "If you knew you were leaving and might never come back, what would be first on your list?"

"A blokey night with the Essex boys I guess," Alan said. "A pint at each of our favorite pubs. I dunno."

I frowned, staring at the colorful tiles on the wall above Alan's head. "Sorry. I need to stop. Like you said, enjoy the time I've got while I'm here. I guess I'm terrified I'll go home and everything will *suck*. And I'll be living with my parents forever in the suburbs and working at some awful desk job the rest of my life. What if I never make it back to London?"

He didn't say anything for a moment and I wondered if I was doing that overly-American sharing too much thing.

"Sounds stupid, I'm sure," I said.

"Not particularly," Alan said with a shrug. "Always wanted to move to the city myself, so I did."

Alan's parents, as I'd learned, owned a massive Grade II listed property in Essex, and university seemed to be more of a way for Alan to pass the time (or stay out of trouble) than anything. He'd admitted once that he'd never held a real job, other than helping out with promoting his older brother's nightclub. His lack of drive in that area didn't bother me; it certainly wasn't my business, and we were only twenty-one after all. But at that moment, it irked me he could coast through life without a second thought and get whatever he wanted.

The Americans continued to yak at the top of their lungs about plans for their new flat—*do we really talk so loudly at home?*— and I stood up abruptly, my heavy wood chair squeaking against the floor. "That's it. We're going to have some fun if it kills me."

"The Boss wasn't fun?" Alan said, sounding more amused than annoyed.

"Yeah, but this place ... I need a change of venue."

He nodded, finishing the last sip of his pint. Somehow he managed to look elegant while doing it, then contradicted himself by leaving the glass with a thud on the table.

"Anything in mind?" he asked, saying "sorry" no fewer than ten times as we wiggled through the crowd past the Victorian-looking mirrored walls to the front of the pub.

"My flat," I said, staring straight ahead and walking with purpose. I could almost feel him raise his eyebrows, but Alan said nothing until we'd emerged outside. Bargoers had squeezed into every available space on the sidewalk, and we had to press our backs against the wall of the pub to avoid the masses.

"Cheeky monkey. Finally bringing me round yours?"

I grabbed his hand. "Just follow me before I change my mind."

Sarah Says

Make Old Ornaments New Again

Why throw something away when you can find a new use for it? Give old or out-of-style glass baubles a second life — and your home a unique look — by making an ornament wreath. An inexpensive wreath form, hot glue and a ribbon are all you need to create a festive craft that looks much more expensive than it actually is.

"AND THAT'S WHAT SARAH SAYS. Have a brilliant day, everyone!" I smiled into the camera, struggling to keep my lips steady, gave a quick wave and walked off set. The rest of the *Good Morning New York* on-air team was already standing around a table chock full of gadgets, ready to do a Christmas gift guide segment after the break. Me? I was desperately trying not to think about breaking the news to my producer about *Stuff*.

Kareena Khan, my best friend at the station, abandoned her post and hobbled over in a pair of painful-looking black boots and a fitted purple dress that probably cost more than my monthly paycheck.

"Awesome segment," she said, patting me on the shoulder. "I'm digging the vintage ornament wreath. Not like I've ever touched a glue gun in my life. But still."

I laughed. "Shocker."

"So, any word from Will? Or Pierce Thompson?" She lowered her voice to a whisper. "You *have* to meet him and see what this is all about, at least for my sake." I hadn't even heard of *Stuff* until Kareena made me watch it with her a few years ago, and she'd almost passed out when I told her about Will's new job with her Home Channel crush.

I shook my head. "I think Mum's pretty pissed off at all of us, and I haven't talked to Will since we got back to the city. Anyway, I can't give him a definite answer until after I meet with Andrew."

"Well what good are you? I need details!" She grabbed her phone, tapped a few keys and then thrust it in front of me. A photo of Pierce appeared on the screen, along with his Wikipedia entry. "Study this. You should be informed before going into a new job. And who knows, maybe you could dip your pen in the office ink, eh?"

"Not interested, although I have to admit, I can see why most people would be ...."

I pinched my fingers on the screen to make his photo larger and studied it for a few moments. Wavy reddish blond hair, a turned-up nose, and deep dimples. Not too shabby, although he definitely seemed like the sort who rode around in a pickup trunk blasting Garth Brooks and liked to take the "g" off the end of words. Scrolling down, I learned that he was thirty-four, attended the University of Georgia, was married to his college sweetheart for seven years, then got divorced after she cheated on him with a Braves player. *Ouch.*

"You could always help a girl out and slip him my number instead," Kareena said with a wink. "Anyway, did you plan what you wanted to say to Andrew?"

"More or less. I'm going to try to point out all the positives and we'll see what happens. And no, I'm not giving Pierce Thompson your number."

"Fine," she said with a huff. "By the way, Andrew told me I had to 'up my social media game.' Can you give me a crash course, Miss Twitterverse?"

"Of course. And let me guess, he found out you made the interns do it?"

"Details, details. I don't even know what a re-twat is, how am I supposed to be posting all of this stuff in my spare time?"

I raised my eyebrows, holding back a laugh. "Um, it's re-tweet."

"Exactly. That's why I need your help."

"Not arguing with you there. But I think they need you back in front," I said, gesturing toward the stage manager, who was frantically waving and pointing at the gift table.

"Don't give yourself a heart attack!" she called out, then turned to kiss my cheek. "Gotta run, babe! We can talk about it over dinner later."

I nodded, watching in amazement as she tossed her glossy black hair over her shoulder and managed to do a little shuffle run over to her place on set without taking a faceplant. Kareena was quite possibly the most uncoordinated person I'd ever met, yet somehow had an affinity for the highest heels possible.

I also was going to have to give her some major tutorials or else the entire city was going to end up seeing blurry pictures of her cat or something. Then again, she'd have to actually take pictures. Despite being the daughter of two Bollywood legends, Kareena wasn't one for curated Instagram moments or airing her personal business online, which I admired but the GMNY higher-ups hated.

Answering some fan emails and Facebook posts and logging a quick blog post about the ornament wreath wasn't an abnormal way to spend the rest of my morning, but really, I could've done it later. I just didn't want to face my producer.

Andrew had been my rock at the station from the start, guiding me with his 30-plus years of TV wisdom and endless cups of strong tea. Other than Kareena, he was the only person at the station who knew about Mum's hoarding, and I could tell him anything without feeling judged. He'd been my biggest cheerleader when I said I wanted to turn my blog posts into a book (and the biggest nag when two years later, I still haven't finished it).

He'd always gone to bat for me when no one else would, and I couldn't help but feel like I was screwing him over. Andrew couldn't defend me forever, and to be honest, lately I felt like he hadn't been as enthusiastic about my segments.

Loads of scenarios ran through my head, and none of them seemed ideal. I wasn't naïve enough to believe Andrew would say "Great news!" and that would be the end of it. Our station manager would have to sign off, even if Andrew was okay with my gig on *Stuff*. And the last thing I needed was to rub my new boss the wrong way; although to be fair, my brother had the same problem.

I silently cursed Will as I headed down the hall to talk to Andrew. As usual, the responsibility fell on my shoulders. If I couldn't be on the show, it would look like Will wasn't good on his word. He hadn't exactly promised Mum would sign on, and I'm sure Pierce understood the mindset of a hoarder enough to realize she might be a no-go, but Will *had* told Pierce I'd definitely do it. Pierce was known in the industry as a humble, salt-of-the-earth type, but being a nice guy didn't mean he didn't have a show to run.

The things I do for this family.

I peeked my head around the corner to see Andrew sitting at his Yankees memorabilia-covered cube, head resting on his hands.

"Everything okay?"

"Sarah! Hey. What's up?" He practically jumped out of his seat, like the time I'd caught him looking at that video of the Victoria's Secret runway show.

"Just wanted to talk about a few things."

He gestured to the chair next to his cube. "Sorry. Distracted. Lots going on today with the new team in place and everything."

"Seems like it. Kareena said she overheard someone saying 'shit's going to change around here, and fast.' Or at least that's what she thought she heard, so who knows how accurate the story is."

Andrew didn't even crack a smile. "She's right. We intend to shuffle some things around."

"Oh wow," I said, secretly wondering if Andrew's job was on the line. Or mine. "Is everything okay with—"

"Nothing for you to worry about." His clipped tone made me think otherwise.

"So ... tomorrow with the mom makeovers and Katie Douglas. Anything else I need to know?"

His eyes brightened at the change in subject. Andrew had been talking about this segment for weeks, and had finally nailed down the latest runner-up on *The Bachelor* to help out with a mom makeover contest. "The ladies arrived today; they're at the hotel now. Tomorrow they'll come on set to do a quick Q&A with you. Katie will take them backstage to do the makeovers, then at the end of the hour we'll do the reveal."

"Perfect! I'm really looking forward to meeting her."

Andrew shuffled a stack of papers on his desk. "Is that it?" he said. "I'm pretty busy, so ...."

I stepped back, surprised at his not-so-subtle attempt to kick me out of his cube. "Actually, I came to speak to you about something unrelated to the show. But if now's not a good time, we could chat tomorrow."

"Is everything okay? I'm sorry. I didn't even ask you about visiting your family. This crap at the station ... it's not an excuse." His expression softened, and in that moment, a glimpse of my mentor was back.

I looked around and the coast seemed clear enough; one of the other producers was on her phone, furiously scribbling notes, and a few cubes over, the interns were having a meeting. I took a deep breath.

"Remember I told you Will was looking for a new job? Well he got hired as an associate producer on *Stuff*."

He clapped his hands together and grinned. "Good for him. That's a pretty big move up. I guess they liked the hands-on experience factor."

"You could say that," I said. "But the thing is, Will's boss wants Mum to be on an episode ... and me as well. Will pitched the idea of me coming on as a sort of organizational consultant and they all loved it."

"Wait, *what*?" It was like a dark cloud moved over Andrew's office and rained all over my parade, replacing his sunny demeanor with raised eyebrows, hunched shoulders and a pissed-off expression. It was like being in England and forgetting your umbrella. "Please tell me you didn't agree to it."

I bit my lip. "I didn't. But Will did."

"For fuck's sake, Sarah!"

I silently thanked the loudness of New Yorkers and the prevalence of F-bombs at the station, because no one even glanced our way.

"Sorry," I said, "I don't know what I'm supposed to do here. At first, I was angry. And embarrassed. But the more I thought about it, I realized I was offered an opportunity that could change my career in a way I never expected, and would help my mother at the same time. So I want to jump on it. Tell me you wouldn't do the same."

"What I wouldn't do, is screw my producer over, and the rest of the team at the station, for that matter."

My fists clenched and my body felt as hot as the steaming mug of English Breakfast on Andrew's desk, but I fought to keep my tone carefully controlled. "I'm not quitting my job, so exactly how am I screwing you over? By taking a role that will give me— and therefore, our show—national exposure? By helping my brother and my mum? I'd like to know."

"Well, to start, who's going to replace you on GMNY while you're filming?"

"It's not like I've never gone on holiday. The taping is only a week or so. You'll survive without me. And Kareena has offered to come up with some extra restaurant and nightlife ideas to fill in the gap for *Sarah Says*."

He tapped his thumbnail against his teeth a few times, which he always did when he was deep in thought. "While we could possibly work with that, what happens when I tell Leslie? You're putting me in a really freaking awkward position here, Sarah. We're all on thin ice as it is."

"I know, and I'm sorry. But it's not like I volunteered myself. Will told them I'd do it, I think partly to entice Pierce to give him the job. I'm backed into a corner here."

He leaned his head against the back of his desk chair and sighed. "I'll see what I can do. But I make no promises."

I blew Andrew a kiss. "You're a star. And I'm happy to meet with management anytime, of course."

"Oh, you can count on that. And Sarah?"

"Yeah?"

"You might want to ask Pierce if that job's a permanent offer, just in case."

❀ Debbie ❀

"MY, MY. If it isn't Debbie, queen of England."

The uneasy feeling in the pit of my stomach hadn't dissipated since Pierce called, so instead of going home after work the next afternoon, my car decided to take me to the antiques store ... and into the path of my not-so-secret admirer, Rich Sullivan.

"Rich. How was your Thanksgiving?" I tried to smile in a friendly, but not *overly* friendly manner. Didn't want him to think I was coming on too strong.

"It was all right, thanks. You know how it is with families." He brushed some dust off his signature chambray shirt and crossed the shop with extended arms, pulling me in for a bear hug.

I'd been shopping at Something Old for as long as it had been on Lancaster Avenue, which was going on five years, but it was only recently that the chatty friendship I'd developed with Rich seemed to have turned into something else.

We'd met at Starbucks a few times for coffee, and then Starbucks turned into a Sunday matinee, and before I knew it, we were ... well, I don't know if you'd call it dating, but we'd been speaking on the phone a few times a week, and I popped into the store often enough. In my other life, Alan's shrink had told me to come up with other ways to pass the time when I felt the urge to visit a shop, but if I had, I would've never met Rich, so what did she know?

A lovely display of red and white teacups, old cookie tins, and other Christmasy items sat just beyond the heavy old door, and I stopped to examine it.

"I know what you mean about the holidays. Always some

kind of drama, am I right?" I picked up a rusty metal birdcage, turning over the price tag. Other than a few terse text message exchanges with Anne (and five missed calls from Will), I hadn't addressed the Pierce situation. I probably deserved a "World's Most Crap Mother" plaque for ignoring my own son's calls, but I wasn't ready to face the music yet.

"Want to talk about it?" Rich said.

"My family? Or the birdcage?"

He chuckled. "I'm guessing that's a no on family and yes on this thing."

"Right you are. And this could stand a coat of paint, but I think it's definitely salvageable." I lifted the birdcage and Rich nodded.

"It would hardly take any work at all to get this looking brand new. What do they call it? You know that style that's supposed to look like everything's cozy and worn but it actually costs out the behind?"

I laughed. "Shabby chic?"

"That's the one. I'm too old for that crap. Call a spade a spade, I say!" He took the birdcage from my hand and placed it on the counter, a long, gorgeous rough wood piece that he once told me used to sit in a French floral shop in the early 1900s. "My treat."

I wanted to protest, but the cage *was* darling, and with some glittery pink paint and a battery-operated candle inside, it was almost exactly what Anne had talked about hanging in Ruby's bedroom. "Rich, you really don't have to, but thanks. That's so sweet. My granddaughter will adore this."

He shook his head and laughed. "No worries. I'm only going to ask one small favor in return. Join me for dinner at Christopher's on Saturday?"

I could almost hear his heart beating in anticipation, but what took me by surprise the most was my own quickened pulse. Dinner at a decent restaurant felt like so much more than a quick coffee or sitting in silence next to each other at a movie.

Like a proper date.

"That sounds lovely. But fair warning: I haven't dated in a few decades. I'm not good at these things."

Rich shrugged as he wrapped the birdcage in pale blue tissue paper and placed it in a raffia-handled bag. "Believe me, I get it. It's been six years since Angela passed and it doesn't get any easier. But you gotta keep on keepin' on, right?"

"KBO," I said, nodding in agreement, and he cocked his head to the side. "Churchill. That was one of his famous sayings, Keep Buggering On." It was advice I could've used myself, but he didn't need to know that just yet.

"I'll have to remember that one. But yeah, that's why I opened the shop. It was something Angela always talked about, and we had all these plans ..." He stopped and cleared his throat, clearly emotional. "Well, after I stopped feeling sorry for myself, I realized I needed to move ahead and not let her dream go to waste. So I KBOd, as you said, and got to work."

I looked at the perfectly kept little store around me in a new light. The weathered wrought iron tables, blue fairy lights, toile wallpaper ... despite our years of chit-chatting about the kids, the weather, and the latest football scores, I never realized he'd created this space all on his own to fulfill his wife's dream. As much as I felt we'd shared with each other, maybe we'd only scraped the surface level. What did he know about my messy house or divorce, after all?

Something about Rich's vulnerability in the moment, or maybe my own lack of vulnerability, made me shuffle my feet in awkwardness. "You have a wonderful shop, and you should be proud."

He beamed at me as he slid the shopping bag across the counter, not seeming to notice my discomfort. "I've got to finish some paperwork before we close for the day, but I'm looking forward to Saturday. Why don't I pick you up around seven? Text me your address."

The hairs on the back of my arms stood up. *Bloody hell.*

"Oh, you know what? I told Anne I'd stop over for a few hours on Saturday, so I'll be coming straight from there. I'll meet you at Christopher's at seven, then."

"It's a date."

Relief washed over me. Crisis averted ... at least this time.

～⌒

Back at home brewing a cup of Earl Grey, I wondered if I'd done the right thing by accepting Rich's dinner invitation. Where did I expect this relationship to go? And what if he eventually asked to come over? One didn't go decades withholding relationships by accident.

It was Alan's fault, of course. Everything was his fault.

I poured my hot water into a floral Emma Bridgewater mug and leaned against the counter, glaring at the basket across the floor. One piece per day. That's what I'd agreed with myself upon. It might take a while, but that was all I could manage at the moment.

My phone buzzed from across the kitchen, vibrating against the laminate countertop. Will. Again. My finger hovered over the ignore button, but I sighed and answered it instead.

"Mum! I've been worried sick. Where have you been?"

"Sorry, darling. I didn't mean to cause a fuss, but all of this has been a lot to take in, as I'm sure you can imagine."

"I was literally about to call the cops. I'm sitting here picturing you crushed under a pile of *Hello!* bleeding magazines, and then I'm like well crap, how am I going to tell this story? I'll be on a date with some guy and he'll say 'Sorry to hear your mother's dead, how did she pass?' And I'll have to be like, 'Oh, you know, CRUSHED BY MAGAZINES.'"

I held the phone away from my ear and let him shout away. It was best to let him get it out of his system. "Are you quite done now?"

"No, not really. But I'm glad you're all right. So I guess you're ready to talk about the meeting with Pierce?"

"I never agreed to a meeting, Will."

He made the weird clicking sound he always made with his tongue when he was annoyed. "Hold on a second?"

The line went silent for about twenty or thirty seconds, and just as I was about to hang up, Will came back. "You guys there?"

Anne and Sarah's voices came across the line. "Yup."

Three against one.

"Oh," I said, startled. "Wasn't expecting you two."

"This isn't how I wanted to go about it," Will said. "But ... well, we had an idea."

"For the record, I had nothing to do with this," Anne said.

Will hesitated for a few beats and then let out a frustrated sigh. "Mum, at the end of the day, this isn't actually your house. It's in Dad's name. If he wanted to sell it, he's entitled. And I can't imagine he'd be thrilled about its current condition."

My mouth went dry and I nearly dropped the phone. *No. They wouldn't. Would they?*

"Mum? Are you still there?"

Finally I opened my mouth. "Is that a threat?"

"No, it's not a threat, it's a fact," Anne said. "We hate it for it to come down to this, but if you refuse to meet with Pierce, Sarah's going to have to speak to our father at Christmas about the house."

Even in my shaky state, I noticed her use of "Sarah." Once again, the twins weren't making the trip to England. Not that I could blame them.

"And what makes you think he gives a rat's arse about me or what I do? He's not sending his mother over to check on me now that he's busy with that little blond twinkie of his. She's barely even legal."

"They've been married for ten years, Mum," Sarah said. "And I think thirty-seven would classify as quite legal."

As usual, Sarah straddled party lines, while Anne and Will

remained silent on the topic of Gemma. At least they had *some* loyalty to me.

"Alan might be many things, but he wouldn't sell the house out from under me and put the mother of his children on the streets." I said this with as much confidence as I could muster, because deep down, I didn't know if I was right. Alan bought that house for his family, but the kids were grown and gone. And he'd moved on a long time ago.

"I don't know exactly what he'll say," Sarah said. "But you know how house-proud Nanny Percy is. And you're on your last warning with her as it is."

"My housekeeping skills are none of her concern." A flush crept across my face remembering the last time my former mother-in-law "popped in for a visit" from England. More than a decade later and I could still hear the swish of her finger along the curio, inspecting for dust.

"Well technically—" Anne started.

"Please, just hear Pierce out," Will cut in. "It will only take an hour or two and then you can be on your way. He's a laid-back kinda guy, not some Hollywood schmoozer. You'll like him, I really think you will."

There was a sharp intake of breath on the other line, and I couldn't tell if it was Will, Anne, Sarah, or all three at once.

"You've tied my hands," I said. "Do what you need to do."

Before any of them could respond, I hung up the phone and tossed it across the counter. It slid off and landed on the tile with a sickening crack. At that moment, I didn't even care. My screen had shattered so many times from dropping it in this place those Genius Bar nerds knew me by name. At least a cleanup would save me some money at the Apple Store.

I let out a bitter laugh and dumped my tea in the sink. Trying to talk me into appearing on *Stuff* was one thing, but using Alan to force me into it? That was the lowest blow they could throw at me.

It's not like I'd be homeless if Alan did take the house; I could probably afford a little fifty-five-plus condo or something. But I surely wouldn't be able to afford to live in Wayne anymore. There would go all of my shopping money down the drain if I had to pay a mortgage, and where would I put everything?

I would have to do *Stuff*. It was the only way.

I squared my shoulders and stepped over a few bags to reach for the basket of Alan, or BOA, as I'd come to call it. Like the snake, it had managed to wrap itself around me and squeeze all of the air out.

"So there, little boa," I said, realizing I probably sounded mad (talking to yourself couldn't be a good sign). "What next?"

It was almost like digging into a bucket of Halloween candy and wondering if you'd get the M&Ms or something crappy like a packet of peanuts. Although to be fair, I wasn't expecting any sweets in this basket. Especially not after the phone call I'd just had.

I took a deep breath, closed my eyes and reached in, feeling a cool, round piece of metal. When I opened them, Diana and Charles smiled back at me, this time from a cheap plastic button emblazoned with OUR ROYAL WEDDING.

～

London, July 1981

Every time I thought about it, I imagined springing out of bed when the alarm went off, jumping up and down like a toddler on Christmas morning. Instead I barely slept the night before. Having to lay on the hard ground for two nights around a bunch of crazy, loud drunks didn't make for ideal shut-eye, and the nervous energy floating in my stomach made it impossible to sleep.

It might as well have been my own bloody wedding day.

Alan, Carol, George and I took our places on The Mall two days before, thinking we'd be one of the first to arrive, but obviously we were mistaken. After the riots a few weeks prior, it seemed England was in the mood to find something to cheer for, and I couldn't believe how many people had actually decided to sleep on the streets just to catch a glimpse of the prince and princess.

Alan, bless him, even painted a flag on his face the morning of the wedding, and the white blazer made a triumphant return along with a red bow tie and a wilting carnation shoved into a buttonhole. To be fair, he also was drunk out of his mind, having not gone to bed after a night out with George, so that helped in the upbeat mood factor. Carol and I had kept watch on our spot while they hit the town; pub hopping was out of the question for us at that point.

"I've never seen anything like this in America," I shouted over the cheers of the crowd as the Horse Guards paraded past in a whirl of red and black, trying to snap a picture with my cheap 110 camera with one hand whilst waving a miniature flag with the other.

Carol nodded, too excited by the day to disagree. "Yeah, England has us beat in the pageantry department."

We'd dressed for the occasion in jeans and matching red polo shirts, and pinned souvenir buttons emblazoned with Diana and Charles's slightly blurry picture on our chests. Sparkly red, white and blue crown brooches attached to a ribbon headband finished the look, a cheap pick-me-up Carol insisted on buying for us after a lousy morning the past Saturday.

Suddenly the volume increased by about a hundred decibels. Carol and I clutched each other's arms. *They were in sight.*

As the clip-clop of horses got closer, the roaring grew so loud that Alan put both hands over his ears, laughing and jumping up and down at the same time. "YEAH ENGLAND!!!!!" he shouted while I tried to stand on my toes and see above the many taller people in front.

"Get on my shoulders," Alan yelled into my ear, but I shook my head no. I wasn't going to be rude and block some other poor shorty's view, and it didn't seem like the greatest of ideas to begin with. I draped an arm around his waist instead and shifted my weight from one foot to the other, the adrenaline rushing through me like nothing I'd felt before.

I wondered what the dress would look like, or if we'd be able to lip-read what they said to each other. Really, all I cared about was seeing the new princess in the flesh; I'd seen Charles that morning on his way to the cathedral, but let's face it, everyone wanted a piece of Diana—poor Chas was just an afterthought.

Finally the royal carriage rolled right in front of us, and I swear Diana locked eyes with me for a second. Her smile looked kind, but hesitant. I smiled back my biggest, most confident grin, hoping to inject a bit of energy and love into her somehow.

Carol and I shouted "DIANA!!!" 'til our voices were hoarse, snapping photos and winding our cameras as fast as possible even though we knew damn well the pictures wouldn't turn out. Alan cheered along and waved his flag, while George snogged a new friend he'd met behind us.

"Look at that gown!" I shouted. "It's massive!"

I squinted to see the details better; looked like some bows and loads of ruffles. Maybe it wasn't the close-up view people were getting at home on their tellies, but for me it was a hundred million times better.

"I can't tell what he just said to her, but she looks terrified," Carol said.

"Wouldn't you be as well? Look at all of these people!"

Once they were gone and we'd seen the rest of the royal carriages (even Alan had been impressed by the Queen) we followed the swarm of people down The Mall toward the palace. Everyone seemed to move in an organized, well-behaved blob, and I laughed, trying to picture people in America do the same without pushing, shoving and acting like hooligans. Then again, I'd seen Alan's beloved Arsenal play, and the fans would definitely give us Americans a run for our money in the hooligan department.

Alan skipped ahead, leading the people around us into a

rousing version of "God Save the Queen." Carol shook her head. "So when are you going to tell him?"

I marched ahead, waving my flag and trying to keep my expression bright. "Don't know. I'm leaving in a week, so what's the point? Please don't mention it."

She sighed but said nothing, although I wondered if that had to do with the lack of sleep and the alcohol versus an actual desire to honor my wishes. Carol could have all the opinions she wanted, but she wasn't in the same situation, and she wasn't about to go home, either.

It seemed like hours, and maybe it was, while we waited for the big balcony kiss.

George was busy "getting to know" his new friend, Carol had struck up a conversation with the group of extremely inebriated, Union Jack beanie-wearing boys next to us, and Alan continued to be the unofficial mayor of the Charles and Di fan club. He marched around, singing patriotic songs I'd never heard of and leading the crowd in cheers of "WE WANT DI" while I sat on a small tartan blanket taking in the scene.

My feet and back ached from hours of standing and all I wanted to do was sleep, but the dancing, cheering and sounds of so many different languages coming together around me buoyed my spirits. The only word I could think of to describe the situation was *surreal*.

"You all right?" Alan said, finally plopping on the ground next to me. He kissed my cheek and then wiped his brow, his skin bright pink from a day in the sun. "Haven't had this much fun in ages!"

I smiled, stretching my feet across his lap. "I'm definitely never going to forget their wedding."

"One for the record books, this is." Alan leaned in to kiss me, and I melted in the embrace, even if he was a bit sweaty and certainly in need of a shower. I think everyone was wrapped up in the romance of the day, and Alan for one was riding high on the excitement and pageantry (most likely something else, too).

Although he always oozed positivity, I'd never seen him *that* buoyant about anything, much less a wedding.

"So," he said, pulling back with a smile. "One week to go. God, I'm going to miss you, Debs."

I patted the side of his face and looked down at the blanket, twisting the fringe on the side. *What was I supposed to say?*

"Alan..." He started tapping on my thighs, and I realized he was leg-drumming to "Born to Run." *Couldn't he sit still for a bloody second?*

"Alan, are you ...?"

He drummed away, lost in a zone.

"ALAN!" I grabbed his wrist mid-tap, the words spilling out before I could stop them.

"I'm pregnant."

Sarah Says

Makeovers are Magic

It's easy to get stuck in a rut, whether it's the same hairstyle or tired shade of pink nail polish. A fresh look isn't just about looking better on the outside, it's about feeling confident as well. So why not go for something new?

COLD WASHCLOTH, WET TEABAGS ... I pulled out all the stops to try to chase the circles and bags away the morning after our call with Mum, but even my top tips did little to help. Thank goodness for makeup artists.

I'd had maybe four hours of sleep after rehashing the situation with Will and Anne at length. Pierce was coming that Saturday, and it gave us a week to get Mum back on our sides.

I didn't see that happening.

I spent most of the ride to the station catching up on social media, since my appearance was a lost cause. My latest Instagram photo, a shot looking down at my new pink slingbacks, already had 400 likes. *You inspire me!!!! Can I be you when I grow up?*

It should have made me feel better, but instead I looked down at the shiny patent pumps and thought, *why would anyone want to be in my shoes right now?* I leaned my head against the town car's window, using my huge wool wrap (the official Diana, Princess of Wales tartan, courtesy of Mum) as a pillow. Who knew what kind of germs were on that door? *Drop scarf at dry cleaner*, I typed into my notes app.

Once I was in the makeup chair and a thick layer of foundation had been spackled onto my ghastly pale skin, I did feel just the tiniest bit better. As I fine-tuned the placement of a few errant curls and pressed my eyelashes into place, Andrew's reflection came into view.

"Morning. I hope you're not still upset about yesterday." He held a Starbucks cup with I'M SORRY scrawled on it in metallic gold marker. "A peace offering."

I took the red cup, grateful for both the caffeine and his change in attitude. "We're all under a lot of stress. It's okay."

"I talked to Leslie."

"And?" I smoothed out my tweed pencil skirt, not because it was wrinkled, but because I needed to wipe my sweaty palms. His expression was unreadable, although if I was getting sacked, he'd probably have said something already.

"It was ... productive. She had a lot of questions, but I said she'd have to ask you for specifics. It seems like everything will work out, though."

It felt like a small chunk of the weight on my shoulders had been lifted, but I'd only accomplished half of the task. "So she wasn't upset?"

"Hard to say."

"Ookay then," I said, shaking my head. "Let's worry about this later. We have a show to prepare for right now. Where's Katie?"

"In the green room. You should go out soon, if you're ready. We're going to play a short clip with their entry videos, then show the before shot, mom comes out, does a little twirl, Katie says some BS about her vision for the makeover, repeat with each woman. Sound good?"

"Fantastic."

As I passed, he grabbed my arm. "We're okay, right?"

"Of course. We're fine."

As I got situated in my chair and mic'd up, Kareena came over and patted my knee, a stack of gold bangles sliding down her arm with a soft jingle. "You kiss and make up with Andrew yet?"

I gave her a so-so hand motion. "Yeah, seems like it."

"He does have a point. You've worked together for a long

time and it's shitty for him to have to be put in this situation. However, and that's a massive *however* ... from what you told me, this could be a good thing for us. So I don't see why the big boss would shoot you down."

"Everything will be fine," I said, making sure to smile after I saw Andrew and a few others watching us. "Let's just forget about it."

"Can you stop shutting everyone out for one second? I'm trying to be helpful here."

Kareena didn't mirror my expression, but I kept the smile planted on my face. "Sorry. I just need to talk about something else right now. Okay?"

"Fine. You'll enjoy this: I saw Katie Douglas and she's pretty much what you'd expect. Platinum bob, lots of bronzer, toddler-sized denim skirt."

I laughed. "I still never get used to seeing people from TV in real life."

"Ironic, yes?"

"You can say that again."

Before we could properly chat about our pseudo-celeb guest, Andrew strode across the set, joking with one of the makeover moms. It always amazed me how he could go from tightly-wound control freak to world's biggest charmer once he was on set. But look who's talking.

The rest of the group followed behind, taking in the crowd of tourists pressed up against the station's glass windows. The bright lights and general craziness could be overwhelming even for TV professionals, but for some middle-aged women who'd never left the Midwest it appeared to be an out-of-body experi-ence.

Katie breezed into the room shortly after, chatting loudly on her cell phone, and plopped down on the chair next to me.

"Hi there! I've read your blog and think it's *adorable*," she said as soon as she ended the call. "I just love British people's ideas."

I wasn't sure whether to take that as a compliment, but smiled anyway. "Clever bunch, we are. But I can't take credit for all of it. My grandmother used to give me DIY projects all the time when I was a kid."

"Nanas are *the greatest*, aren't they?" she said. "But enough about that. I heard you were going to be on *Stuff*? Spill, girl-friend."

Andrew, who was chatting with another producer off to the side, met my panicked gaze. *Shit.*

"Wait. How do you know about *Stuff*?" I lowered my voice as I leaned in toward her. Was Pierce gossiping all over the industry when I hadn't even signed on yet?

"I used to date Pierce back in high school. His mama's friends with my mama … you know how it is. We had dinner last week and he seemed really jazzed about meeting you."

I don't know why this caught me so off guard; TV was inces-tuous as it was, and they were both from Georgia. It made sense. Still, I stared at her blankly for a moment before regaining my composure. "What a small world. I haven't signed anything yet, but yes, we're meeting Saturday."

"You'll adore him. Such a nice guy, we've been friends for ages. It takes a special kind of person to deal with hoarders, as I'm sure you know!" She said each sentence as if it were written in all caps with an exclamation point at the end, with volume to match.

"It does," I said, giving her a tight-lipped smile. The last thing I needed was for Andrew to think I went behind his back and agreed to do *Stuff* without the station's okay.

Luckily, we got the cue that the show was about to start, so I took a deep breath and faced the cameras, pushing my problems down and bringing a confident smile to the surface. "This morn-ing, *Sarah Says* makeovers are magic! We're transforming five deserving mothers from an Indiana book club, and we've got Katie Douglas, the most recent runner-up from *The Bachelor*, to help us."

Katie flashed her megawatt veneers at me, then the camera.

"I'm so happy to be here. And y'all will definitely want to have those tissues ready as we meet the winners of our makeover contest!"

Our contest? I meant to tap my foot on the teleprompter paddle to keep it moving, but it came down more like a stomp, and the screen skipped two lines too far ahead. *Shit.* The station had finally installed a system for the anchors to control their own teleprompters, instead of having the interns work them. To be fair, I was still getting used to the new technology. But I couldn't afford to mess up, not with Leslie watching my every move.

I caught a glimpse of Andrew off to the side of the camera, waving his hand frantically. He mouthed, "keep going."

"Well, I don't know about y'all, but I'm ready to take a look at these ladies!" Katie said, not missing a beat. Andrew gave a thumbs up.

She continued the overly enthusiastic routine as we went through the segment, ad-libbing way more often than Andrew would've ever let me get away with, even when I wasn't screwing up the teleprompter. Soon enough it was over, and Katie turned to me and gave a quick wave.

"Nice to meet you. I'm sure we'll be seeing more of each other real soon!" She hopped down from her seat and ran off to talk to Andrew.

"Well," I said to Kareena, who'd appeared at my side almost instantly after Katie's departure. "That was interesting."

"Indeed. Charming girl, but you don't think she's after a job here, do you?" Kareena flicked her eyes in the direction of Katie, who was deep in conversation with Andrew. He tapped something into his phone and nodded a few times.

"I thought I was being paranoid, but I guess not. I felt like she was trying to talk over me the entire segment."

Kareena pursed her lips. "Yeah, that was weird. But I wouldn't think too much of it. I heard she got a gig on *E! News,* anyway."

"Let's hope that's true." While Kareena kept a close ear to broadcasting gossip, she always seemed to mix up the details, like the time she insisted Tom Cruise was going to be a guest on GMNY, but it ended up being Tom Selleck (who was lovely, by the way).

"Sarah! Can we chat?" Andrew gave me a get-here-this-second kind of wave.

"Good luck," Kareena whispered.

I stepped down from the carpeted risers and cleared my throat. "What did you think of the makeovers?"

"Good energy. Glad Katie can think on her feet." He gestured to the hall, guiding me out of the studio. "Why don't we step into the conference room?"

He opened the door, took a seat at the scratched faux wood table, and pulled out his phone before I could even step into the room. "Leslie should be on the way."

I crossed and uncrossed my legs, tapped my foot, then out of lack of anything else to do, got up and fixed myself a cup of coffee from the Keurig machine in the corner while we waited for the station manager. The awkward silence as Andrew tapped away at his phone made me want to spurt out small talk about the weather, but I sipped the terrible coffee instead.

"All right guys, I only have like five minutes," Leslie said, breezing in a couple of minutes later. Her shapeless black trousers and white button-up (complete with coffee stain) made her look like a catering waitress, not the manager of a station in the number-one market in America.

"Sarah, I understand you don't want to pass up this opportunity at *Stuff*, and I don't blame you," she said. "I think it would be some nice exposure for GMNY, if you can plug the show. But we'd have to consider how you're presented and what that would mean for our viewers' perceptions of you."

I nodded. I saw this one coming, and used my most professional, collected tone. *I've got this.* "That was exactly my concern when my brother pitched the idea to me. You know how seriously I take my image. But I do think this would be wonderful for our viewers to get a look at the real person behind all my tips."

"What I can't work out," Leslie said, "is whether people will think you're a fraud, or they'll admire how far you've come from your background. I know personally, I was shocked when I learned your mother was a hoarder. You give off this vibe like ..." she paused and smiled sweetly, clasping her hands in front of her like a goody-two shoes student. "You know, the perfect girl from the perfect family whose mother was wearing a 1950s apron walking around with a feather duster."

Andrew covered his laugh with a well-timed cough. "I think what Leslie is trying to say is we're worried how this might impact the *Sarah Says* brand in terms of you being an aspirational figure."

"You know, we want people we admire to be *just* a little bit unattainable," Leslie said. "If celebrities are exactly like us, then it takes away some of the dazzle, no?"

"So you *don't* want me to be on Stuff, then?" First the show was good exposure, then it was bad for my image. I couldn't quite work out which way they were going to go in the end.

"That's not what we're saying," Andrew said, running a hand through his cropped gray hair. "But if you do the show, I think it's a good idea to come up with a plan to make sure you come off in the best possible way."

"Andrew, you know as well as I do they could edit me to look however they want. But I'd do whatever it took to control my image, and show GMNY in a good light, obviously."

He nodded. "I know. And I think you'd do a great job. Do you know anything specific about timing yet?"

"Pierce Thompson is coming to my mother's house on Saturday for an initial meeting. I suspect we'll have more concrete details then, but from what my brother said, the filming should last about a week." I left out the part how Mum hadn't technically signed up for the show yet. No need to leave an air of uncertainty around the project.

"All right. Why don't we regroup Monday?" Leslie said, already tapping away at her phone. "Andrew, can you send me that list of potential replacements for Sarah when you get back to your desk?"

The contents of my breakfast threatened to come up. "Wait a second. I'm not leaving the show, I—"

"Calm down," Andrew said. "We just need someone to cover for you if you're out, that's all."

My heart was still pounding so loud I could barely hear the words come out of my mouth. "Okay, but I told you Kareena and I already worked out a plan where she'd cover during my absence. I have a list of all the segment ideas and proposed guests I can send you."

"I appreciate the effort, but Kareena has her own stories to worry about," Leslie said. "And we thought it would be a nice ratings boost to bring in some fresh blood. I'm guessing *Stuff* wouldn't start filming until after the New Year, so a celebrity guest host would be perfect if we could line it up with sweeps."

I locked eyes with Andrew, silently pleading for him to take my side. Don't know why I bothered, because he wasn't going to throw himself under the bus.

"This is a solution we think will work well for everyone," Andrew said. "And luckily, I spoke with Katie Douglas after the show today and she would be happy to come on board if we asked."

To my credit, I didn't let my mouth drop to the floor. Instead, I gave them a surprised little smile, like it was a pleasant interruption in my morning to hear some twenty-six-year-old reality star could mean the end of my future at the station.

❀ Debbie ❀

London, August 1981

"IT'LL BE FINE, you'll see, Debs." Alan fluffed his pillow, then reached over to pat my stomach. "And since we're getting married, now you can stay after all. We'll get a flat together, push the baby around Regents Park in his pram. It'll be great."

Not exactly my idea of *great*, I thought. But Alan was at least partially right. Now I didn't have to leave him. Or London for that matter. Plenty of girls I knew from my hometown already had babies. If they could do it, surely I could, too?

"How are you so sure it's a him?" I asked, resting my hand on top of his. It was pointless really, since it was far too early to feel anything move, but somehow I was convinced if I held my hand on my belly long enough that something would happen.

"Dunno, just do." He pulled his hand back and rolled out of my bed. "Now all we have to do is break the news to our parents."

He said this as if he'd uttered a perfectly commonplace sentence, then pulled on the t-shirt and jeans that had been crumpled up on the floor. I still hadn't told my own parents, but at least an ocean separated us. I knew they didn't have the funds to fly overseas and wring my neck. The thought of Alan's upper-class (and nearby) family giving me the stare-down sent chills up my spine.

Hopefully they wouldn't think I got "up the duff" on purpose to take advantage of Alan's trust fund. The only thing that happened on purpose was the amount of alcohol consumed at my flat after the Springsteen concert, and a frantic need to take moving home out of my mind.

I padded out of bed and took the fourth pee break of the morning before collapsing on the sofa. The constant exhaustion still took me surprise, and I couldn't help but feel envious of Carol, who was off at her new job in the City. She was probably having a fancy lunch meeting, sipping wine while I was holding back vomit and planning a shotgun wedding to my baby's father. On the bright side, at least I wasn't going back to Pennsylvania, so there was that.

"So," I said, thumbing through the phone book. "I'll call and find out what we have to do to get the marriage license and my visa sorted and everything."

"Brilliant," Alan called out from the kitchen, where he was fixing himself (and hopefully me) a cuppa. "George can be our witness. Or I could ask my brother, I suppose."

"What about Carol? She *is* my flatmate, and the only one who knows about the baby, after all."

He walked in with a single steaming cup and placed it on the coffee table without a coaster, splashing tea on the glass top. "That's fine. Whatever you want to do, Debs."

I nodded. "Yes. That's what I want to do. And thanks for the tea, by the way."

"Oh. Erm ... sure." He made a hasty exit to the kitchen and turned the kettle back on. I might've loved him, but he really *was* a wanker at times, despite his proclamation at the pub the first night we met.

I shimmied my way into a seated position and watched him humming away to the radio as he fixed his tea. You'd think he didn't have a care in the world. And, other than the whole "my American girlfriend got pregnant and now I have to marry her" situation, he didn't. His parents would be angry at first, but from what Alan had told me, they'd probably still pay for everything. Then our baby could end up just like him, expecting everyone else to sweep in when things became difficult. Fantastic.

"Keep calm. There's nothing to worry about," Alan said as one of the poshest houses I'd ever seen came into view. We'd made the hourlong drive out to Brentwood to see his parents, and keeping calm was the last thing I could do. Alan broke the news to them the previous week, and while they obviously weren't pleased, he said they didn't freak out. Then again, they were English.

The driveway leading up to the house had stretched on forever, and I guessed that for every extra second in the car, the grander the house would be. I wasn't wrong. When we passed a lake complete with a bridge and gazebo on an island in the middle, I decided I'd shut up and let Alan do the talking, because I was clearly out of my league.

The gravel crunched under my feet as we got out of the car and walked up to the house, all classic brick and perfectly symmetrical lines. White columns surrounded the massive red front door and three pointy turrets of sorts at the top of the house faced the immaculate green lawn sloping down to the water.

"So," Alan said, "this is Percy Hall."

It wasn't just morning sickness that had my stomach twisted tighter than the Queen's knickers. I'd been nervous enough about Alan's parents' reaction to meeting me, but now that I'd seen where they lived, it was a hundred times worse. My parents' one-story house with yellow siding and overgrown grass seemed absurd in comparison ... almost like the picture you'd see in a dictionary next to "trashy American suburbia." The Percys' home was a legitimate old-timey English mansion.

I wondered if there was one of those "Queen Elizabeth I slept here" plaques somewhere, like Carol and I saw on some of our field trips to stately homes during uni.

Alan pressed the doorbell and a tiny brunette woman, who I assumed was his mother (or a really well-dressed maid) opened the door. "Alan, my dear." She said this with an almost imperceptible sigh, as if the greeting had taken some sort of effort.

Still, she smiled at us, so I stood there attempting to look pleasant, not sure if I should introduce myself first, or what. The rules of the English upper class baffled me, but then again, I'd already gotten myself knocked up ... any other infractions would surely pale in comparison.

"It's nice to meet you. I'm Debbie. As you probably have guessed." She shook my hand with the limpest of handshakes possible, then smiled tightly. "Sarah Percy. Come in now, don't want you waiting outside all day in your condition."

She led us into the most typical stately home drawing room I could imagine, where old-as-dirt-looking paintings of ancestors framed in gold hung on the walls next to heavy burgundy drapes. The only undraped window was made of shimmering stained glass, with a massive Percy family crest that looked like something out of the Tudor age. Deep red Oriental rugs covered the hardwood floor, and mismatched, but definitely antique furniture, filled the room. Mr. Percy sat on a floral chair next to a roaring fire (even though it was September) and smoked a cigarette.

"Well then. I suppose we should get down to this whole nasty business," he said by way of introduction.

My heart felt like it'd dropped into my stomach. So he was going to play hardball.

Alan grabbed my hand and led me to the overstuffed love seat across from his father. "Dad, like I told you, we've got this all sorted. Debbie and I are getting married straightaway. She'll be able to stay here, and give birth in London. We'll raise him together and get a flat."

"I see," Mr. Percy said. "And what will you do for work? How do you plan on supporting this child?"

In typical Alan fashion, he leaned back with a lazy smile and folded his arms. "I'll figure it out. I can always work for Mark's club."

"There are ... *options* in these situations. Have you thought about that, Alan?"

At least Mrs. Percy shot her husband a horrified look, so I knew she wasn't entirely terrible.

"Options?" I said, holding a hand up before Alan could speak. "I'm sorry, I'm really not trying to be rude, but I'm the one who's pregnant, not your son. And I'd appreciate it if you could at least pretend I'm sitting in this room."

"Debs, calm down. It's just his way." Alan put his arm around me, and I was glad for the comfort, but my hands still shook.

"It's because of you that we're in this mess, is it not?" Mr. Percy crossed one gray trousered leg over the other, tapping his fingers on the chair's armrest. *Now I know where he gets it.*

"Henry, it takes two to tango, as they say." Mrs. Percy put a hand on her husband's shoulder. "These two are scared enough. The poor girl's shaking. And we're talking about our future grand-child."

My mouth turned up in a tiny, but grateful smile. "Thank you, Mrs. Percy. We want to do the right thing and get married and be a family. Alan's not trying to shirk responsibility, and a lot of other guys our age would probably have run off. You've raised a good son."

"And what do *your* parents think about this?" Mr. Percy said, looking at me for the first time. When he wasn't scowling, I could see the resemblance to Alan. Same nose, same glint in the eye ... although instead of cheeky, his glint was a bit more calculating and hard. I wondered what had happened to Mr. Percy over the years to take the sparkle away.

"They weren't pleased. As you can imagine. But I'm an adult, and they'll have to accept it." I didn't want to add that my mother had hung up, then airmailed me the world's biggest guilt trip, going on and on about how their only daughter had humiliated all of them, and that none of her friends' daughters would *ever* do something as dumb as getting pregnant by a guy they barely knew. In another country.

Mr. Percy let out a deep sigh and stood up. "Do what you want to do, Alan. I've said my piece. Your mother can take over from here." With that he stalked out of the room, a puff of smoke drifting over Alan and me as he slammed the door.

Messes are an inevitable part of life, but cleaning them up doesn't have to be a bother. Create your own cleaning spray with a half cup of distilled white vinegar, a half cup of water, and about twelve drops of your favorite essential oil. Simple and cheap, and the best part—it works a treat!

"ON THE BRIGHT SIDE, you didn't get sacked," Will said, biting his lip. We'd met for coffee after work, since I desperately needed to talk to someone about the Katie situation.

I grimaced. "I'm sure I will be once Little Miss Sunshine takes over. What if they see a big ratings boost and want to keep her on? They even mentioned sweeps."

"Darling, I can barely hear a word you're saying," Will shouted, leaning in closer across the tiny high-top table. Between the tourists, holiday shoppers and office worker crowd, the café was so loud I initially complained about meeting there ... until I realized it was probably a good thing that half of New York wasn't going to overhear our conversation.

"Anyway," I said, leaning closer and raising my voice just slightly, "Even if she sucks, I'm still screwed. If the ratings are worse, it'll be my fault for leaving."

"I can always talk to Pierce and let him know you couldn't take the time off ...."

I shook my head. "I've already put this plan in motion at the station, plus Mum needs the help. The only problem is Anne."

It was a subject to approach carefully, since Will would either defend his twin to the death, or join in on a massive vent session.

There was no way to tell which direction the wind would blow. Fortunately, he nodded.

"Agree. I'd like Anne to be fully on board before we give it a go with Mum this weekend. We need to show a united front."

"Definitely. If I'm going to put myself out there and risk my job, I think it's only fair for her to be on the show as well. We're a family and we should stick together."

"I'll sort it all out this afternoon."

"Well, if you want me to sit in on the phone call with you, I can," I offered, crossing my fingers under the high-top table. Hopefully he'd turn me down. She was *his* twin, after all.

"That's all right, I got us into this mess. And she usually listens to me, anyway." He might as well have said, "She'll get pissed off if you lecture her about what's fair," because let's face it, that was the truth.

Back at my apartment, I kicked off my heels and changed into a pair of monogrammed silk pajamas, then plopped on the bed. I decided to spend the night putting together a rough plan to show Pierce: organization products, a diagram of the house, the works. I was an hour into preparing the binder when Will called.

"She hung up on me."

I fell back on my pile of pink pillows with a soft thud ... and a loud groan. "I can't say I'm surprised. What did you tell her?"

"I suggested we all needed to be involved fully on the show, and she got increasingly shouty, like 'What will my in-laws say?' blah blah blah."

"Shit. So what do we do?"

"Can you speak to her? I know I said it wasn't necessary before. But maybe she just needs to hear another perspective."

I sighed. "I can't imagine there's anything I can say that would change her mind, but if you really want me to, I'll try."

"She'll come round." I could hear the doubt in Will's voice, though.

We chatted a few more minutes, and I hung up with a twitchy

feeling in my legs. I loved my brother, and I wanted Mum's house to get clean, but wondered if this job was really worth the drama.

I wanted to give Anne some time to cool off, so I went back to the organization plan. But after staring at the same list of ideas for five minutes, I couldn't see myself concentrating enough to finish. I debated whether to write a blog post about handling tricky family situations, but decided against it. Despite her snobbery and other faults, Anne was a loyal *Sarah Says* reader.

What I needed was some escapism. I turned on my IP address blocker app, which I'd bought specifically to watch all of my UK shows that were blacked out in America. A moment later I was watching the latest episode of my favorite guilty pleasure reality show, *Essex Girls*. Since Dad owned half the clubs in Brentwood, he showed up on screen from time to time, even though it was totally cringey watching him chat up twenty-somethings who wore more makeup than a TV anchor (and that's a *lot*). There was no sign of Dad this time, but Lolly and James had broken up yet again, which helped take my mind off my own drama. They were in the middle of a massive row outside a restaurant, with her screaming "DON'T MUG ME OFF!" when a buzz came from my phone. Anne.

"I'm taking it you want to speak about this whole reality show mess?" I said, pressing pause on the computer. So much for giving her time to calm down.

Anne made a weird tutting sound. "I'm being put in an extremely awkward situation here."

It didn't surprise me that the only thing my sister was worried about was putting *herself* in an uncomfortable position. What about Mum? Or me? Or my boss for that matter, because he'd said the same exact thing to me a few days earlier.

"I understand that, but all of us are out of our comfort zones. I think you can make some sacrifices, too."

"Oh, because I don't have anything better to do than have people film me hauling out trash?" Anne said, raising her voice enough for me to hold the phone away from my ear. "I don't have two kids under six? A mother's group to run? A husband who's never home?"

Here we go again. "Not at all what I meant. But I'm putting my career on the line to do this for Mum, and for Will. If I can leave New York for a week, you can drive the five minutes from your house and help clean up."

"Just because I don't have some flashy job, it doesn't mean I don't have a life. Who'd watch Ruby and Charlie if I was off filming?"

"What about Rob's parents? They're retired. Or could he take a day or two off?"

I don't even know why I said it, because my brother-in-law had flown back to Philly in the middle of their Disney trip last year because of a client problem.

"Right. Because he's going to take time off work so I can embarrass him on TV and, quote-unquote, ruin the business reputation he's taken thirteen years to build."

"It's not like you're going to be standing there wearing his company T-shirt, Anne. How would anyone even know unless they A) happened to watch the episode and B) also knew you were Rob's wife?"

"Bad news travels fast on the Main Line. You know that as well as I do." I thought about the mothers at Ruby's $30,000-a-year private elementary school and the field day they'd had when Anne's neighbor went to prison for a ponzi scheme. Ending up on a hoarding reality show was probably more embarrassing in their minds than making a few "teensy little business mistakes," as the neighbor's wife had put it.

"Well unless Rob tells people you're going to be on *Stuff,* I still don't see how anyone would be the wiser," I said. "Plus, how are we supposed to convince Mum she shouldn't be embarrassed to do the show if you're too ashamed to participate yourself?"

"Seriously? Don't touch your brother's nose!" Scuffling noises and the sound of running water ensued on the other line, then Anne's voice came back. "Sorry. Yeah, I get what you're saying.

And I'll be there Saturday, but as for being on TV, it's up in the air. I don't want to end up D-I-V-O-R-C-E-D over this."

"Is he really going to divorce you for helping your family?"

"Can you just leave it, Sarah? Like I said, I can't guarantee a thing. But I've considered what you said."

A tiny wave of relief washed over me. "Right, well I'm off to take care of some things. I'll see you Saturday?"

"RUBY! Honestly, I told you not to ..." Click.

Why were my siblings incapable of properly ending a conversation?

I set the phone on my nightstand next to a worn copy of "Get Rid of Your Accent." I'd bought it when I first started preparing my reel to interview for TV jobs; who wanted to hire someone the viewers wouldn't be able to understand?

Andrew agreed if I was going to keep my English accent, stations wanted to hear inoffensive, proper BBC English, not Essex girl banter (the first time I said "think" as "fink" I thought he was going to pass out). Now I could barely remember what my real voice sounded like, except when I visited Dad and Nanny, or if I was stressed. After that phone call with Anne, I probably could've been hired for the cast of *Essex Girls* straight away.

As for going back to my roots, there were only two weeks until my flight to London for the holidays. Would I have to bring Dad into this whole mess, too? Will might've suggested using the house as leverage, but considering he hadn't spoken to Dad since Ruby was born, I knew the dirty work would be left to me.

I turned the show back on and tried to do my calming yoga breaths, but all I could think about was stuff ... as usual.

Sarah Says

Meet Your Boss Like a Boss

It can be overwhelming to meet a new
manager for the first time, but there's
no need to freak out. Show your personality, speak up, and prove that you're
a valuable member of the team with ideas
and input on key projects. Most impor-
tantly, don't forget to smile!

"SO HAVE YOU HEARD FROM ANNE?" I put my phone on speaker
and tapped my nails on the stack of Jane Austen novels piled on
Mum's kitchen table. Pierce was due to arrive any minute, and I
had no idea if my sister had even spoken to Rob about *Stuff*, since
my texts had gone unanswered all week.

"She said she'd meet me at the restaurant," Will said. "Are
you sure you're okay there alone? I can come back if you feel
awkward."

"No, no. I'm fine. You just enjoy and keep Mum calm. Order
some wine if you need to."

Will and Anne had offered to take Mum out to lunch so Pierce
could take an initial look at the house without interruption, so it
was up to me to stay behind and give him the grand tour. Will
said it would be for the best; we didn't want Mum to go into
panic mode the second she saw someone's reaction to the hoard,
then refuse to go through with the show. But I wondered if we
were protecting her too much, considering she was about to have
an entire crew come to her house for the sole purpose of throwing
things away.

I said goodbye to Will and stepped into the carport to get a
breath of fresh air. Twenty minutes in Mum's house and my chest
already felt tight; how was I going to manage an entire week?

I sat on the bench and wrapped my arms around my thin cashmere turtleneck, inhaling the scent of fresh pine. The wreath on Mum's door, complete with glittery Union Jack heart baubles, reminded me of simpler days when it was just us kids, Mum, and Dad watching the Queen's Christmas message and going caroling with our friends. Before everything got so complicated and a Christmas visit with family required crossing an ocean.

Suddenly Mum's attachment to these old things didn't seem quite so silly. But whether or not I could relate was irrelevant, because a shiny black BMW pulled into the driveway. Everything was about to change.

I looked at my watch ... precisely eleven. Part of me hoped he'd get tied up with some sort of important business and have to cancel, but Pierce Thompson was a man of his word, like Will said.

The driver-side door opened and I got my first glimpse of my new boss when a pair of long, denim-clad legs swung out. Pierce looked like a cross between a lumberjack and an old-school Abercrombie and Fitch ad in a plaid shirt and a red puffy vest as he walked up the driveway. Not exactly the type of guy who drove a luxury convertible.

He flashed a slightly lopsided grin at me and held out his hand. Even though he wasn't wearing gloves and it was forty degrees outside, Pierce's grasp felt toasty warm.

"You're tinier than I expected."

"Sorry?" I felt my cheeks redden, and not because of the cold.

"I just mean I've seen your show. Everyone looks taller on TV, don't they?"

I looked down at my ballet-flat clad feet. "It's probably the heels. I needed something a bit more sensible today. And I have to disagree, because you're even taller than you look on television."

He laughed. "Touché. And I'm sorry, I probably sounded rude as hell. Let's start over. Sarah! It's great to meet you."

"Lovely to meet you, too. I'm guessing Will told you he's at lunch with our mother and Anne, and they'll catch up with us after we do a little tour?"

"He did. You can go ahead and lead the way if you're ready."

I put my hand on the doorknob and closed my eyes for a second. *You can do this.*

We stepped inside and I waved my hand like Vanna White. "So, what do you think? Obviously you can be honest here."

Pierce took a long look around, turning in a circle and rubbing the scruff on his chin. "Honestly? It's not as bad as I thought."

A part of me felt relieved, another part wondered if I needed to throw some extra royal wedding magazines on the floor.

"Surely this would be the first, and probably last time anyone would refer to the house as such, but it's not too 'clean' is it?"

He laughed. "No, we're good. This is perfect actually. It's not often we see places with quite a ... theme."

I'll give the man credit, he didn't so much as flinch, even when he almost tripped over a bag of Kate and Pippa paper dolls as we shimmied through the path to the living room. Then again, that was Pierce's job, wasn't it?

With the exception of my last relationship I'd never brought a boyfriend, or even a friend, to the house, so it wasn't like I was used to processing anyone's reactions to the hoard outside of our family. Inexperience in handling a social situation was a new phenomenon for me; people wrote in to *Sarah Says* looking for answers, and I always delivered. What if I didn't know what I was talking about after all?

"How does she even afford all of this on a school secretary's salary?" he asked, leaning in to examine the contents of one of the many curio cabinets in the living room.

"Family money." He probably knew all the details from Will, or would find out from Mum soon, anyway.

Pierce picked up a few of the knick-knacks from a shelf, his mouth opening in a wide "O" when he saw the hand-painted, newborn baby-sized Prince George doll.

"Now *that* is something special, isn't it?" His mouth twitched at the corners.

"Go ahead, laugh if you want." I snatched the doll from him, cradling it almost like he was a real baby. Secretly, I did kind of like it, but I'd never tell Pierce that bit of information. "This doll was actually really expensive."

It felt like the old days when someone made fun of Anne at school. Even if she stole my Barbies and said I had bad hair, it was only okay for *me* to tease her.

"You can't come in here and ... and ..."

"And what?"

His perpetually relaxed posture and easy smile riled me up even more. I put my hands on my hips and finally spit out the words. "Just come in and start criticizing her Prince bloody George doll. I thought your job was to help people, not take the piss out of them. Not that you even know what that means."

He threw his hands up. "I'm sorry. I wasn't taking the piss. And I actually *do* know what that means, because I took my parents to London on vacation last year."

I raised my eyebrows.

"Okay, maybe I was taking a *tiny* bit of piss. But you've got to admit, not many people have one of these hangin' around."

I reached up to lay George back on his shelf. "Actually, 4,999."

"Huh?"

"It's a numbered, limited edition of 5,000," I said, smoothing George's christening gown. "So you could go in thousands of other homes and find one, in fact."

"Interesting. Well I'm definitely eager to get to know more about your mother. And you, too. Checked out the blog a few times and I was definitely impressed. That post about the ornament wreath, now *that* was something."

Based on his permanent "I look like I'm about to burst out laughing" smirk, I honestly couldn't tell if he was being sarcastic.

"You enjoy a bit of Christmas DIY at the weekend, then?"

He laughed. "You could say that."

"Fantastic. But I'm assuming you're not looking for me to create holiday décor out of people's household junk."

"Now do I sense some hostility here, Miss Percy?"

"Not at all. Just curious what's going to be expected of me," I added in a more polite voice. I didn't know what had come over me, because defensiveness over Mum's house was the last emotion I expected to bubble to the surface. *No need to piss off your potential employer within the first five minutes.*

Pierce smiled and nodded in a way that most people would reserve for someone in a mental institution and gestured toward the back of the house. "Why don't we take a look at her room?"

We climbed, ducked and side-stepped our way back into Mum's bedroom, where Pierce took a seat on the carpet, moving a plastic bin labeled "Early 80s Diana-replica fashions" aside so there was room for two. He patted the empty space next to him.

I hesitated for a second, wary of both the proximity to Pierce and the condition of the carpet ... although probably more of the former.

"I'll try not to bite, but I can't make any promises."

Uh oh.

"So," I said, lowering myself to the dusty pink carpet. "As you can tell, she's not sleeping in here anymore." We both looked up at the windowsill, where she'd at least had the sense to replace the old fire hazard candles surrounding her framed Diana photos with those new, battery-operated ones. Thank you, QVC.

Pierce said nothing for a minute as his eyes scanned the room, and I wondered if he was silently judging Mum, or me for that matter. Wasn't I supposed to be the expert here? He stretched out his legs, his boot catching on the handle of a plastic bag marked DIAMOND JUBILEE TEA TOWELS.

"It's sad when someone you love is crying out for help like this," Pierce said.

Anger bubbled to the surface and I turned back to Pierce with gritted teeth and a raised voice. My perfectly in control newscaster façade was falling away by the second. "Do you know how many times we've tried to clean this place up over the years? How many times I'd come back the next month and the house looked exactly the same, if not worse? It's not like Will, Anne, and I sat back and let her house become a storage shed while we lived our happy little lives."

He reached out and touched my shoulder. "I'm not blaming you. I just feel for your mother. I understand what you're all going through, as much as you think I don't."

"I'm sure you understand a lot—that people like Mum pay for your mansion and fancy convertible." I shrugged off his touch and he let out a low whistle.

"Good Lord, you've got a big old chip on your shoulder. And believe me, those start to get heavy. Oh, and not that it matters, but I drive the same beat-up Jeep from college. The rental place mixed up my reservation and the BMW was the only car they had left. I felt like an ass driving that thing here."

I looked down and tugged at my sweater, feeling my cheeks burn. I constantly advised people not to make flash judgments, and here I was making assumptions about someone I'd known for less than an hour. This guy was never going to want to work with me now.

"I'm sorry. That was uncalled for, and I'm the one who should feel like an ass."

"Don't you mean arse?" Pierce gave me a small, tight-lipped smile. "I know it's natural to protect your mother, but I'm not the enemy."

"I know you're not. This is just … it's a lot to process."

Pierce shrugged. "It's fine. I've dealt with worse."

"Like?"

"Do you want to know how I got the idea for *Stuff*?" He paused a few beats, like he wasn't sure if he should continue. "My best friend growing up, well I found out when we were in high school that his mother was a hoarder. I had no idea."

"Let me guess, he wasn't allowed to have friends over?"

"You got it. So when I developed the show, she was my first

ever case. I didn't expect much of anything, but then *Stuff* got picked up on the Home Channel. Suddenly, Luke, my friend, wanted nothing to do with me. His mama was humiliated that the neighbors all knew her secret. She thought I'd used them for ratings and to get my show off the ground. Meanwhile, I was still so broke I couldn't even afford to pay attention."

He closed his eyes for a second, then shook his head. "Anyway, I never would've done that to hurt them. But Luke didn't want to hear it. Wouldn't return my calls or texts ... haven't spoken to him since."

"Wow. I'm sorry. Will and I worry about that, too. It would kill us if our mother thought we were only using her for our careers."

Maybe he did know what it was like to be me, just a bit. I couldn't imagine how bittersweet it must've been to finally break through and find success, but lose your best friend in the process. Sure, I sacrificed holidays and time with family to be on GMNY, but no one had shut me out because of it. Yet.

"You gotta do what you think is best, Sarah. I was really cut up over Luke for a long time, but my mama always says if someone won't stick with you in the long run, they ain't worth the salt in their bread."

I picked up a tiny pewter replica of Tower Bridge, twisting it between my thumb and forefinger. The pain was evident on his face, and I felt the overwhelming urge to make it disappear. A subject change seemed in order. "She's still holding on to the memories all of these years later. It's not healthy."

Pierce didn't respond, but he reached out and took the bridge from me, examining it while I carried on blabbering on about Mum. "My mum's family was, as they say in Essex, 'well jel' of our posh life in England."

He threw his head back and laughed. "Sorry. I like that term. Going to adopt it immediately. But continue."

"Anyway, we hardly ever saw my grandparents in America, and my dad's parents ... well, at first they thought she'd trapped him. Got herself pregnant so she could marry him for the money and not have to come back to the States. Horrible, right?"

"I'm guessing that wasn't the case."

I shook my head. "God no. Mum was barely out of college. Imagine being in another country, casually dating a guy for a couple of months and suddenly you're twenty-one and pregnant."

Pierce handed the cheesy souvenir back to me. "From what Will told me, it wasn't a great marriage from the start. Do you talk to your father much?"

"I hear from him maybe every few months, and I visit once a year. I'm going over for Christmas soon. Anne and Will ... are a different story." I kept my tone light, but the sadness in Pierce's eyes told me he read right through it.

"It's all right. You don't have to talk about him."

I folded my arms. "It's not that I don't want to talk about him. I just don't have a super close relationship with my father, so that's all there is to say."

"All right then."

We sat there for a few moments in awkward silence as I tapped the stupid Tower Bridge on the carpet. *Honestly, Sarah. How are you going to deal with this guy for a week?*

"My mother really does need the help," I said.

"Help is exactly what she's going to get. And you're the person we need to pitch in most of all. Are we good?"

I couldn't help but feel like a major bitch. Yes, he thought mum's collection was ridiculous, but most of the time he *had* been kind to me, and I knew he was a great boss to Will. And all I could do was argue like a spoiled child.

I sighed. "We're good. And you're not as bad as I thought."

"You're not so bad either." He smiled down at me (honestly, I felt like a dwarf compared to the man) and my defenses started to very, very slowly back down.

I tried to articulate a clever response but instead just nodded, keenly aware of Pierce's continued stare and the mere inches between our denim-covered knees. If I twitched even a bit, we'd be touching. How easy would it be to just ....

"You guys in here?" Will called out, and the bubble surrounding us popped as if my niece had shoved her sticky little hand through it.

❀ Debbie ❀

"HI THERE, you must be Debbie. It's a real privilege to meet you."

No one warned me how startlingly attractive Mr. Thompson was in the flesh, and I shook his hand limply, staring at him much like an animal in a zoo. Also, I couldn't be certain, but it seemed like we had interrupted a "moment" between Sarah and Pierce, and I hung back, unsure if I should've just shut the door and let them go about their business.

Will and Pierce exchanged a blokey kind of handshake/arm slap, then Pierce turned to give me a bear hug. "Thank you for letting me into your home, ma'am."

"Well, that was Will's doing, but you're welcome, dear." I wondered if he used this Southern charm thing to trick unsuspecting people to go on his program. I could see how it worked.

"How about we sit down in the living room and have a chat?"

Sarah cleared her throat. "Sorry, I'm a bit stuck." She pointed to the bins next to her, and lifted her ballet flat like she wasn't quite sure where to step next.

"Sorry, didn't realize you were back there," Pierce said, and in what seemed like two seconds he'd managed to not only traverse around the boxes but lift Sarah into the air and whip her around the corner. "There you go."

Sarah's expression was a mix of confusion and appreciation, like she wasn't quite sure what to make of the guy. I couldn't blame her.

"Whatever Sarah says is fine with me," he said with a wink.

"Haven't heard that one before." Sarah rolled her eyes but I saw the hint of a smile.

Oh dear.

I marched ahead of the group, not wanting to see Pierce's reaction. I'd spent the night before clearing some things out of the kitchen, but the bins were just too heavy for me to move, and shame washed over me when I thought about Pierce looking up at the wall of containers lining the way to the living room. The man had found a loaf of bread with bugs crawling in it on the last episode (I'd broken down and watched a few while I cleaned) so I don't know why a few dusty bins bothered me, but they did all the same.

"Let's have a seat and get to know each other first," I said once we reached the clearing. Having a stranger tromping through my house was bad enough, I could at least know what kind of family he came from first.

Pierce plopped down on the sofa without a second of hesitation. "Hmm, well you probably know I grew up in a small town in Georgia. My mama stayed home with us, Daddy was a contractor, so I learned pretty much everything I know about houses from him. My mama, she always dreamed of being an actress, but you know—population of 1,400 people in our town, Hollywood was kind of a pipe dream. But she always wanted my sister and me to aim for something bigger, so she's been my biggest cheerleader."

"She sounds lovely," Sarah said. "Right, Mum?"

I heard the door creak open and for a moment my heart jumped. Was he already bringing the camera crew in? Then I realized by the heavy footsteps it was just Anne, who'd had to take a call after lunch. The girl was incapable of doing anything quietly.

"Hey, guys." Anne stepped into the living room and leaned down to put her bag on the floor. She paused, looked around, then placed it on my Topshop dress instead.

"Anne, this is Pierce," Will said.

Pierce jumped up to give her his seat, but Anne waved him back. "Sit, sit. I've been in the car for a while so I'm fine."

Lie. But I kept my mouth shut, and smiled tightly. "Thanks for coming, dear."

"Why don't you tell Mum and Anne how you got involved in

all of this?" Sarah suggested.

He launched into the story of how the show started, and his best friend's mum being a hoarder. "People like to keep those things a secret, as I'm sure you know, so I can definitely relate to you guys."

"You don't have to tell me twice," I said with a short nod. I pressed my nails into my leg to keep myself from saying anything else. Who was this man to think he knew what it was like to be us, just because he liked to invade peoples' homes and some friend twenty years ago had a hoarder mum?

"Anyway, I won't bore you with my TV career but when it came time for me to set out on my own, I always knew I'd do something with compulsive hoarders. That it took off like this was beyond my wildest imagination. Anyway, why don't you tell me some more about yourself, Mrs. Percy?"

"Windsor, actually. Got rid of the Percy after the divorce. But please, call me Debbie. And I suppose you know nearly everything from Will, so I'm not sure what to say. Born and raised here in Pennsylvania, studied in London, met a guy, got myself pregnant, raised a family there, divorced, moved back to America, filled my house with collectibles. The end."

"Fair enough," Pierce said. "I won't force you to tell your deepest secrets or anything, but I've got to warn you, we do have a personality profile you'll need to fill out. It gets pretty in-depth."

"Great," I said, thinking I'd rather sit through my school's holiday band concert every week than deal with a sodding personality profile.

"So, Sarah, what we want is for you to come in and assess the house, which I know you've done already, but we need it on camera," Pierce said. "Talk about not only what your mum can do, but what steps the average person watching at home can take to organize. Will showed me the ideas you two came up with, and that works fine with me."

"Sounds great," she said. "Are you sure there's not anything you had in mind?" They continued talking about organizing plans, schedules, and cleaning crews like I wasn't even in the room until I coughed a touch louder than necessary.

"Considering this is my home, I hope I'll have *some* sort of input."

"Of course, Mum," Will said. "Sorry, we're just trying to work out some of the nitty-gritty stuff here first. Do you think you could extend your Christmas vacation at school by a few days? Sarah will be back from Brentwood the day after Christmas, and it would be nice to shoot the episode over the holiday break."

"You mean, as in a few weeks from now?" My throat tightened. I was expecting the filming to take place in a few months, not *this* month.

"Yes ma'am. I apologize for the short notice, but it turns out we actually have an opening in the filming schedule because something else fell through. And the added bonus is your house will be clean much faster than we expected, instead of having to wait 'til the spring."

Pierce looked at me like I should jump up and hug him, but I pursed my lips.

"I see."

"You'll see if you can take the time?" Anne folded her arms.

"I don't know if the request will be approved with such short notice. But I suppose I can ask Monday." Why did they think I could drop everything? Didn't I have a life, just like them?

We chatted some more about the logistics of taping—or more like Sarah, Will, Anne, and Pierce chatted while I nodded and stared at the floor—but with each decision made, my sense of dread grew. The cameras, the cleaning crew, Pierce ... all of it seemed like an abstract idea when Will first mentioned being on *Stuff*. Now that words like "release form" were being thrown around, the enormity of what I was getting myself into was starting to become real, and terrifying.

"I suppose everything's sorted then," Pierce said. "We just have some paperwork for you, Debbie. And our team does a short psychological assessment first. Standard procedure."

I knew I was going to have to do the show; I didn't have a choice if they were going to blackmail me with the prospect of Alan selling the house, after all. But I needed time to process the information. Someone waiting for my response and talking about profiles and assessments amped up the anxiety factor.

"Can I have a day or two to ponder all of this before you start sending a shrink to my house? Despite the mess, I am quite normal, I assure you."

Anne closed her eyes and exhaled, as if the thought of even replying exhausted her. It was startling how much she reminded me of her grandmother sometimes. "Do you know anyone else's house that looks like yours? If this was normal, there wouldn't be an entire show devoted to helping people with clutter."

"I think I realize that, dear."

"No, I really think you don't. Do you think any of us want to be here? I can't even let your grandchildren come over because I'm afraid they'll get hurt. Enough is enough. You're being ridiculous."

Anne's response hurt, possibly even more than the threat of the house being sold. It was silly for me to think she'd be on my side.

Pierce held up a hand. "We can have a frank discussion, but let's try to keep it civil. Now Anne, I know part of your mother's issue with being on the show is that she doesn't want to be embarrassed. And I hear that's your problem, too. What can I do to assure you this isn't going to be some kind of sensationalized nonsense?"

I had to admit, Pierce was good.

"You're not going to edit Mum to look like she's some kind of nut-job obsessed with Princess Diana, right?" Anne said.

I screwed up my nose. "I hardly think—"

"Of course not," Pierce said. He turned to Will and clapped him on the shoulder. "And with your brother on board, I can assure you we'll be as sensitive as possible in putting this episode together. We're all a team here. And we want the same thing, which is for Debbie to have a nice, safe place to live. Are you in?"

Anne looked at the ceiling and expelled about an entire balloon's worth of air. Finally she nodded. "I'm going to be on my husband's shit list, but yeah. If this is the only way to get Mum to sign on, I'll do it."

"Now I don't want you getting your marriage in hot water over me," I said. After my disaster of a union, the last thing I wanted was for one of my kids to wind up divorced, too.

"It's fine, really. This is my decision. He's going to have to live with it."

After a few more details had been nailed down, the four of them made their way out the door and I was alone again. Anne said no one wanted to be at my house, and the funny thing is once they left and I climbed over all of the ridiculous boxes and bags and tunneled my way into the living room, I realized I didn't want to be there, either. My knees ached, I was out of breath, and all I wished for was to curl up in bed and take a nap. Except I couldn't. Because my bed was covered with plastic bins.

I woke up the next day and winced as I rolled to my right side. My back and tailbone ached from yet another night on the sofa. Staring at the ceiling, I pictured twenty, maybe thirty more years like the night before. And by that point, I wouldn't even be able to lift the boxes off my bed.

What if one fell on top of me? With Sarah and Will in New York, and Anne busy being supermom, it might be weeks before anyone would find my body ... and worse, I'd end up in the news like some kind of freak show. "Woman crushed by commemorative royal family plates" sounded like a headline no one would be able to resist clicking on.

I picked up my phone before I lost the nerve.

"Mum!" Will said. "Just the person I wanted to speak with. I'm guessing you need—"

"I'll do it."

"What?" he said, sounding, for once in his life, genuinely shocked.

I swallowed hard. "I said I'll do it. I don't have much of a choice, do I?"

"I know it probably seems like we're ambushing you ...."

"*Probably*?"

"Fair enough. But it's all in your best interest. Even if it wasn't for this job ... well, I'd actually nominated you for an episode before. We want you to get help and have a safe life. I hope you understand that."

I believed Will, of course. But part of me still wondered how much of this plan was tied to making sure Will's career took off. "Just don't make me look like a fool, will you?"

"Oh my God, of course not. You'll see, it's going to be amazing. I promise. I'm actually getting on the train now, but I'm going to call you later and we'll go over the details. Going to need to send you some paperwork. All good things!" He rambled on for a few more minutes, barely comprehensible in his excitement, before I ended the call.

Well, that was that. No turning back. It almost felt like a box of china had been lifted off my shoulders, now that a decision had at least been made.

I looked around the room, wondering what they'd make me throw out. I'd have to do some initial sweeps before the show, of course, to make sure anything important didn't end up on the air. Definitely not anything in the BOA, that was for sure.

Ugh. Might as well open it then if I was going to get broody.

I made the trek across the room to the basket and stepped gingerly over a few things until I reached the stupid thing. One piece per day. Would that be enough time before they started filming?

I reached in and felt the soft cotton and satiny edge of what I knew was a baby blanket. Sarah's blanket. I rubbed the edge against my cheek, remembering the day we bought it, and wondering if things would have been different if that blanket had been another color.

∼✺

Brentwood, Essex, February 1982

Baby shopping with Alan's mum was about the last thing I wanted to do at seven months pregnant, but there I was in some fancy boutique oohing and aahing over onesies (which she called babygrows) on a Friday afternoon. Dragging myself off the sofa away from a bag of crisps and my beloved *Coronation Street* had felt like torture, especially since I had to "look presentable."

Stuffing my swollen feet into the white pumps wasn't going to happen, so I resorted to the trusty Hunter wellies Alan's parents had given me for Christmas. More like his mum gave me for Christmas, but still. If I paired them with an ivory cashmere jumper (my other gift) and my dressiest maternity trousers, I looked decent enough. I stared down at my boots, secretly thinking how pleased I was that she bought me the exact pair Princess Diana had been photographed in, and how exciting it was that Diana and I were pregnant at the same time. I'd started saving all the magazines I read about her. In a way it felt like documenting my own—albeit very different—love story. I wondered if she had as much trouble relating to her in-laws as I did. The Percys were bad enough, but it must've been a thousand times more stressful to have the Queen as your mother-in-law.

While Mrs. Percy had grown on me—or I'd grown on her, along with my belly—Alan's father remained aloof as ever. "Give him time," was her trademark phrase over the months since our pregnancy announcement, and I just smiled and nodded.

Yeah right.

Once we'd chosen a suitably obnoxious number of embroidered and pintucked white and yellow baby outfits, most of them looking like something a child in Charles Dickens' age would wear, we left the shop to meet Alan for lunch at the pub. He'd been talking business with his brother there, since he finally admitted he needed to work full-time if we were to make our own life together and not rely on his parents. But whether or not that would actually happen was another story.

As Mrs. Percy and I walked into the quiet, wood-paneled dining room upstairs, I spotted Alan and his brother, Mark, laughing at a table in the corner. Good sign.

"My darlings," Alan's mum said, leaning in for a cheek kiss. "How did your little meeting go?"

"Good, thanks," Mark said, all smiles as usual. "Alan's got some ideas for the club that I think will be massive for us." Despite the rest of his family's stiff upper lip, Mark had an easy, laid back charm about him you simply couldn't resist.

"Sounds great," I said, relieved that Mark actually liked Alan's pitch for a fancy dress theme every Thursday night. "We can start with superheroes, maybe do an 'around the world' theme, won't that be amazing?" he'd said to me that morning, while I used my good old smile and nod tactic.

We said goodbye to Mark, who was going back to work, then settled in at the table and ordered our usuals: fish and chips for me, shepherd's pie for Mrs. Percy, bangers and mash for Alan. "So," Alan said, taking a leisurely sip of his pint. "I think helping Mark with the club is going to work out well."

His mother smiled and said she was pleased, but I noticed she was holding something back. I figured she was used to years of Alan having these ideas and not following through. Hell, I'd known him for not quite nine months and already felt that way.

"Ooh," I said as the baby kicked me hard in the ribs. "Sorry. The little one is being quite active today."

"Future football star, I know it!" Alan grinned.

"As long as he supports Arsenal," Mrs. Percy added.

I held back any further comments and stuck with "We'll see." Their obsession with having a boy had grown over the weeks, and frankly, it was annoying. I was nervous, plain and simple, and whether it was a boy or a girl wouldn't change how hard it would be to raise a child.

"Speaking of," Mrs. Percy said, pulling out one of the glossy carrier bags from under the table. "I couldn't resist. Perfect for the next little Percy heir." She removed a beautiful snowy white wool blanket with a pale blue satin trim. I hadn't seen her buy it, and my mouth dropped open. "Don't worry, we can still use it if it's a girl!"

I felt a wave of nausea and excused myself to the ladies' room to regain composure. This must've been what Anne Boleyn felt like back in the day. *Make an heir or else.*

Even though I was barely speaking to my own mother, I wished I could've called her to vent. What would happen if Alan didn't have this baby boy he dreamed about? Even Mr. Percy might have warmed up to the idea of a little boy to show how to do all of that proper English outdoorsy stuff. Then again, the words "warm" and "Mr. Percy" didn't really go hand in hand, in any case.

I took a few calming breaths and headed back to our table, just in time for the food's arrival. Alan had already tucked into his plate, although Mrs. Percy had waited for me to return. "So," I said, trying to think of anything pleasant to talk about, "you know my roommate, Carol? She's thinking of throwing me a baby shower next month."

"What's that?" Alan said, totally oblivious as usual, while Mrs. Percy chewed her food with a bit too much vigor. "I'm afraid we don't do those in England, dear," she finally said. "It's a very American tradition."

"Yeah, and I'm American. And so is Carol." As much as I loved England, and honestly, didn't care much about a baby shower, I felt my defenses rising.

"Isn't it a bit ... vulgar? To ask people for gifts? Surely we can buy you anything you need. And we have already, in fact."

"That's not the issue. It's a party to celebrate the baby. But that's fine. It'll just be for our friends from uni. No worries about offending your family with our *American* nonsense."

"Come now, Debs," Alan said, patting my leg under the table. "She didn't mean anything by it." Mrs. Percy just cleared her throat in a huffy sort of way and continued eating. *Typical.*

As hard as I tried to fit in, and I thought I fit in pretty well (at least in London), every time I was with Alan's family I felt like an outsider. And if I was an outsider back at home, and an outsider abroad, then where exactly did I belong?

Sarah Says

Always Have a Backup Gift

During the festive season, we've all found ourselves in the situation where someone gives us a present … and we haven't bought anything for them. Avoid this situation by keeping small, affordable gifts like bottles of wine, scented candles, and pretty picture frames on hand. No more awkward Christmas visits!

"MERRY CHRISTMAS, I guess I won't see you before then." Andrew pulled a tiny wrapped box out of his drawer and pushed it across the desk. It was my last day at the station before heading to Essex, but nothing felt merry.

The NBC affiliate had snagged Michelle Obama as a guest, and everyone in New York was talking about it … and that meant no one was talking about GMNY. The news I'd be filming *Stuff* much earlier than expected—and right after a vacation—couldn't have come at a worse time. But since it was Christmas anyway, Andrew announced I'd be taking a short leave of absence, instead of disappearing for a week, coming back for a few days, and taking off again. I couldn't decide if "leave of absence" was code for "we're getting rid of her and she doesn't know it yet."

When Andrew wasn't stomping around cursing the competition, he wouldn't stop talking about how exciting it was to work with Katie while I was filming *Stuff*; of course they'd offered her the job, and she'd accepted. Everyone was so excited, in fact, they'd brought her in for a test run before I went on holiday. Katie was already parading around the station in a dress that looked like it came from Frederick's of Hollywood and talked over me every chance she got during that morning's "decorating on a dime" segment. But what was I supposed to do? I was the one who was inconveniencing everyone by taking off to film another show.

"You didn't have to get me a gift," I said. "Especially since ... well, you know." I hadn't bought anything for him, considering we were barely on speaking terms, but I still felt that awkward, nagging feeling when you've committed a social faux pas. Why did I bother giving anyone advice when I couldn't even follow it?

"No, I wanted to. I owe you an apology for how everything's gone down here. This is to say thanks for everything."

I pulled a corner of the paper and held back a grin; the paper had been cut too short and Andrew had tried to cover up the mistake with a giant red bow. Inside was a silver frame with a photo of the two of us holding our Emmy last year. Back in the good old days before the ratings dropped. When I felt like Andrew was proud of me, and I was still the star pupil.

I wanted to ask if it was some sort of parting gift, because it sure felt like it. But I wasn't brave enough.

"I feel terrible, I've been so busy I didn't get you—"

Andrew raised his eyebrows. "Can you stop protesting for once and just say thank you?"

"All right. Thank you. Truly. This will look lovely on my desk. It's a nice memory."

"You're welcome. I hope you enjoy the break." He put his tasseled loafers up on the desk and glanced at the news monitors on the wall across from us for a second. "Oh, and when you get back from England we can really map out how this is all going to work at the station."

That uneasy feeling I'd had about not giving him a gift morphed into something else. Panic.

"I thought we did work it out. Katie's here, the segments are all lined up. What else is there?"

"I know. But I just want to make sure your transition goes as smoothly as possible. And we'll need to figure out when Katie will hand the reins back."

"I thought I was returning January 5? I don't understand why we're going over this again when we sat down with the team the other day."

Andrew stared down at the pen he was tapping on his desk. "About that ...."

"Oh my God. Andrew, please don't tell me you've hired her for real."

"Nothing's finalized. But there's a chance we might bring her on full-time. We're going to treat this as a trial."

"And no one thought to consult me? What does that mean for my job?" My throat felt tight, like I'd swallowed a hard candy whole, and I struggled to breathe. This could be the end of my career, and all because of *Stuff*.

"Nothing. We're adding another host on GMNY. Why are you freaking out?"

"Because no one wanted me to be on *Stuff* in the first place, and now you're bringing in this new girl as a replacement and telling me you're going to hire her permanently?"

Kareena ran past his cube just then, clutching a giant makeup case the size of a small carry-on bag. Three Chanel lipsticks flew out and rolled into Andrew's cube. "Sorry! I've got a lunch date and need to do some touching up." She bent down to stuff everything back in her bag and paused, looking back and forth between us as she stood. "What's wrong with you two?"

"Just a misunderstanding," Andrew said. "Nothing to worry about."

"Did you know they're thinking of hiring Katie Douglas full-time?" I asked.

Kareena pursed her lips. "I'd say I'm surprised, but I'm not. Told you."

"Enough, guys. I'm only doing what the higher ups tell me. I'm not out to get anyone."

"Really? Because I feel like you used to be in my corner. And now ..." I looked at the picture frame and sighed. Andrew had always talked me up to the station manager, made sure I had the biggest guests, and coached me through every up and down. He always knew what was best ... or at least I thought he did.

"You know what, Sarah? Ratings are down. Kareena's segments have been more popular than yours. Half the reason the station has kept you on is because *I* fought for you." Andrew grabbed his phone before marching past us, then stopped and shook his head. "I have a job to worry about, too. And I don't know how much longer I can fight for yours."

·ᵒᵉ Debbie ᵉᵒ·

MY BIG BEN KITCHEN CLOCK chimed for the third time since I'd started the personality profile, and I tossed my pen down in defeat. Should it really have taken three hours (or a few weeks, for that matter) to get through the silly thing? Sure, the upcoming holiday was a good excuse, but all I had to show for my Christmas procrastinating was a messier house, a lower bank account, and a wreath on the door. There wasn't even room for a tree, no matter how many times I tried to rearrange the boxes.

I flipped through the papers Will had emailed me again, as if I'd somehow discover different questions this time. I'd never seen such an invasive document in my life, and I work in a school office, for God's sake. Beyond the usual suspects like address, age and marital status, they wanted to know if I'd ever thought of hurting myself or others ("Not really, unless you count Alan"); have I ever been in a domestic dispute ("Define the word dispute?"); and how much I spent per month on shopping ("It definitely varies, but it's not like I can't afford it").

I answered all of the basic bits, but as I moved on the questions got tougher. I ticked the "no" box with glee when asked if I thought there were any dead animals in the house, but had to think about some of the others. *Do you feel a compulsion to acquire things? Can you sleep in your own bed?* There wasn't a "sometimes" box, unfortunately.

How difficult would it be for emergency personnel to move through the house? I made an x through the "difficult" box, but then I took a look at the path to the kitchen. With a sigh I crossed out my answer and chose "very difficult." Sarah and Will could barely get through, and both of them were New York City skinny.

107

I should've been pretty pleased with myself for making some sort of progress, but the final part of the profile remained ... the personal statement. I was supposed to write a "brief, no more than one-page statement" about my hoarding and how I think it started. I needed far more than a page to open that can of worms, and probably an international flight while we were at it. I had one sentence so far:

I would have to say my collecting began a few years before I left England (5 years maybe?!) not long after which my husband took off to behave like a singleton running out to nightclubs.

What else could I say? Maybe some pictures of the house would suffice, although then I remembered that was already required separately from the personality profile.

"What on earth have you gotten me into?" I asked after speed dialing Will.

"It's all standard procedure!" he said, and I could picture him with his feet up on the coffee table, book in hand as usual. "I'm sure it's probably more than you're used to revealing about yourself to strangers, but don't worry."

"More than I'm used to? I don't think Dr. Brown knows this much about me, and I've been seeing him since the nineties. I bet your father probably wouldn't have even—" I stopped myself when I heard the sharp intake of breath on the other line.

"Look," I continued. "I'm sure it's all well and good but I just had some concerns. That's all, darling. It's fine. I'll let you get back to your busy city life! Kisses."

I hung up the phone and frowned. Five more pages, front and back, of interrogation awaited me. What was this, eHarmony?

Everyone in town would think I was a fraud, for God's sake. I could imagine the gossip at school. *Neatnick Debbie with her lint roller obsession is actually a hoarder.* But then I remembered the feel of the sofa springs poking me. A bad back would only get worse if I couldn't sleep in my bedroom some day before Prince William became king.

Deep breaths. You can do this. I decided to put the essay section aside and at least finish the remainder of the other questions.

Do you have an emotional attachment to objects in your home?

Oh dear.

I threw the paper down and dialed Rich's number. It was seven o'clock, not too late to ask someone out. And I needed an out, big time.

"I was just thinking about you," Rich said in place of a hello.

"Fancy meeting me at Bookville? I could use a new read, and we can have a coffee after and chat a bit." I crossed my fingers and made a bargain with myself. If he said no, I'd have to finish the profile and stay home.

Luckily, he didn't hesitate a second before saying he'd meet me there in fifteen minutes. "How about a half hour?" I said, making an excuse about cleaning up from dinner. There was no way I could've got out the door and to the bookshop that quickly.

Luckily, I had some makeup in my purse, so I did a quick job of making myself look somewhat presentable, threw my coat on, and made my way down the path. Ever since that first time the kids came to visit, I'd been trying to shave my time out the door to under five minutes, but the addition of a few new bins and an antique desk from Something Old had impeded my progress. It would all be straightened up when the TV crew came, at least, which should've given me some small comfort. But instead I felt a sick rumble in my stomach, kind of like the sensation when I ate too much Mexican food. Will assured me I'd get the final say in everything, and they wouldn't toss anything without my permission. But I'd seen the show, and they didn't hire dumpsters for no reason.

As I trudged along the path to the door, another thought flashed in my head. I was going to have to tell Rich about the show. I'd been seeing him more often, and between dinners, movies, coffees, and a Christmas shopping trip to King of Prussia Mall, I'd say I could change my Facebook status to "in a relationship" with some confidence. I almost slipped once, when he'd complained about having no time to clean. I'd had two glasses of wine, and next thing I knew I'd said I was sure my house was an absolute disaster compared to his, but then the conversation turned to kids, and asking questions about Sarah's show, and I lucked out.

The problem was, I didn't know if I had, in fact, lucked out. If he knew straight away about the house, wouldn't that make life easier? He could make a quick exit before things got too serious or either of us got attached. Worst case scenario, he'd think I was a slob. The more time we spent together, the harder it was going to be to hide all of this from him.

Screw you, Alan, I thought, pushing past the final stack of bins and leaning against the kitchen wall to catch my breath. I made it out of the house in six minutes, twenty-seven seconds (worst in a while) but at least I pulled up to the store a few minutes early. Rich was waiting in the front, examining a display of e-readers.

"Call me a fuddy duddy, but give me an old-fashioned paper book any day." He greeted me with a kiss on the cheek.

I nodded, lifting a tablet off the table and flipping it over. "I've got so many books, I don't even know where else to put them, so I suppose I can see how an e-reader is appealing. But how do you even turn this thing on?"

He laughed. "You're asking the wrong man. And I didn't know you were such an enthusiastic reader."

"Oh you know me, full of surprises." *You don't know the half of it.*

"So where to? New releases? Cookbooks? Romance?" he said the last word with a cheeky lilt to his voice.

"Rich Sullivan, is that a proposition?"

He put his hand on the small of my back and led me to the escalator. "Pleading the fifth."

A table of historical fiction with a sign promising an "ESCAPE TO THE DAYS OF CHIVALRY" came into view as the escalator climbed to the second floor.

"Wouldn't that be nice?" I thought I'd said it under my breath, but Rich let out a low chuckle. "Point noted," he said, linking arms with me. He made a dramatic flourish with his arm and bowed like a courtier when we reached the top of the escalator. "My lady."

I'd almost forgotten what it was like to blush.

We must've walked down every aisle, talking about our favorite authors and which books we loved reading to our kids, and then I saw the clearance table. After sifting through the selection, *A History of Royalty* ($5.99) jumped off the table and into my hands, joining a London travel guide. Not that I was planning on going anytime soon, but it didn't hurt to have a browse.

"Ah, you do love yourself some England," Rich said, stacking the rest of the books back into neat rows. "Always talking about the royals."

A few violent coughs escaped before I said. "*Love* might be an understatement. Coffee?"

Two cups of coffee (Rich), a decaf tea and a scone (me), and a pile of purchased books (both of us) later, we realized the employees in the café were starting to sweep around us, and the registers had closed down.

Rich checked his watch. "Ten o'clock? I hate to sound cliché but time really does fly when you're having fun."

I stifled a yawn. Chatting with him was fun, but I promised Will I'd finish the personality profile, and that meant a late night ahead. "Guess we'd better hit the road."

Rich shuffled along next to me, passing his car on the way to mine. "So ..."

"This was nice," I said, clutching the books to my chest. It must've been twenty degrees outside; not exactly the best conditions for dithering about.

"May I? I mean, would you mind if ... oh, hell." Rich swooped in and planted a proper kiss on me, not the usual quick peck on the lips we'd been exchanging after our dates. If I hadn't been so shocked, I probably would've enjoyed it instead of dropping my books on the sidewalk.

"Oh!" I said, bending down to pick them up. "Sorry, you caught me off guard. In a good way."

His cheeks flamed and he looked down at his loafers. "I apologize if that was out of—wait. You're not upset?"

I cleared my throat. "Not at all, actually." Relief, and maybe a little surprise showed in his face, and I had to admit I'd surprised even myself.

"Good night, Rich," I said, squeezing his hand.

I drove home, still feeling completely off kilter after that kiss. A *kiss*, me! In a parking lot of all places. What was I, sixteen? I burst out laughing at the absurdity of it all, but at the same time, my heart soared and my hands trembled on the steering wheel. Maybe it wasn't too late for me. But then the reality of it all slapped me in the face when I got home. Rich would never stay with me for the long-run.

After the usual climb through the house I plopped on the floor, rubbing my knee. Adrenaline and some strong tea weren't going to be enough to carry on through the pain; it felt like another three-Advil night.

After taking my pills and finding the *Stuff* application, I realized I hadn't touched the BOA in a few days, and wondered if looking inside would help trigger some sort of compulsion to finish that essay; I already had the compulsion to acquire things, after all.

The piece of yellowing cardstock I pulled out felt heavy in my hands for more reasons than the weight of the paper: the thickest they'd carried in the invitation shop near our old house in Brentwood. "Join us for a First Birthday Garden Party in Honor of Sarah Percy" was printed in swirly embossed letters. I waved the invitation in front of my face a few times. I already needed a makeshift fan after the snog fest at the bookstore, and would definitely need to cool down even more if I was going to force myself to think about that afternoon again.

∾

Essex, May 1983

"Happy birthday, little one," Mrs. Percy said, plopping a pink paper birthday hat atop Sarah's wispy blonde curls. We'd gathered on an unusually warm Saturday afternoon in the Percys' garden for Sarah's first birthday party, and it felt like a major milestone for me, not just Sarah. I'd made it through one year.

White lace bunting strung through the trees and tiny pink rose plants decorating each table set the scene for an adorable little garden party, not that Sarah knew the difference since she was content to test out her no longer shaky walking skills at every opportunity. It felt like a new start, a new opportunity to wipe things clean and be a better mum in the year ahead. But I had to get through three hours in the company of our fifty guests first.

As long as Alan's father didn't make any snide remarks, and my parents, who Mrs. Percy flew out as a surprise, acted like normal human beings, I decided I'd be fine. We were a motley group including various extended members of the Percy family, Carol (who now lived solo in the flat since Alan and I had moved closer to his family), George and a few of Alan's other friends, but thankfully no Wanker Guy. And then there were my parents, looking like the stereotypical American tourists staring at everything in awe yet trying to appear nonchalant at the same time. I brought a glass of water over to Mom and a beer for Dad, trying to think of some neutral conversation topic we hadn't already exhausted.

"So ... this is some place," Dad said. "Now I know what you saw in Alan. Sheesh."

"Bill!" My mom slapped his arm and then withdrew her hand just as quickly. She held it against her heart with a guilty expression, like she'd realized she committed some sort of "you can't do that at a stately home" faux pas.

We'd only seen each other once since Sarah was born, when my mother flew out a few weeks after I left the hospital. Relations were still strained with Dad, but at least my mom had met Alan and Sarah and knew a bit what my life was like in England. Translation: she knew how much I was struggling with motherhood, and with Alan. Our quickie courthouse marriage went off without a hitch (no pun intended) but Sarah's arrival in our lives had turned our already tenuous relationship upside down.

"Alan has a lot of great qualities," Mom said. "He's just young and trying to find his way in the world, like Debbie. And Debs had no idea his family was so wealthy when she first met him."

"Of course I didn't," I said, glancing over at my husband clinking glasses with his friends on the lawn. To be fair, he'd made a real effort at doing something useful with himself, and was now working full time in his brother's nightclub business. But that meant late nights rolling home reeking of cigarettes, beer, and the perfume of tipsy girls. Add a move to Essex, where I didn't know anyone except his family, and you had a recipe for disaster.

I tried to push any unpleasant thoughts out of my mind. *Focus on the happy.* "Can you excuse me for a moment? I need to get Sarah her milk."

I headed off to the house to find our nanny, Annie, a recent addition to the family. I tried to act like I didn't need her, but the truth was, I was so grateful for Annie I could cry every time I saw her. Mrs. Percy had hired her after the "I think I'm going to throw myself and possibly Alan out the window" incident of December '82, and although Annie wasn't live-in, she made my life a hundred times easier.

I knew the early months were never easy for a new mum, but Alan slept all day due to his night owl job, and when I was most in need of a break, he was getting ready to leave for the club. And hoping Alan would wake up with her at 4 a.m. was pointless; the man slept like the dead, and unfortunately our daughter did not.

What else was there to do to ease my mind but go shopping? I'd started hiding the carrier bags, or even asking stores not to give me one, since he got cross when he saw I'd brought home something new. Clothes and things like that were easy, since he was the least perceptive person on earth when it came to what I wore. The collectibles were a different story, since I was starting to run out of room for everything. But now that the baby was a bit older and I had help in the form of our proper British nanny, I almost felt like my old self again. Maybe I wouldn't need shopping to fill the void.

The problem was, resentment and almost a year of postnatal depression couldn't be waved away just like that, or in my case, bought off with a pair of diamond earrings and a mini break to Paris.

Mrs. Percy bustled into the kitchen, which always reminded me of the type you see in a PBS drama, complete with massive copper pots hanging from the ceiling and maids gossiping in a corner. She rattled off some orders to the caterer as I took the cup of milk from Annie.

"Debbie, you all right? You look tired again." Mrs. Percy turned to Annie. "Is she still taking naps during the day like I suggested?"

Annie nodded, looking up from the strawberries she was chopping for Sarah's lunch. "Sarah and I took a nice long walk at Thorndon Country Park yesterday and chased the ducks. Debbie was still sleeping when we got back."

"Lovely," Mrs. Percy said. "Where *is* Sarah, by the way?"

I gestured outside, proud that I actually knew the answer. "She's sitting on your cousin's lap."

Alan's mum seemed satisfied with this and hurried out of the room, leaving me with Annie for a second of quiet. I sighed and leaned against the stone countertop.

"I'd love not to be under the microscope for a minute."

Annie smiled in a motherly sort of way, which was funny because she was only four years older. Still, she had way more experience taking care of children than I did, which in my mind made her more of a mum.

"Give that to Sarah and I'll finish lunch," she said. "And you're doing just fine."

It was sad that "fine" felt like a victory, but I needed all of the encouragement I could get. Annie gave me a gentle push. "Go on then, I'm sure she's hungry."

As I crossed the lawn to find Sarah, Alan ran over. "Debs! There you are. Guess what?"

I continued walking, forcing Alan to fall in step with me. "I haven't a clue. But go ahead."

"Mark's going to make me a partner in the business!" He lifted me off the ground and I saw a blurred version of his brother give us a thumbs-up as Alan spun me around.

I tried to make sense of it all in my dizzy state, and blinked slowly after he set me on the ground next to Sarah. "Well done, but what does that mean? Will you be out even more?" Panic threatened to take over at the mere thought of it.

"What it means," he said, "is my brother wants me to do more behind the scenes work instead of promoting like I am now. Yeah, I'll have to show my face at the club sometimes, but more often than not, I'll be home with you."

I'd heard the whole "I'll try harder to be home more" line before, but this time his ear-to-ear grin looked sincere. I also wondered if Mrs. Percy had given Mark a push in the "give your brother a less demanding job" direction.

Alan picked Sarah up and did a little dance as she squealed with delight at her father's attention. "Everything will be different, I promise. Who knows, Sarah ... maybe you'll even have a little brother soon?"

The cup slipped from my hand and Sarah yelled "Uh oh!" as milk puddled around Alan's feet.

Sarah Says
Keep Calm at Christmas

Tensions tend to run high during the holiday season, but there's no need to lose your cool with Uncle Teddy for drinking the last eggnog. Step outside, take a break, and remember it's the season of charity and goodwill toward men—surely you've done something to annoy a family member over the years, too?

"AND I SAID, 'Honestly Agnes, we've already taken you to Marbella three times this year, and you want two weeks' vacation?' But then I remembered how my mother-in-law always said to consider the staff part of the family, so of course I gave it to her."

I looked at Dad with raised eyebrows while my stepmother continued to babble to her friends about staffing woes. He motioned for me to come with him to the dessert table across the room, and a string quartet struck up "Joy to the World" behind us as a hundred or so of the Percys' nearest and dearest sipped champagne and nibbled on apps in the expansive marble-floored ballroom.

Yes, my family's home has an actual ballroom. And no, I did not think this was normal.

Just another Christmas at Percy Hall.

I should've been relieved to escape from the drama with Mum's house, and at the station, but a few hours in Gemma's company reminded me how much I stood out in Essex. Her spray-tanned, big hair, big teeth, big boobs look—as well as her big personality—fit right in with the *Essex Girls* crowd Dad had invited to the party (I nearly died when I saw Lolly and James in the flesh). Meanwhile, I felt like a grandmother, or at the very least a Kate Middleton wannabe, in my long-sleeved, high-neck midi dress and beige pumps, nursing my champagne in the corner. I was wearing a brooch, for God's sake.

"I'm not trying to be horrible, but I don't know how you manage to keep anyone on staff," I said.

Dad set an empty crystal flute on a tray and grabbed a new one, all in one swift, practiced motion. "Don't worry about Agnes, she can hold her own. And you know Gem. I let it go in one ear, and out the other."

I shook my head. "Right, well I suppose you need to do a lot of that to grow up in the Percy household."

"Do I detect a hint of snark, Saz?" Dad asked, although he said it with a smile.

"Who, me?" I popped a tiny chocolate pastry into my mouth and examined the Swarovski crystal snowmen on the twenty-foot Douglas fir next to the table. "New ornaments this year?"

"Probably. Gem takes care of that stuff, and I get the bills."

"Right. Of course." I took a deep breath. "So, I have some news about my mum." I'd chosen a very loud, and very public place to talk to dad about the show. He wasn't going to get upset in front of all those important people, and especially not at Christmas. Was that a bit manipulative? Perhaps. But I didn't have it in me to deal with another mess.

"Oh? Do ya?" Dad said it in such a casual way, while straightening the collar of his black blazer, it made me think he was pretending not to care.

"Well, it's about Will, too. He got a new job as a producer on a reality show. A really popular one."

"Well done. Tell him I said congratulations, although I doubt he cares what his old dad thinks either way." He looked down at his champagne. "Anyway, what's going on with Debbie?" It was more than an ocean that separated him from Will (and because of that, Anne, too), but as usual, every time I brought one of them up, he swiftly changed the subject.

I sighed. "The house has gotten a bit worse."

"Define worse."

"So Will's job, it's on that show, *Stuff*. You have it in the UK, right?" I knew very well they did, but maybe I wanted to downplay its popularity.

"Yeah, we do actually, but I don't care to watch it for obvious reasons. What does that have to do with ..." His eyes widened in recognition. "Jesus."

"I know. It's not ideal. But I think being on the show could really help Mum. And they've asked me to come on board as an organizational consultant as well. So I'm afraid you're no longer the only Percy on reality television."

Dad touched his glass to mine. "Cheers, then. Although I can't say I'm jumping up and down over my family—or my house—being on a hoarding program."

"It's not like anyone knows it's yours. Although I did almost have to call in a favor. Will thought if Mum refused to do the show, we—or, well, I—could ask you to tell Mum you were selling."

"What's New York done to my kids? I'm surprised at you, Saz. Although I suppose I've got to admire the cleverness."

I would've said I felt like a kid being scolded, but I never really did anything to get scolded for growing up. The shameful sensation washing over me was a new one. And Dad was the last person I expected to be on Team Mum, especially considering they'd hardly spoken in fifteen years, but maybe I wasn't giving him enough credit. Since Gemma he'd calmed down and grown up by miles, even if the shiny shoes, tight jeans and sculpted hair remained.

"What about Anne?" Dad asked. "Is she involved, too?"

I shrugged. "She says she is, but I don't know that I believe it. She had a pretty big row with Rob over the whole thing. He doesn't want to embarrass his family."

"Can't say I blame him."

Gemma came over and wrapped an arm around Dad's waist, breaking the awkward silence. "Look at the pair of you! Thick as thieves." In her exaggerated accent, it sounded more like "look at tha pair-a-ya."

"Hi, Gemma. You look nice." Her outfit consisted of a red off-the-shoulder dress with cut-outs at the waist and a pair of black crystal-encrusted platform heels that must've been at least six inches high. Diamond chandeliers swung from her ears as she tossed her wavy extensions over one shoulder. Mum would have simply died at the sight of her, and I made a mental note to keep any pictures of Gem off social media.

"Sarah was just sharing some family news," Dad said stiffly. "Will's got himself a job on that show, *Stuff,* and the kids are going to be on an episode with Debbie."

"That's amazing! I'm sure you have loads of experience to bring to the table. And you must be proud of your brother."

Gemma, the perpetual glass half-full type, clearly wasn't reading any of Dad's signals that the news might not be so welcome. I shrugged. "At first I was fuming, to be honest. I won't bore you with the story but things haven't been going well at GMNY, and I don't think this news helped. But we've all come to accept it. Even Mum, to a degree."

Dad choked on his sip of champagne and tried to cover it with a cough. "I hardly think Debbie's letting that ship go down without hanging on 'til the bitter end."

"I don't know, Alan. People can change. Who'd think a hairdresser from Dagenham, the daughter of a plumber, would end up at Percy Hall? Anything can happen."

I smiled at Gemma, feeling an unusual fondness for her. It wasn't like I hated her, but my feelings were more like resigned tolerance. I kept in touch regularly with my half-brother, Richie, but he was a little kid, innocent in all of this. That Gem had stepped into Mum's shoes and was living our old life wasn't something I could wrap my head around even a decade later. Why was she good enough, but we weren't?

But at the end of the day, despite her brashness and love for leopard print, Gemma had brought out Dad's softer side. Anyone who could manage to tame my father was someone with quite an impressive skill set, and one none of the rest of us possessed, since we couldn't get him to stay.

"Anyway, it sounds like this is all a bit of you, babe. Cleaning up and telling people what to do is basically your dream job."

The fondness level dipped a bit, but she wasn't wrong. "I've got some plans for the house, yes. So it should be exciting."

"But how is all of this going to play out?" Dad said. "You'll all come in and clean up the house and expect it won't be filled up again in a month's time? I'd love to see Debbie finally get some help, but let's call a square a square here."

I bit my lip. What was I supposed to say to the man whose marriage was turned upside down by all of Mum's stuff? "Nothing in life's a guarantee, but it's worth a shot, don't you think? And the show has a therapist on staff who specializes in hoarding, so she'll be working with Mum the whole time. They even pay for follow-up counseling after the show's over."

Dad nodded. "That's all well and good, but I don't want anyone to expect a miracle and have it all go tits up."

"I happen to think it's a lovely thing you're doing for your mum. Ignore this old bore." She gave Dad's arm an affectionate shove and he cracked a grin, but it didn't reach his eyes. "Well I'll leave you to it. I'm going to say hi to Lolly and James. See ya in a bit, yeah?" She cheek-kissed both of us and scuttled off to join the *Essex Girls* squad.

I turned back to Dad with an amused smile. "I forgot to ask, but how's the dog thing going?"

I didn't mean anything rude by it, but Dad instantly raised his defenses. "I know you think Gem's all fur coat and no knickers, but she's actually got a great business sense. People pay good money to buy stuff for their pets. And the boutique's slated to open in the spring."

"Good luck to her. I'm sure it'll be successful." An image of Gemma flashed in my mind, fawning over Chihuahuas in tiny coats and convincing their owners to go for the diamante polka dot leash. I let out a little snorty-sounding laugh that probably came off the wrong way.

Dad's eyes turned cold. "I wish you would just give Gem a chance."

"When have I ever been rude to her? I thought what she said earlier was nice. But you've got to admit, doggie couture *is* a bit funny."

"I mean a proper chance. Not this 'hi, you look nice, good weather we're having, eh?' kind of relationship. You keep everyone at arm's length, Saz."

"Considering we live in different countries, it's a bit hard to build a friendship with someone I see once or twice a year. When was the last time you came to the States?" Annoyance flowed through me, but hurt, too. For ages I'd accepted the state of our family as it was, but for Dad to insinuate it was my fault Gemma and I weren't closer? He was the one who'd left us, not the other way around.

"And why would I do that? To visit the twins, who won't take my calls? To see Ruby and Charlie, who don't even know who I am?"

"Is that their fault? How's a one-year-old supposed to reach out and form a bond with someone on his own? And what about me? Family is a two-way street, you know."

The more heated I got, the stronger my accent came back, and for a second I realized I sounded exactly like Gemma.

"Whilst we're at it, for you of all people to act concerned about Mum? That's rich."

"Lower your voice, will you?" Dad said, cocking his head toward a few guys in novelty Christmas jumpers who'd appeared next to us, scoping out the biscuits. I put my TV smile back on and said "Merry Christmas" to them before pulling Dad into the corner next to the tree.

"Sorry. I didn't intend to have it out with you in general, let alone at this party. But I feel like nothing's gone right lately, and when else will I have a chance to get this off my mind?"

"It's fine. And about your mum, ask her sometime how often I called or wrote her over the years. You might find there's more than one side to this story." He patted my shoulder and went over to greet the sweater guys, leaving me with a sense of regret and loneliness that felt crushing, like the massive tree had fallen on top of me and each crystal ornament had poked a hole in my heart.

Had Dad tried to fly over and see us and Mum shot him down? All these years I thought he was being distant, preoccupied with his new and improved family and content with our Christmas vacations funded by Nanny. But maybe Mum's bitterness was so powerful she'd been willing to sacrifice our relationship with our father to get her revenge.

The idea that Mum had lied to me, or at least purposely omitted information, sat about as well as Gemma's fruitcake. And just as Dad and I were finally having a proper heartfelt conversation, poof, it was over.

I searched around, desperate for a friendly face, but short of Agnes (who was yelling at a waiter, gesturing toward his crooked bow tie then back at Gemma), and the Essex reality stars, I didn't recognize anyone. Nanny had taken Richie up to bed, with excuses she couldn't stay up as late as she used to. It was one of those moments when I wished Anne and Will would get over it and make amends with Dad, but that was wishful thinking, even during the season of miracles.

I forced an appropriately cheery grin on my red lips as I made my way through the crowd to the balcony doors in the back of the room. No one even noticed as I slipped behind the curtain and pushed the doors open, revealing the rolling lawn leading down to the lake. I took a deep breath of the cold night air, tinged with the scent of burning wood.

I could hardly remember the girl who brought books down to the water's edge and watched as her brother and sister chased each other. And it wasn't because the house had been Gemmafied (although the addition of a black lacquer dining table wasn't high on my list). I just couldn't recall the last time I'd felt happy there. Or at all, if I was going to be honest.

I stared out at the grounds with my arms wrapped around me, lost in thought until I heard the creak of the door. "He'll get over it," Gemma said, leaning against the wrought iron railing. "After ten years I've figured one thing out, and it's your Dad's a passionate man."

That was a mental picture I definitely didn't want to see. "No offense, but TMI."

She threw her head back and laughed. "No, not in that way, although—well, nevermind. I mean he's passionate about the people he cares about. And when he's got something to say, he believes in it. Sometimes your dad's got his head halfway up his arse, but generally he means well."

I was grateful for the kindness, but that didn't mean I wasn't pissed off at my father. Even so, bitching about him to Gemma seemed like some sort of betrayal. I stuck with a simple, "Thanks for trying to make me feel better."

She nodded and rubbed her arms, shivering. "Right. Well it's freezing out here, so I'm gonna get back to the party." She paused at the door and turned back to me. "You're all he's got left of the three of you. Talk to him, yeah?"

"I will. I just need to regroup and get some fresh air. This view never gets old." Fortunately, Gemma didn't know my TV voice, and she smiled and stepped back inside.

Once she was gone, I slumped against the railing. I'd already managed to alienate myself in one country, and now I was on the outs in another. Maybe it was better if Katie took over my show, because I clearly didn't have the answers. Not anymore.

✺ Debbie ✺

THE WREATH WAS DOWN, the presents put away, and Pierce, with his incredibly white teeth and infectious laugh, had arranged for an appraiser to come to the house and have a browse to see if anything was worth money before we started filming. It was like antiques bloody roadshow, minus the film crew, but obviously that would come later.

It was even weirder than I thought to have a stranger look through my collectibles, picking things up and examining them to see if they were "worthy," and the appraiser and I had butted heads over half of my china collection already.

Even worse, Rich texted me just as the appraiser showed up and asked if I could meet for a coffee. How could I explain this to him? He knew nothing about my hoarding, and I had planned on taking the slow "getting to know you" route ... i.e., not inviting him to my house until I absolutely had to do it. But with filming stretching ahead of me, excuses were going to run out quickly.

Sorry, the kids are visiting from NY and you know how often that happens! I'll try and pop in the shop this week!

I thought about it for a moment and then added a smiley face to make the text seem extra friendly. We *had* kissed, after all.

"These particular teacups are quite rare, actually," the appraiser said, holding one of my Queen Elizabeth coronation cups in the air, one pinky out as if he was enjoying a civilized afternoon tea himself. I could see it was almost physically painful for Sarah, who was standing next to him, to restrain herself from telling the man it was improper etiquette to stick your pinky out.

"Of course they are," I said, my chest puffed up with pride.

"Found them in an antiques shop on holiday up in Maine, and couldn't believe my luck."

He set the cup back on its shelf and turned to me. "You could definitely make some money from what I've seen so far. When and if you're willing to sell, here's my card."

After chatting with Pierce for a few minutes, Mr. Appraiser was on his way.

"You were right, guys," Pierce said with an ear-to-ear grin. "If this pans out well, maybe we'll do it on every episode."

"Wait, the appraiser was *your* idea?" I said, turning to my kids. *Traitors.*

"I didn't mean any harm," Sarah said. "An idea that Will and I had talked about to change up the show was maybe, and only if you were open to it … we could sell some of the things. Not all of it, of course."

"Of course not," I said. "Don't want to upset your old Mum, do we? I'll be lucky if there's a chair left to sit on by the time this show is over."

Will, always eager to please, (bless him) put his arm around me. "Don't get cross with Sarah. We're all trying to help, and the money would be used to improve the house. We wouldn't sell anything without your okay."

"Will's right. The rest of the team will be here to guide you, but ultimately the decisions made will be yours." Pierce held out a hand, which I gave my limpest handshake.

"I'll think about it. Now if you'll excuse me, I need to use the ladies' room."

I stepped around one of my stacks of tea towel bins and past Pierce, refusing to make eye contact as I made my way to the loo.

Everyone wanted to help clear out the house, but how about what I wanted? Cleaning, sure, but no one said anything about selling. Once the door was closed, I took a few deep breaths and tried to regain composure. Surely Sarah had some kind of tip about dealing with pushy organizers on her blog, but who could remember them all? She started that thing long before she was ever on the telly, and I'd have to search through years of posts about color-coding and how to hire the right professional for the job.

I pulled one of my lint rollers out of the cabinet under the sink and gave myself a quick once-over, then fluffed my hair with a brush. Who knew when a man with a camera would come jumping out from around a corner, so it was best to be prepared. When I finally made my way back into the living room, I saw Sarah and Will poring over a pile of papers on the sofa, while Pierce perched on the worn arm next to them. I stopped and watched from the entrance to the hall, wondering when they'd realize I had come through. Sarah highlighted something on the page, clearly against Pierce's wishes because he yelped and tried to steal the highlighter from her.

"Why are you so annoying?" she said, wrestling with the Sharpie until Will snatched it and handed it over ... to Pierce. *Oh dear.*

I cleared my throat, and all three of their heads turned.

"Mum, we were just going over some ideas," Will said, motioning for me to join them on the sofa.

I stepped around the bins that hid the BOA, which they hadn't spotted yet, and eventually squeezed through the path to the clearing in the living room. Panting, I sat next to Sarah.

"You all right?" she asked, alarm crossing her features. "Do you need your inhaler?"

"Fine, fine, although it's nice to have someone fussing over me for once," I said. "Now what do we need to discuss that's made you practically break out into a WWF fight?"

Pierce choked back a laugh, causing Sarah's head to whip around so fast I made a note to give her the number of my chiropractor.

"Do you take *anything* seriously?" she asked, whacking him in the knee with her bright pink Sharpie.

"Ouch, that hurts," Pierce said with a wince. "Both physically and emotionally."

Will just shook his head. "Can you please get along for more than thirty seconds?"

Sarah let out a small humph and turned back to me. "So, I know this aspect of the show isn't something you've seen, but like I said we had to kind of spice things up for the new season. Basically, we'd have a massive yard sale and invite the community. And then use the proceeds to help renovate the house and make it really lovely, instead of just the basic clean-up they usually do on the show."

I took a long swallow and stared at her in silence. It wasn't just the whole selling things bit, it was when she used the word "community."

"Everyone would know ...."

Pierce opened his mouth, then closed it and bit his lip like he was about to choose his words carefully. "Not to sound like a jerk, ma'am, but you do realize you're going to be on national television, so that kind of comes with the territory."

Sarah scowled. "Pierce, you realize that you could be a bit more—"

"It's all right. I appreciate his directness. And he's not wrong. I signed up to do this, so it's my problem to face."

Will's arm was draped around my shoulders, and I could feel his muscles tense up. He'd always hated conflict.

"Don't worry, Mum. It'll all be amazing and the house will look so nice, we promise. Right, guys?" He shot Sarah and Pierce a look.

"Right," they said in unison, although Sarah's response sounded slightly more reluctant than her new boss's. Pierce leaned down and tugged one of Sarah's blond curls. "Don't sound so enthusiastic, Miss Percy."

"Pull my hair again and you're a dead man."

If they didn't fall into bed within a fortnight, I decided I'd eat a stack of *Hello!* magazines.

Once my house was blissfully free of children, appraisers and attractive TV hosts, I settled down on the carpet next to the BOA. Suddenly a terrible thought, and shockingly one I hadn't imagined before, came to mind: What if Alan saw my episode of *Stuff*? It wasn't like international TV boundaries kept me from watching *Essex Girls*.

I closed my eyes and dove into the basket. The red tartan blanket tucked into the side had brushed my hand a few times on other occasions, but I hadn't wanted to go there. This time I yanked it out, spreading the soft wool across my lap. It was barely faded, a testament to the quality of days gone by, and, to be fair, spending quite a lot of money. I always told the kids, you get what you pay for. I ran my finger along the fringe on the ends, wondering how the Debbie who laughed and picnicked and hid under this blanket ever existed.

What did it matter anyway if Alan saw the show? He was off living his carefree life in Essex with his new family while I was in essentially the same place as I was more than 20 years ago. Reaching into a basket of memories.

∿

Devon, England, March 1984

"I don't know why I thought this was a good idea." Alan kicked the side of the car, rubbing his hands on his temples. "Stupid. Sodding. Car."

I sighed and looked up from my magazine with a frown. "Actually, it was your mum's idea."

He'd been tinkering with the engine, or Lord knows what, for the better part of twenty minutes. Traveling on the M5 for three hours with a backache and what felt like 80,000 pounds of water weight eventually took its toll, so I took a seat in the grass and started reading.

At least Diana was pregnant again, too.

Alan's mum had suggested taking a romantic break by the sea in Salcombe so the two of us could have some quiet time together before the twins arrived. Which was kind of her, don't get me wrong. I was fortunate that my in-laws—read: mother-in-law—could babysit Sarah and cared about us getting some time away. But what would've been nicer was my husband actually suggesting it himself.

To my shock, Alan was fully on board with the plan, and booked us at some posh hotel he'd heard about from one of his regulars at the club. It all sounded grand, until Alan's Aston Martin started rattling. His solution was to turn the volume on his Springsteen cassette way up ... until the rattling grew so loud it rivaled the crowd at our long-ago concert. Alan took the first exit off in hopes of a mechanic (or a pub), and then the car just up and died.

"Wouldn't it be amazing if cars had built-in phones?" he said. "Would solve half of the world's problems, I bet."

"Half?" I didn't even bother looking up from the article showcasing Diana's pregnancy news. I was a good four months or so further along, as the palace just announced her news on Valentine's Day, but it felt nice that we were in it together again ... even if she had no idea who I was.

"Well, maybe not that high of a percent. But still." He slammed the hood closed. "Looks like I'm going to have to go find some help. I saw a sign that said *village centre* a ways back, so it can't be that far."

I just nodded, dreading sitting by myself on the side of the A381 for who knows how long. At least he hadn't said *we* needed to walk and find help, although I was sure a massively pregnant woman waddling down the road might've gotten us assistance faster.

"Wait in the car then and lock the doors. Hopefully I'll be back in an hour or so." He kissed my cheek and then he was off, hands shoved deep into the pockets of his Member's Only jacket.

Even though I couldn't see the water yet, a stiff sea breeze whipped through my permed hair, and I pulled the tartan blanket around me a bit tighter. Alan's insistence on me getting inside the car seemed pointless: without the heat working, it wouldn't be much warmer. And the smell of the salt air and view of the rolling green hills stretching out toward the bay had calmed me down when Alan's shouting at the car should've set my nerves on edge.

Diving into the magazine provided a welcome escape for a good twenty minutes; that is, until a fat drop of water plopped down on Diana's head. And then another.

I jumped up as quickly as someone could at six months pregnant with twins, throwing the blanket over my head to protect me (and, honestly the magazine). I pulled on the car's shiny handle, ready to dry off and continue reading ... but it wouldn't budge. I wiggled it some more, swearing under my breath, and then realized something.

He.took.the.bloody.keys.

I leaned my head back against the door and slumped all the way down in slow motion until my arse hit the ground. *You've got to be kidding me.*

I held the blanket up like a tarp, cursing Alan, his mum, English weather and just about anyone and anything else I could think to curse. How did I end up soaking wet, alone and up the duff (again) on the side of a road in Devon? The pregnant part would normally be easy enough to explain in a normal marriage. Ours ... not so much.

Alan's job really had improved, like he promised. He was home more in the evenings, but even though he was physically present, he wasn't always *there*. I could tell he wanted to be out with his brother, chatting up the regulars and enjoying a few pints rather than playing blocks and singing ABCs, which he actually did do on occasion.

But most of the time, when he wasn't glued to the telly, he was at his parents' house with Sarah. And why would I want to hang out there? I wasn't *un*welcome, but not exactly welcomed either. Mr. Percy loved Sarah in his own way, but no matter how much time had passed or how nice his wife was to me, he still kept a guard worthy of Buckingham Palace up when I was around. Plus, I didn't feel like hearing the annoying questions about when the "next Percy heir" would be on the way. We did have a blue blanket to use, after all.

Maybe it was the familial pressure that finally got to me, or perhaps I was just in a good mood that night when Alan and I had shared a bottle of wine, but I thought why not have more kids? He'd been talking about it for ages, and maybe part of me thought if Alan had a son to kick the football around with and do "manly things" that he'd be more engaged at home. At the very least, another child would provide me with something to focus on and keep busy with when Alan was at work, other than finding places to store my growing pile of royal-watching magazines and china.

But twins? That definitely wasn't in the plan. Alan seemed excited, though, and things were going much better with us, so I just embraced it. It was nice to have old ladies smile at my belly in the shops and exchange friendly chit-chat about babies with Alan's friends' wives. Plus, we had Annie this time, and Alan's mum said she'd pay for a night nurse as well, so I wasn't terribly worried. It had to be easier the second time around, right?

The rumbling of a truck (I still couldn't force myself to call it a lorry) splashing down the road startled me out of my contemplative state. I pulled the blanket off my head, waving wildly at the driver, when I realized Alan was in the passenger seat. *Finally*.

"Jesus Christ!" Alan yelled, jumping down from the truck. His jeans were soaked and hair matted to his head, and running through a muddy puddle to our car didn't make the situation any better.

"Are the babies all right? Why are you sitting out here in the rain?" He grabbed my arm and pulled me up in a drippy hug.

"Oh, just thought it would be a bit of fun," I said, ripping the keys out of his hand and unlocking the door. "Why do you think?

You locked me out of the car!"

"Shit, Debs. I'm so sorry. I mustn't have—"

I slammed the door shut behind me and watched him throw his hands up in defeat, then join the truck driver to tinker under the hood some more. After what seemed like hours of him in and out of the car playing with different things, he hopped into the driver's seat and tested the ignition once more. The car sprang to life, not a rattle to be heard, and he pumped his fist in the air with a loud, "Woohoo!"

After Alan got out and thanked the trucker, slipping a few folded-up twenties in our saviour's palm, we were on the road again. "Right. Now that's over and done with, let's get to our hotel."

I tried to control my temper by staring out at the scenery, but the countryside was barely visible through the rain, and my blood had rolled to the steady boil you get just before the kettle whistles. Pregnancy hormones were a bitch—or at least made me into one on a regular basis—and eventually I couldn't keep my mouth shut.

"If you had thought about someone other than *yourself* for a second, you would've given me the keys and I wouldn't need to get dried off in the first place."

I might as well have slapped him, judging by the pained look on his face.

"And who else was I thinking about when I walked three miles in the rain to find help? I was worried sick that something would happen to you or the babies when I was gone. I try my best to provide for our family, but it never feels good enough, Debs. I'm out late working every night building this business so we can have a good life and nice things. Isn't that what you want?"

Not by a longshot. What I should have told him was I'd rather have his time than his money, but I knew it was pointless. As much as he claimed to be doing it "for us," I knew he loved his business as much as (if not more than) his wife and daughter. I took the easy way out.

"I know. I'm just tired … and overly pregnant. Try not to strand me on the side of a road again and we'll be peachy keen." I tried to make my tone light and jokey, but it didn't seem to work. The air between us felt as strained and uncomfortable as my stretched-to-the-limit belly.

I couldn't force myself to make stilted conversation, so we drove in silence for a few minutes until he cranked up the heat and turned to squeeze my hand. "I'm sorry you had to sit out in the rain. We'll get you warm and dry soon, don't worry."

I remembered an article I'd read about resolving arguments with your partner, and it said to try and remember all of the positive things that you drew you to them in the first place. So I focused on the night we met at the pub. That ridiculous white blazer, the Diana and Charles postcard, his easy charm that made it impossible not to like him.

Suddenly I felt my annoyance dissipating. Yes, he forgot to unlock the car, but the old Alan probably would've sat on the side of the road right with me, waiting for someone to bail him out. Maybe this new, take-charge Alan was here to stay. And maybe I needed to cut him some slack.

"It's fine," I said as the coast finally came into view. "Everything's going to be fine, I promise." I wasn't sure if I was convincing him, or myself, although it was probably a bit of both. Just then one of the babies gave me a sharp kick, followed by the other, as if to say "Try harder, Mum."

Sarah Says
Dress to Impress

Even when you're going to a casual event, or just tidying up your house, it can't hurt to look smart and presentable. Sweatpants scream, "I've given up on life!" whilst crisp trousers and a blouse announce, "I've got something important to say."

"I SIMPLY CAN'T THROW THESE AWAY, Pierce. And don't shoot me that look, I'm immune to your Southern charms." Mum yanked a stack of magazines out of Pierce's hands, showering the floor with dust, whilst my brother shot her a death stare and Anne stood in the corner texting.

This was the scene I walked into at Mum's on day one of the cleanup, and it almost made me want to fly back to Essex, or at the least run right back out the door and go home ... although, to be fair, in this situation I literally couldn't. "Climb back out the door whilst tripping over plastic storage bins and narrowly missing things falling on my head" would've been more like it.

I should've known that this idea wouldn't go down like tea and cakes at the Ritz, but for some reason I thought Mum's quick agreement to sign up for the show meant she'd finally decided to turn over a new leaf.

"Good lord. The cameras haven't even been turned on yet, but at the mere suggestion of getting rid of a pile of old paper that made me slip and fall flat on my face, she goes completely off her rocker. Will make for great TV at least." Pierce stomped off to retrieve his coffee from the counter. I wondered what crawled up his arse (other than the gossip mags).

I opted to avoid him for a bit. Being friends with Kareena

had taught me not to speak to coffee freaks until at *least* the first cup had been consumed.

Instead I introduced myself to the cameramen, Trey and Jon, who were hanging out at the newly cleared-off kitchen table surrounded by a bunch of paperwork, bags, laptops, and lighting equipment. I knew they'd have the inside info that would make my job easier, and Will told me they were super laid back, cool guys.

"So, what do I need to know about Pierce?" I whispered, leaning across the pink floral tablecloth.

Trey let out a deep laugh and rubbed his red goatee. "Hmm. Well, you've probably already noticed the caffeine thing. And he's a stickler about being on time, but something tells me that won't be a problem with you."

"*Sarah Says*: punctuality is perfection," Jon said in a faux English accent, causing my jaw to drop to the ground. "Hey, we did our research on you just like Pierce did."

After my cheeks stopped burning, Jon offered up some actual useful advice. "Pierce: Nicest guy in the world, but screw him over and he'll screw you times a hundred. Get on his good side by bringing some Nutella. Anything with Nutella. Eats it off the damn spoon. Never mention his ex-wife. Oh, and he loves Broadway musicals, but don't tell him I told you that."

"Got it," I said, trying not to laugh while I imagined Pierce singing along to *West Side Story*. "What about the others?"

"The rest of the team kind of stays out of the way. It's the therapist, Molly, who you need to watch for," Trey said. "That lady is crazier than any of the patients she treats."

I raised an eyebrow but kept my response neutral. "I see. Well, thanks for the heads up."

Pierce strolled over before I could ask anything else, and his mood looked like it had improved to at least a five out of ten. "So, I hear you're on your producer's bad side now?"

"How did you know about ... oh, wait. Let me guess. Katie?" I pulled my phone out and pretended to scroll through something important (well, my Twitter feed *was* important). The last thing I felt like discussing was my fight with Andrew. We hadn't spoken since my last day at the station.

"Yeah, we spoke the other day," Pierce said. "Do you think he's threatened by your new gig?"

"No, I think he's just doing whatever he can to suck up to the new station manager and keep his job. But he'll eventually come round, I'm sure."

The camera guys got up from the table to fiddle around with some equipment and Pierce took one of their empty seats.

"I'm over the moon that you've decided to join us, but let's be clear, I don't want you to get in trouble at work or lose your livelihood." He reached out and touched my arm, eyes crinkled with concern. "Are you *absolutely* sure you want to move forward with this episode? It's not too late to bail, even though I'd be pretty bummed if you did."

It took a few moments before I nodded in slow motion. *Do not let him throw you off kilter with one stupid touch.*

"I'm sure. I want to help my mother and if this is what it takes, it's what we've got to do."

"And you don't care if your real job's on the line?"

"My job's not on the line. I'm just on hiatus."

Pierce shrugged. "I'm just the messenger here, but Katie mentioned they've been talking about keeping her on the show. She was concerned they might be keeping things from you. Not trying to butt into your business, but I'd keep your ears and eyes open, that's all."

My mind felt like mush. All I could think about was that everyone at GMNY must've been thinking I was a complete and utter joke, and Katie was taking over for good.

Pierce paused a moment, then added, "Or, you know, you could always stick with me permanently."

After seeing my confused expression he doubled back, red-faced. "I mean, on the show. Of course. Like, a job? Depending on how everything goes, of course."

"I knew what you meant," I said with a laugh, even though part of me had briefly wondered if he meant otherwise. Which was crazy. It took one of my trademark cleansing breaths to pull myself together.

"That's sweet of you to offer but I don't plan on leaving my job. I mean, at least not now."

I tossed my beaded red cardigan on the table. "Why is it so hot in this house?"

Mum's muffled shout called from behind the wall of boxes. "It's winter! No need to freeze."

"Proof that she's actually *not* English," I said to Pierce. He smiled, but it faded in an instant.

"So, back to GMNY ...."

I folded my arms. "Just be assured I'm one-hundred percent committed to being on *Stuff*, and that's all you need to know." With that I stood up and tied my cardigan around my shoulders, then went to figure out what Mum was doing.

Ignore him, one side of me thought. *He's just loyal to his friend, and how would he know if she was trying to manipulate him into making me feel threatened?*

The other side worried Pierce (or Katie) was right. Even though the station approved my absence, and participation, it felt like they were trying to gently push me out the door. At least I had this potential offer of a permanent job on *Stuff*, but was Pierce just trying to be nice?

With all of these thoughts racing through my head, I almost didn't notice the enormous pile of garbage bags in front of me. That is, until my shoe hit the slippery plastic and I ended up on my arse.

"Between you and Pierce, it's like an emergency room's wet dream," Trey said, setting his camera down and extending an arm to help me up.

"I'm fine, thanks," I said, brushing the dust off my black trousers. "I should've worn trainers."

Mum was kneeling next to an oversized wicker hamper, but

as soon as I looked at her, she snapped the lid closed in a rush. "Our Sarah is usually more into function than fashion, but I suppose national television is as good a time as any to get gussied up."

I felt Pierce's presence behind me before he spoke. "You got dressed up just for us? I feel special."

I whirled around. "I'm always dressed up, in case you haven't noticed."

"Defense mechanism?"

"What's that supposed to mean?"

"Well, it's something people do when they're trying to mask—"

"I know what a defense mechanism is, Pierce."

"Actually," he said, folding his arms, "that armor of yours is so damn thick that I don't think you do."

﹉ Debbie ﹊

AS A LITTLE GIRL, I never imagined I'd end up on television. Not in my wildest dreams. I always thought I'd be an artist or something, maybe a school teacher. But a reality TV star? I'd have thought someone was absolutely mental if they'd told me ... not that reality TV even existed back in those days.

As they set up their fancy equipment and the crew did sound checks and all of that stuff, it started to feel real for the first time. Maybe it was the heat from the lights, or the anticipation, but I tugged at the collar of my sweater and wiped my face. *There's no backing out now.*

Those kids could really get me to do anything, and that's what it came down to in the end, although the threat of going to Alan about the house certainly helped. How could I let my son lose his shot at this new job? Sarah had been roped into participating, just like me. The perks of being on a national program couldn't have hurt, I'm sure, but I knew she was only doing it because of her loyalty to Will. Especially since *Stuff* wasn't doing her any favors when it came to her actual job.

I wondered who she was frantically typing to on her phone, but peeked over her shoulder and realized she was twittering, or whatever you call it. Something about taking stock of what you've got in the house before ....

"Mum, it's rude to look at someone's phone." She held it against her chest. "I don't go reading through your papers and personal business."

"I thought twits were public?" I said with a huff. "And what does it look like you're doing here, silly girl?"

Sarah opened her mouth and then closed it, looking a bit

like a fish out of water. "Yes, technically ... but, it's not, I mean I don't want you to read about the organization plan before we talk about it."

I'd become a bit of an expert about knowing when I'm not wanted over the years, so I stood up and made my way into the kitchen. "I'll leave you to it, dear."

As I waited for someone to tell me what to do, Will rushed past me with a thin highlighter shoved behind his ear, carrying a clipboard and an iPad balanced precariously on top of a stack of papers. I had a new appreciation for Will's career. Due to their production assistant not showing up that morning, Will also had to juggle Pierce's errands, the crew's travel arrangements, updating everyone on the schedule, and a million other jobs. Whilst most people would be running around like a chicken with their head cut off, my Will was never without a smile and a helpful opinion.

Other than Jon and Trey, who were both lovely, so far I'd also met Molly, the show's psychologist, a woman whose opinions were nearly as big as her hair. She'd been nice enough to me in our brief encounter, but I had a sinking feeling Sarah wouldn't be as keen on her. Two strong personalities were bound to clash, especially Molly, who seemed like a know-it-all.

"Is everyone ready? We'd like to film the kick-off chat part now if that's all right." Will popped his head around the corner, giving me a quick wave.

"I'm ready," Anne said, hopping up from the blanket where she was sitting on the floor. "Been waiting round here all morning for something useful to do." She headed outside with Jon and Sarah, who stared at her phone the whole time (it's a miracle she didn't trip) while Will and Molly stayed behind with me, along with the redheaded cameraman.

"So, today we're going to take things a bit easy and if anything gets overwhelming, just send off the alarm," Molly said, squeezing my hand so tightly I thought it was going to break. "I want to know your feelings throughout the process, that's *very* important.

Stay true to Debbie."

"All right then, I will," I said, trying to subtly release myself from her grip. *This woman was intense.*

"Trey's just going to film a few seconds of the team, Mum. Molly will speak to everyone about goals. Kind of a pep talk." Will pointed at the cameraman. "Just be yourself, pretend he's not even there."

"Easier said than done, I'm guessing, but I'll try my best."

We all ventured outside, where I was supposed to stand out front and act cheerful and excited about the day ahead. Luckily, I'd had some experience in theatrical performances during my Bedford College days.

Three of the cleanup company employees chatted loudly about traffic on I-76, shivering in their WE TAKE JUNK long-sleeve tees. I knew they were going for brand recognition, but couldn't the boss have at least bought the poor men some logo jackets?

After a few things were situated with the equipment, Molly spoke in an even more animated voice than before.

"All right, we all know why we're here. Debbie has been brave enough to come forward for help, and we know it's a long road ahead. With your hard work, we can get Debbie's house back, and she can start a new life. Can I get a cheer?"

An enthusiastic "woo-hoo!" came from our little group, with Pierce shouting the loudest and doing a little jump. I clapped politely.

"Sarah, can we film your intro now?" Pierce said, his tone returning back to normal. "We'll do it in the backyard."

She followed him around the back with Jon in tow, and Will gestured for me and the others to come inside. "Let's get this show on the road, I suppose!"

Once we headed back indoors, Molly sat with me on the sofa and Anne perched on her blanket again, where she'd set up a little fort of sorts with some pillows. "Debbie, let's start off this first day by sharing some of your fears about the cleanup. I want to get them out in the open, and then talk about how we can overcome them."

I took a deep breath and tried to pretend there wasn't a camera in my face. "Well, erm ... I suppose I'm afraid of giving away something that's important to me. That the memories attached to those things will be gone as well."

"The memories disappearing. You've touched on something vital here." Molly leaned in, her eyes wide. "MEMORIES! Powerful stuff, huh? People who hoard take those past occurrences and attach them to physical things, and somehow the object becomes magical."

I thought about the BOA, and even though this woman seemed to have a screw loose, I completely understood what she meant. If Sarah's blanket, or the Charles and Diana postcard, had suddenly disappeared, would there be any proof that those moments had even happened? I bit my tongue to try and keep the tears at bay.

"You're getting emotional about this. What are you thinking, Debbie?"

I looked around the room at the things that made up my life over the past thirty-some years. "I'm grateful to get a new start and a clean space to live in, but I'm worried about what will happen when I'm alone."

"Elaborate a bit about what you mean by that."

I sighed, trying to figure out how to explain what had been nagging me since Alan left. "Since I moved back to America, I've had the kids, and my lovely things, and they all filled my house. Then the kids grew up and left, and all I've got here is ... stuff. And memories. And when they're gone, what will I do?"

Will frowned and Anne pulled at a thread on the blanket while Molly spouted off more psycho-babble. I hadn't meant to make Will feel guilty about moving to New York, or Anne getting married and moving on, but it looked like my little confessional had hit a nerve. All I wanted to do was help my kids, and now being on the show was upsetting them. Talk about a lose-lose situation.

Eventually Will squeezed behind Trey and I heard the screen door slam.

Trey put the camera down. "What's his issue?"

"Obviously his mother's revelation has caused some of Will's own feelings to come to the surface. That's normal, my dear." Molly pursed her neon pink-painted lips. "Too bad he can't be on screen. I'd love to delve into that mind right there."

My mother bear alarm rang. "What do you mean by that?"

"Oh, nothing. I'd just imagine his feelings about his sexuality are somehow tied into his childhood, and yada yada."

Anne stood up, fists clenched. Mess with her twin, mess with her. "Listen, I don't know who you think you are, but you've got *some* nerve trying to talk about my brother like that!"

"I don't know what you're insinuating, but if you think I'm homophobic, you're absolutely wrong," Molly said, folding her arms and remaining in her seat. "I'm not saying it's your fault he decided to take this path, Debbie. But—"

"But what?" I got up and joined Anne. Standing over Molly felt intimidating, at least, since I've never towered over anyone in my life.

"Ookay, I'm gonna stop you right there. That's enough, ladies," Trey said, rushing over to stand between us and the sofa. "Geez. Talk about things we wish could be on camera." I was instantly grateful for Pierce's decision not to let Will actually take part in the episode, since it would be a conflict of interest as a producer. At least we were saved from having this mess show up on TV.

Anne stomped out of the room, heading for the kitchen (or most likely, the door) and shouting, "*Never* talk about my brother like that again. Full stop."

I took the path to follow Anne, not bothering to wait for Molly's response ... not that I thought she'd apologize. It was going to be a long shoot if I had to deal with this woman for another week. I didn't care if Will dated men, women, or sea creatures, as long as he was content, so why was she trying to stir up drama knowing it wouldn't even be on the show?

The frosty morning air slapped me in the face like a welcome jolt of sanity after the heated discussion inside. I found Sarah and Pierce sitting on the wrought iron chairs I'd bought at Rich's shop. Jon had the camera pointed at her while Will and Anne stood off to the side watching. With all of their backs to me, I decided to just stay quiet and observe.

"I've always loved cleaning and organizing, and being in my grandmother's house pretty much taught me everything I know. But I also knew growing up that I didn't want my life to end up like my mother's."

"So in a way, you chose the complete opposite path to try and prevent that from happening," Pierce said. "To appear perfect would hide the embarrassment of having a mum who's a hoarder."

I recoiled as if Pierce had smacked me across the face. *Was that actually how she felt?* I held my breath waiting for her answer.

"Not really. I mean, this is what I'm meant to be doing. But yes, it's embarrassing when people find out your 'dirty secret,' as you can imagine. I suppose it's all tied together if you want to get psychological about it."

Pierce laughed. "That's Molly's job. But let's talk some more about what you've got planned for the cleanup."

Sarah's voice brightened as she went over organizing, talking with her hands while Pierce turned and beamed at her. If he saw me, he didn't react. I took this as my chance to slip back inside before they could notice, an overwhelming need to be alone washing over me.

I was an embarrassment and a fool.

I trudged through the kitchen, pushing stray boxes out of the way as I went. It shouldn't have come as a shock that she was humiliated about the hoarding. The kids had told me this more than once over the years, but usually during those horrible teenage "I hate you for no reason" arguments. I'd never heard her say it to anyone else, not in person at least.

This was precisely why I didn't tell anyone. If my friends—or worse, Rich—came to the house, my entire world would come crashing down. Neatnick Debbie would be replaced with some insane lady living in a house of filth. Maybe Sarah and I weren't so different after all. Both of us had put up these personas to the outside world to keep everyone from finding out the truth.

As if he could read my thoughts, my pocket vibrated with a text from Rich. *If you're not busy, want to meet me at Minella's for an early dinner? 5:00?*

I tapped the screen, trying to think of an excuse. He knew Minella's was my favorite diner, and I never turned down an opportunity for their turkey avocado BLT. But the crew was at the house until 5, and then I had a dinner with the kids. Normally that would've sufficed as a reason not to go, but what if he wanted to meet the next day, or the one after?

Would love to but I'm feeling like I've been hit by a bus. Can barely move off sofa. Don't want to spread my germs to you! Let's meet up when I've recovered xx

Honestly, I would've rather been sick than dealing with that fiasco of a TV show. I said a quick prayer that my lies to Rich wouldn't catch up to me.

Since Molly was taking a phone call in the corner and Trey was nowhere to be found, I slipped over to the BOA, ready for my fix. It felt like I was a drug addict or something. Once I'd opened the can of worms, I couldn't stop.

This time, I pulled out a yellowing newspaper advertisement. A photo of an impressive brick home sat underneath the headline "Grade II property for sale."

The house that changed everything.

Brentwood, January 1987

"You awake, Debs?"

I rolled over, careful not to whack Will and Anne in the face.

They'd climbed into bed with me after both insisting that they had monsters in their closet, and the bed had become a pile of tangled brown curls and tiny limbs thrown in different directions over mine.

"Shh," I said, sliding out from under the covers inch by inch. I tiptoed over to the bedroom door and motioned for Alan to step outside. "It's three in the morning, for God's sake."

"Sorry," he said, running a hand through his new, shorter and spikier haircut. "I couldn't wait until morning to tell you. We've got the deal!"

"Wow, well done," I said, reaching up for a hug. Alan and his brother had been hoping to open a second location of their most popular club, Beats, after the success of the first club. After two different properties had fallen through, he'd been waiting to hear about a converted factory space that seemed perfect for their vision.

"You must be so pleased," I said between yawns.

"Long night with the twins again?"

"The longest." I padded out to the kitchen and put the kettle on. "Might as well since I'm up now. You want some?"

Alan shook his head no and sprawled out on the sofa, kicking off his shiny black shoes. "Can't believe it. This is actually going to happen."

I busied myself getting the milk and lemon out, but really I didn't know what to say. Was I happy for my husband's success? Surely. We'd come a long way from our early days in the flat, and with business booming, money was never an issue. But a second location would only bring more nights out clubbing ... oh, I meant *working* ....

"It's quite exciting," I finally said, pulling out one of my Buckingham Palace mugs. "When do you think it'll open?"

He shrugged. "Anyone's guess, depending on how soon we can get the guys in for the renovations. But by the spring, hopefully."

"Well, just make sure you keep your promise to Sarah about

that holiday for her birthday. She'll be gutted if you don't follow through."

I could've added "again" to the end of my sentence, but decided to refrain. It was too late, or in this case, early, to start a row.

"The cottage is already booked," Alan said. "My mum took care of it the other day. Right by the sea as requested. And I'm not going to cancel, I promise."

I thought he'd drifted off to sleep since I didn't hear another peep from him as I finished preparing my tea, but when I carried it over to the sofa, his eyes popped open.

"What do you think about moving?"

"Moving?" I said, nearly choking on my Earl Grey. "To where?"

He reached into his briefcase and pulled a newspaper out. "Here. In Brentwood. Just a bigger place."

I scanned the advert, eyes growing wide when I spotted the cost. "Can we even afford this?"

"Course we can. You know we've been doing well lately, but with the second location of Beats it's going to change everything. Why live somewhere average when you can have a home like this?" He took the paper back from me, staring at the picture with a far-off, dreamy expression. I could tell he'd already bought it in his head. Seven bedrooms, four baths, a huge garden ... it was like a mini version of Percy Hall.

"I don't know. The kids love it here, and do we really need that much space?" It had taken me years to feel at home in our cozy three-bedroom, and it was decorated exactly the way I wanted, although Alan bemoaned that I'd taken over the back corner of the living room with the overflow of my collectibles that couldn't fit elsewhere.

"This house is getting to be too tight for all of us. You have to admit we didn't move in here expecting to have three kids. Or all of your stuff."

"You're right," I said. "But I still don't want to relocate."

Alan set my cup on the coffee table, putting his arm around me. "But just imagine what you could do with your collection. You could have an entire room just for your royal wedding souvenirs if you wanted."

We settled on the house the following month.

Sarah Says
Do You REALLY Need It?

Tackling a big organization project takes time and effort, but no one thinks about how emotionally draining it can be, too. We all cling to belongings that we think are useful for whatever reason, but remember the one-year rule: if you haven't used it in the past year, and can't think of an occasion in the coming weeks when you'll definitely need it, that item needs to go. Clutter is a Sarah don't!

"SO YOU CAN DEFINITELY be back next week then?" Andrew said. I could hear the day's headlines blaring and someone shouting, "Where the hell is Kareena?" in the background.

"Yes, like I told you a hundred times, I'll be—"

Just then a much more pleasant voice called out. "Sarah, we need you inside." I held my finger up in the universal "just a minute" gesture as Pierce rounded the corner into Mum's garden. He exhaled deeply, grinning at the puffs of air that blew out of his mouth on the chilly winter morning, and I held back a laugh.

"Don't sound so excited," Andrew said.

At first I was relieved to get Andrew's call to finalize scheduling, but that feeling quickly passed. No, I wasn't looking forward to getting back on set at GMNY, and Andrew's curt tone wasn't making me more enthusiastic. I had another show to shoot, and right then they were the ones who needed me on set. As a producer, Andrew had to have understood that.

"Look, I've got to film the bit about me going over the organization plan with Mum, so I'll speak to you later, okay?"

Andrew mumbled, "Fine. Good luck then," as I stood there

in the dismal garden, shaking my head.

"Sorry for interrupting. That sounds like it went well," Pierce gritted his teeth.

I tucked the phone into my coat pocket and shrugged. "He's just a bit grumpy about me missing all this time from the show, that's all."

"I reckon you're entitled to time off though? It's not like a host has never gone on a vacation." Pierce zipped his black down jacket up to the top, pulling the collar over his mouth. "Sorry. It's ridiculous out here. Don't know how you manage these East coast winters."

We trudged around the side of the house, the faded, sad brown grass making crunching noises under our feet. "I take it you're used to a more hospitable climate down south."

"You could say that again. But I travel all over for the show, so I had to suck it up and buy this coat. Makes it harder to bring just a carry-on when you've got all these big old things like boots and sweaters."

"So are you used to packing lightly when you travel?"

Pierce paused, and for a second I thought he wasn't going to answer. It was a simple question, wasn't it?

"Yeah. I used to go on a lot of island vacations ... when I was married. Kind of done with those now."

It was the first time he'd brought her up, and although I wanted to ask more, the cameramen's warning echoed. *Never bring up his divorce.*

Not that I could blame Pierce, because I'd had my fair share of disastrous couples' trips. A memory of packing for the last island holiday my ex and I took together flashed in my brain. The bikinis, strappy sandals, and sundresses never even got worn, because there was an emergency at his office and we flew home after the first day. I vowed I wouldn't holiday like that for the rest of my life, but here I was stressing out over taking a week off to *work*.

"Sarah? You going in?"

I snapped out of it and stepped inside the door Pierce held open for me. "Sorry, was just thinking about what I wanted to say to Mum."

"Just remember what we talked about. Not too pushy, because she'll instantly raise her defenses. Just focus on how we could display her collection in new ways, yadda yadda yadda."

"I don't think that will be an issue since Mum's all about admiring her stuff. The biggest problem is getting rid of everything that doesn't fit in the plan," I said as we snaked our way through the path into the living room. "And as much as I love the yard sale idea, I'm nervous it's going to backfire on us."

"It'll all work out. You'll see." He reached behind for my hand as we got to the last turn before the clearing. I grabbed it without hesitation, stepping over the last of the bins, but then thought ... *is this weird*? The feeling of warmth and support certainly felt like it.

There was no time to ponder after we saw what was happening on camera. Mum was working with Anne and Molly on a bin marked "Prince William collectibles," the contents of which were laid out on the carpet around them. I dropped Pierce's hand when I saw the defiant expression on Mum's face.

"No, no. Definitely keeping that," she said, snatching a stuffed bear wearing an "Our prince has arrived" t-shirt from Molly. "Ruby would love this."

"Ruby has enough stuffed animals," Anne said, stepping over a coffee table book with the young royal family on the cover. Trey turned his camera to get my reaction and I stopped like a deer in headlights.

After working in television for the past five years, you'd think I'd learn when I was going to end up on screen. I took a deep breath and tried to save face.

"Anne's right. I think it's great you're thinking of things to put away for the kids, but Ruby has loads of toys she never plays with. Maybe you could put a few things aside and then ask her if she wants them. If not, we can use those items for the yard sale."

"I can assure you she won't want another bear, Mum," Anne said. "Why don't we make this one a donation?"

Mum tossed the teddy at me. "I like Sarah's plan. Go ahead and make a pile over there if you want."

I turned to put the bear on the sofa, but Anne grabbed it out of my hands. "Don't you think that's the wrong approach? By encouraging her to hold onto more stuff, you're just going to set her progress back even further."

I pulled the bear out of her grip and hugged it to my chest. "Sorry, but I disagree. By forcing her to throw things away, you're only going to alienate her. You know how Mum is, she'll just replace them all as soon as we leave."

"I *am* in the room here, you know," Mum said, folding her arms.

"That's where you and I differ, I suppose." Anne turned to Molly. "And what's your input?"

"I see Sarah's point. If this process starts out on the wrong foot, all of our work will be pointless. However, if we allow Debbie to keep doing this, we won't get rid of a single item."

"Exactly," I said, whipping my phone out of my pocket and opening the notes app, "The majority of hoarders simply fill their houses back up after a forced cleanout. Unless they're active participants and making decisions, you can pretty much guarantee we'll be back here within the year. Plus, a traumatic clean-out can lead to some dangerous emotional consequences for the homeowner."

I smiled at Molly, waiting for her impressed reaction. "I've done my research."

Molly's mouth formed a tight line. "That's great, but after twenty years in the field, I would consider myself an expert. Please, tell me more about your Internet research. I'm sure you could take my job now, so clearly I'm no longer needed here."

"Molly, come on now. Calm down," Will said, following her across the room. I heard him mutter something under his breath, and suddenly she headed down the path with Jon chasing behind.

I wondered if Will purposely told her to storm out. More conflict meant more drama (and juicy teaser commercials), which meant more viewers.

"Without meaning to, you've made this episode about ten times more exciting," Pierce said, draping an arm around my shoulder. A zing traveled down my arm, and either I was imagining things, or he felt it too, because his head jolted back a bit and he looked at me with confusion.

"What was I saying?"

"Um, something about the episode being dramatic because of Molly?"

"Ah. Yeah. I can see Molly storming off and the door slamming in our faces just as the screen fades to black with the logo. Good stuff." He let his arm fall, dragging his hand along my back a bit slower than necessary, and winked as he walked away.

What was that about?

Mum remained so silent throughout the whole ordeal, and I was so distracted by Pierce, I almost forgot she was there until she finally spoke up. "All of this fuss over a teddy bear? Honestly, what's wrong with you two?"

"What's wrong with me? I'm on *your* side." I finally let go of the bear, tossing it on the sofa, and Anne swiftly picked it up and put it in the donation pile. Trey turned back and forth, following the action like a wildlife documentary ... which was appropriate, because it felt like I was in one.

Mum marched over and tossed the teddy right back into the bin. "You all told me I'd get to have a say in what stays and what goes, and I say I'm keeping the bear. And all of the rest of this container. You know royal baby souvenirs are worth money."

"You're right," I said. "That's why we should consider putting out at least a few of these items for Ebay or the sale. They'll bring in the money we need to make the improvements on the house and buy the display pieces to make your collection look gorgeous."

"I see where you're coming from. You know I'm not completely unreasonable. But I just don't want to let go of these things quite yet. Okay?"

"Fine," I said, throwing my hands up in defeat. "Let's move on to another box since Molly obviously doesn't want to participate right now. We can chat about the organization ideas I have whilst we work. Anne, are you in?"

"Fine. Whatever." She pursed her lips and grabbed the highest container off the pile. "Assorted London tea towels. That should be easy."

Mum opened the box and looked inside. "These are all useful, so they stay."

My fingers started twitching and I bit my tongue hard to keep my composure. "I want to hang some of the towels up on some pretty ceramic hooks in the kitchen, and I think we only need about ten in total. There's at least ... what, fifty in here?"

"We'll sort through them later," Mum said, her tone turning increasingly huffy.

"What about this one?" I bent over and lifted the big wicker hamper Mum had been looking inside earlier. She was next to me in an instant.

"Don't touch that!" Mum said, panting. I swore I could see little blurry lines behind her like a cartoon, that's how fast she'd moved across the room.

"Tell Pierce and everyone else that this is off limits, all right?" She snatched it out of my arms, setting the container gently back on the ground. I felt Trey's presence behind me, capturing the whole embarrassing thing on camera.

Anne stepped between us. "Mum, honestly! Calm down. And what the hell is inside that thing?" She reached down to move the basket out of the way, but that's when Mum *really* lost it.

"Do. Not. Touch. This. Basket." She enunciated each syllable so sharply that it was like she was spitting out knives. The audience was going to just eat this up.

"Fine, lovely. Let's not touch any of your things. You're only on a show about hoarding, what did you expect was going to happen?" I knew I shouldn't have said it, I should have been "keeping calm" and whatnot, but the words poured out before I could stop them.

Mum's eyes looked wild and her hair had frizzed out like she'd stuck her finger in an electrical outlet. For a second, I was almost scared. "What did I think would happen? I thought my children would support me."

"We *are* supporting you. What does it look like I'm doing here?" I gestured at the binder with my organization plans, sitting on the sofa untouched. "I risked my job to come here and be with you. But how can any of us help you if you refuse to even listen?"

"If you knew what it was like to be thrown away with the morning garbage, you wouldn't want to toss anything out either, would you?"

Here we go again.

Ever since Dad left, everything was his fault. Of course I was team Mum, but decades of hearing the same excuse, and the same line, got old. Especially after what Dad had said to me in Essex. Weren't we all in charge of our own destinies? Hadn't she listened to anything I'd ever said on TV?

"I know it was a traumatic experience for you. It was for all of us. But sometimes I wish you'd stop blaming Dad for all of your problems. It's been over 20 years. Can't we move on?"

Anne shot Will a desperate look, and he said, "Sarah, I don't think you should go there." But I kept talking.

"Do you know Dad told me he tried to call and talk to you, to write to us, but you ignored him? You kept us away from our father on purpose because you wanted to punish him for the divorce. But you know, everything is all *his* fault."

Mum's mouth drooped, and she stared at the ground. "You have no idea what I went through with your father. He left us because he couldn't deal with some boxes around the house. Was that fair?"

Mum was being so irrational that Anne, who was the last

person anyone would expect to defend Dad, spoke up. "A few boxes? Mum, you've got to understand it was more than that. And you fought all the time, even before your collection got out of control."

"You were children. But please tell me more about my marriage." Mum's eyes said *go ahead, I dare you*. So I did.

"Your marriage ended because you're a hoarder, in part. But also because it was a shaky relationship to begin with. And news flash: you can choose to stop collecting, but you won't. It's like you're a prisoner in the Tower of London and they've thrown away the key. But guess what? You do have the key. And a passport. You can leave whenever you want! So what's keeping you here?"

⁂ Debbie ⁂

"POUR SOME BAILEYS IN IT, I think that'll help." Rich slid a tiny bottle across his equally Lilliputian kitchen table.

"Might as well at this point." After the kids, Pierce and the rest of the crew had wrapped up for the day, I immediately picked up the phone and called Rich. I couldn't explain what made me do it, but maybe I just needed to talk to someone who was completely on my side. Of course I couldn't tell him what had *really* happened, other than a fight with my kids about their dad (which wasn't technically a lie).

And although it required me to fake a miraculous recovery from being sick, he immediately invited me to his house for a good, long heart-to-heart. Or in this case, alcoholic hot chocolate.

"Can you believe her? My own daughter," I said, pouring a wee splash of Baileys onto my spoon and dumping it into my floral mug. I might have been open to a drink, but it was five-thirty on a Tuesday, after all.

"It sounded like she got pretty heated. And that's not fair, since you're always there for your kids. But ..." He twisted the paper napkin in his hand.

"Go ahead, I can take it."

"You've been divorced since the nineties. Maybe it's time to step aside and let your kids form whatever relationship they need with their father. Wouldn't you be hurt in the same situation if you found out your father had wanted to come see you more often, but your mother kept him away?"

His voice was kind, but that didn't take the sting of his words away, and I took my time swallowing the hot chocolate before responding. Normally the warmth traveling down my throat would feel comforting, but it just burned. *Why was everyone trying to change me?* If I wanted to hear criticism, I would've stayed home.

"You've obviously never met Alan, but what I went through with that man ... let's just say it turned my life upside down. He was always so immature, and obsessed with his work, I didn't want him to blow into their lives and make all of these promises and disappoint them. He couldn't always stay true to his word when we were in the same house, let alone across an ocean. Does that make me an overprotective mum? I guess so."

"I get that. And I'm sorry if I'm overstepping. Like you said, I've never met him. But I thought I'd be remiss as a friend—or well, boyfriend, if I can call myself that—if I didn't try to get you to see it from your kids' point of view." He cracked the tiniest of smiles, like a chip on a teacup.

Although it *was* slightly thrilling, I didn't know how to react to the boyfriend comment (and it seemed ridiculous using that term at our age), so I stuck to the topic at hand instead.

"Thanks. I know you're not trying to be a jerk, but this is just tough for me. It's easier said than done putting all of the bad stuff behind and thinking of him independently of the Alan I used to know. Like Sarah will say, 'well you know how Dad is about so-and-so,' and honestly I don't, because he's not the Alan I was with. And that almost hurts even more, if that makes sense."

"It does. But you're not the same Debbie, either. I wouldn't want you to be."

"Fancy that," I said. I knew his heart was in the right place. But how was I supposed to explain my marriage to someone like Rich, whose dearly departed wife was practically a saint? And if I'd ever thought of breaking the news about my house to him, stepping into his perfect little townhouse, where the only clutter was a stack of unopened mail and some newspapers piled on the coffee table, would've changed my mind lickety split.

"Every family has their ups and downs. But it's how we handle the downs that matter," Rich said. "I don't talk about this much ...

but my youngest daughter, the one out in California, we're barely on speaking terms. I didn't approve of the man she married, and it's caused a lot of heartache in our family. I see my grandkids once a year if I'm lucky. So I can see where Alan's coming from, even though that probably annoys you. And I don't want you to end up in the same situation, too."

"I'm sorry, I had no idea. You always talk about your kids so fondly ...."

Rich dumped some more Baileys into his drink. "Have you never sugarcoated something to try and feel normal?"

I swallowed the last sip of my drink with a loud gulp.

"Of course," I said with my best goody-two-shoes smile. "Everyone likes to put their best face forward, especially when they're just getting to know someone." If this went any further and he asked if *I* had any little secrets, I'd have to tell a bold-faced lie about the house. To my kids, or Pierce, or Molly, it didn't make sense, but I wasn't ready to tell Rich about my collection, let alone about *Stuff*, and all their voices in my head telling me to do it just made me push back even harder.

I wanted to run out the door, but forced myself to take a seat back at the table and check my phone instead, hoping he'd take that as a cue to end the conversation. Sarah had called and texted. I deleted both messages.

Rich took my hand across the table. "Whether you know it or not, you're a tough act to follow, Debs. You seem like you have it all together, and please don't take this the wrong way, but I was almost relieved when you told me about the argument. I thought 'well thank God, she's just like the rest of us.'"

I threw back my head and laughed, but inside I was cringing. How could anyone think I, of all people, had my act together? "Thank you, but I'm not perfect. Trust me on that one."

Rich shook his head. "Practically. You're like Mary Poppins with all your little gadgets in your purse, and you're always dressed impeccably, and you make me feel ... well, special."

I squeezed his hand back and said a simple "you too," because

I would've been lying if I hadn't said it back. His face lit up, a far cry from the forced grin earlier in the evening. When was the last time I'd made someone feel special, not counting the kids? Hell, I couldn't even count the kids, as apparently I only embarrassed them. We sat there smiling at each other like fools, and it should have been an opportune moment for a kiss ... but with a table and a stack of lies between us, I stayed in my chair.

Rich must have gotten the hint because he stood up, and on his way into the kitchen, kissed the top of my head. "So, I bought a cheesecake at Wegmans and it isn't going to eat itself. You in?"

Relief washed over me. "You sure know the way to a woman's heart. And thank you. For everything."

We made an impressive dent on the cheesecake and a few more hot chocolates, sharing stories about growing up, and our kids, and just life ... and for the first time I felt like my burden wasn't so heavy, even if I still carried the brunt of it.

"I know it's getting late, but do you want to stay and watch a movie? What do the kids call it? Netflix and hang out?"

Luckily I had no idea what he was talking about, because he most likely had botched the term. Either way, the thought of getting close on a sofa didn't seem like the best of ideas. "I've got an early morning ahead and a lot of emotions to deal with. I hope you understand."

Rich grabbed my things from the coat rack. "Of course. You're not upset with me, right?"

I might've answered differently a few hours earlier, but I shook my head. "No, not even remotely. Just tired and a bit overwhelmed. But you've been a big help."

"Good." He leaned in for a long kiss, making it a bit harder to resist staying and just watching the film after all.

Rich made the decision much easier when he took a step back. "I have a request, though. I think you should smooth things out with Alan. Maybe give him a call, or at least send an email. If you let go of the past, I really think it will help move things in the right direction for you."

I'm sure he meant it would improve my relationship with the kids, but wondered if the subtext was "get you to hurry up and move this relationship along." He'd never complained about the speed before, but you never knew with men.

"I think it would be easier to arrange a meeting with the Queen." I said it with a nervous chuckle, hoping to lighten the mood, but Rich's lips had formed a tight line and wouldn't budge.

"Seriously, Debs. Consider it?"

"I know you're probably right. And I'll think about it. Have a good night, okay?"

I rushed over to my car before he could stop me.

The visit had ended much differently than I could've ever expected, but then again, who expects their sort-of boyfriend to stage a surprise intervention over Bailey's and hot cocoa? I'd made one of my biggest breakthroughs by confessing my troubles with the kids and my divorce to him; the added step of calling Alan felt like too much, too soon. And frankly it *was* overstepping a bit for him to suggest it.

Even so, on the drive home I thought about what would happen if I called Alan. I even went as far as rehearsing a few things I could say. Somehow, "So, I know it comes a shock, but I'm participating in a hoarding reality show and think I need to forgive you to move on" didn't sound like a great opener. Surely I'd think of a better way to bridge the gap with the kids.

Later, safe in my living room, I was engaged in a stare-down with the BOA. Deep down, I knew opening it probably wouldn't have given me any flashes of inspiration, but things couldn't have gotten much worse, either. I'd torn enough things out of that basket so far and I was still standing, and that was a miracle in itself.

I reached in, hoping for something not too traumatic, since it'd already been a *day*. The smooth paper box in my hand seemed ordinary enough, then I lifted it out to reveal it was one of those Christmas ornament boxes with the top that folds in to protect the ball.

"Buckingham Palace, 1989" read the white ball with sparkly red lettering and a painted rendition of the palace. That was the year my parents actually came to England for the holidays ... the year stuff began taking over my house.

And my marriage.

~~

London, Christmas 1989

"Grandma, come see the tree! Look at the carolers!"

Sarah grabbed my mother's Isotoner-gloved hand and led her toward the crowd in Trafalgar Square, cheeks flushed from the cold and the excitement. It wasn't every day her grandparents came over from the States, after all, and her friends were simply dying of jealousy that she had "a cool American family." Sarah had accordingly started speaking in an almost painful-sounding American accent, which drove Alan mad.

What *didn't* drive Alan mad?

"This is beautiful, isn't it, Bill?" Mom said, nodding at Dad vigorously and widening her eyes as if to say, "you'd better agree with me." Despite a decade of me living in England at that point, Dad still fought the idea of international travel tooth and nail.

"It's definitely festive," he said, switching Anne from one hip to the other with an *oof*. "And crowded." He scanned the bundled-up tourists taking pictures and oohing and aahing over the towering, brightly lit tree in front of the fountain. "Might as well go ahead with it."

To be fair, after cramming through the mob of toy shoppers in Hamley's with Will and Anne fighting over teddy bears and Sarah begging for a toy vacuum (typical), I couldn't exactly blame him.

I tugged my snowflake-print hat down over my ears and shot Dad my best enthusiastic daughter smile as a choir of school-age boys belted out the first lines of "O Holy Night."

"It's a popular place to visit at Christmas. But if you haven't been to London at this time of year, it's one of those must-sees. Why don't we sit down and listen to the carolers for a bit?"

I turned to motion Will and Alan to hurry up; as usual my son was dawdling behind, interested in some obscure detail like the pattern in the sidewalk. "Come on, luv! Let's listen to the nice Christmas music."

Will let go of his father's hand and raced to join me, jumping up and doing a crazy spin that only a five-year old could pull off without falling flat on his face. "Do you think Father Christmas will be here? Dad said he only comes round on Christmas Eve, and that anyone else is just an old man dressed up in a red-and-white suit. But I think he might come say hello. If I were him, I'd want to come here."

"Daddy is so silly sometimes," I said, shooting my husband The Look. "Sometimes people like to dress up and pretend to be Father Christmas, but you never know who could be the *real* one."

"Whatever your mother says." Alan ruffled Will's hair absent-mindedly, staring off at the tree's twinkling lights. The Trafalgar Square tree was a gift from the city of Oslo each year, and I wondered if Alan was thinking about his own connection to Norway: namely, Hedda, the blonde bombshell who'd recently joined the staff at Beats as a cocktail waitress. I didn't have proof of anything untoward going on, but that didn't mean I wasn't on the lookout for her flirty glances on the rare occasions I did step into Alan's club.

He didn't show much interest in the kids, or in me, so he had to have an interest in *something*, didn't he?

My parents had corralled the others and were sitting shoulder to shoulder on the steps leading down to the tree, the tartan blanket that Sarah had insisted on bringing in her "just in case" bag draped across their laps.

"After you," I said to Alan, touching the small of his back.

"Oh. Yeah, of course." He took the steps two at a time, his red scarf fluttering behind him in the chilly wind, and took a seat next to my father. "Should we skive off and go to the pub?" I heard him mutter as I stood behind them. *You've got to be joking.*

Dad chuckled. "I'd kill for a beer, but Debbie would never let us hear the end of it, and I don't want to even go there with Sarah."

"To be honest, I'm scared of her, and she's eight years of age." Alan said just as Will and I took a seat to his left.

"Who're you scared of, Dad?" Will climbed on to my lap. "Mummy said if I'm scared, I should just come and sleep with her at night. Maybe you could try that, too."

My father cleared his throat and turned to look back at the stage, suddenly extremely interested in the performance.

"You know Dad's out working late at night sometimes, and if you're asleep in bed with Mum I'd rather leave you to it and not wake anyone by tripping in the hall," Alan said. "I think I know a little boy who hates being waken up early, right?"

Will giggled. "I wish I could sleep allllll day!"

I leaned my chin on his stiff blue cap and hugged him, hoping my damp eyes wouldn't mean a mascara stain on the Phillies hat my parents had brought him. At least Sarah would've known exactly how to clean it.

Will hummed along to the music and I squeezed him tighter. My clever, funny boy. I thought that once he came along, Alan would be thrilled to have his little protégé. But the two of them didn't quite connect, as hard as I tried to encourage it. Will would rather sing with me, play with the animals, or look at the pictures in my magazines than kick a ball around with his father. Now Alan had two girls, and a boy who had no interest in anything his dad wanted to do. It was like I'd failed the Percys yet again.

The carolers had moved on to an upbeat version of "Jingle Bells," and I tried to arrange my expression into a more cheerful one as well. As long as Alan didn't see my tears, the night wouldn't be ruined. I didn't need to get into a row when my parents were finally visiting.

Mom leaned forward to get my attention. "Debbie, what time

do you think we should head back to Brentwood? It's getting late."

I shrugged. "This is your holiday. Whenever you'd like to head back to the car is fine with us."

"Why don't we let Debbie and Alan listen to the rest of this song, since we're the old folks ready for bed," Dad suggested. "We'll bring the kids up by the museum and wait for you." He patted my shoulder as he left, which I knew was supposed to be reassuring, but instead felt humiliating. My father wasn't supposed to get involved in my marriage problems. I wasn't supposed to *have* marriage problems, for that matter.

Alan tapped his trainer against the steps, probably to a Springsteen tune, but who knew what was going through his head anymore. "Debs, I know we need to talk, and this probably isn't the time ... but I guess your father thinks it should be, huh?"

"Listen, I know the house is a mess, but things have been so crazy with the kids and getting settled—"

The tapping increased speed. "We moved in nearly two years ago. There's only so long I can use the 'we're still settling in' excuse when people want to come round ours. Frankly, it's embarrassing."

I almost had to laugh at the contrast of the cheery Christmas tunes and the tone of our conversation, but what could I do? He was right about everything. I knew that. Sarah had been bugging me for ages to let her move all of the boxes into our spare bedroom and set up a display. If my eight-year-old knew there was a problem, that wasn't a good sign.

But when Alan was out working, and the kids were in school, I relied on shopping more than ever to pass the time. The few friends I'd made all lived on the opposite side of town now, and were too absorbed with their own school runs, kids' sports and family dinners. I wasn't posh enough to be living in our historic pile, and I knew it—and so did the neighbors.

"I'll try harder." I inhaled slowly to take a deep, cleansing breath and count to five like Mrs. Percy had taught me, but struggled to find enough air. *Not again.* My heart raced and every-thing closed in around me. *You won't lose all of your stuff. Don't panic.*

"Honestly Debs ..." *Tap. Tap. Tap,* "at this point any effort would classify as harder, considering you're not trying at all."

"Will you STOP the bloody tapping?" My brown boot came down on top of his trainer hard enough to feel his toes squash under the leather, and for a moment we just stared at each other. I'd seen that wide-eyed look—a cross between surprise, confusion and anger—once before, when I went mental on a girl at Beats who'd asked for his phone number. Just like that night, part of me wondered if I'd crossed a line. The other part didn't care. But I did pull my foot back.

"I've just worked really hard to find some of these things ... I can't bear to give them up. And as my husband you shouldn't make me."

Alan winced and rubbed the back of his neck. If only it was that easy to get rid of the tension between us. "Make you? Just organize everything better. No one's forcing you to bin all of it. Anyway, it doesn't matter. Let's just leave it."

English to American Translation: This matters quite a lot and I'm furious, but desperate to change the subject so people won't stare at us.

It was bad enough when my own father lectured me about the stuff in my high school bedroom; I didn't need my husband doing it, too. "You know what? Maybe—"

"Daddy!" Both of our heads turned to find Will racing down the steps with my mother chasing behind him in vain. "Sorry," she mouthed.

"Grandma and Grandpa told me when we get home that we're going to do puzzles and read books before bedtime, and that we can't be naughty because Mummy and you need some private time." He blurted this out in one rapid-fire sentence without taking a breath, as children often do. I turned my head to the side for a second to wipe my eyes, and then smiled my most genuine fake smile before turning back to Will. I knew he'd be studying my reaction.

"Ah, that sounds like fun, doesn't it? Why don't we hurry home so you can get to your games then." I took his mittened hand and led him back up to my family, turning to take one last look at the perfect winter scene before me once we reached the top of the steps. Perfect families and perfect carolers, all celebrating a perfect Christmas around the stupidly perfect Norwegian tree.

Fa la la la, indeed.

Sarah Says
Make the Most of It

When you find yourself with some unexpected free time, why squander it away on the Internet or reality TV when you could be doing something productive? Tackle that pantry organization project, print out your holiday photos, or finally meet up with that old friend for lunch. Doesn't that feel better?

THERE'S SOMETHING about hotels that turns even the most Type-A person into an absolute lazy arse. Since they didn't need me for filming the day after the blow-up with Mum, I slept until a luxurious 7:30 (which in my world, was like noon), and two hours later I still hadn't budged from under the fluffy white duvet.

Perhaps it's the whole "your entire house is a bedroom for the time being" feeling, but all I'd ever wanted to do in a hotel was watch silly rom-coms and eat fast food off a room service tray. I once read a story about over-the-top kids' parties, and these little girls were put up in a suite and served candy on silver platters. That seemed like the ideal sort of party to me (and one Nanny Percy would've let me have) but I'm sure Mum would've been horrified.

She was already horrified at what I said about her hoarding, and I couldn't blame her. After we wrapped up shooting, I tried to apologize, but Mum wasn't having any of it. An ignored phone call and text message on my phone reminded me that she was a champion grudge holder. Not that anyone ever questioned that aspect of her personality.

One person who *had* texted was Pierce. Just to check in if I was okay after the argument with Mum the night before. Even invited me to grab a drink in the hotel bar. Was that crossing some sort of personal/professional line? I couldn't decide, and since I had already changed into pajamas, I let my outfit make the decision for me. I was fairly sure that the good folks at Marriott frowned upon pink silk heart-print pajamas in the lobby.

My phone buzzed around 10 a.m. and Kareena's name flashed on the screen. "Thank God you answered. Why do you always have to leave New York when I have a crisis?"

"What now?" I said. Kareena thought losing her favorite coffee cup was an extreme crisis, so I didn't even blink at her opening line.

"My parents disowned me. Again. It's not my fault that those photographers saw us and I ended up on Page Six. They said I was an embarrassment to the family and they'd already given me plenty of chances after … you know. The last time."

I groaned. Kareena's last boyfriend leaked info about her parents to the Bollywood gossip media, but they eventually forgave her.

"Exactly what did you do?"

She took a deep breath. "Well, you know that guy I met when we did the segment about clean-eating restaurants? I ran into him when I was out for drinks, and he introduced me to one of his friends … and I kind of might have gone on a date with Rod Pump."

If I'd been drinking a glass of water, I most definitely would have spit it out like a fountain. "That guy who was on the news for insider trading? Please tell me you're joking."

"Why would I joke about something this embarrassing? It was stupid, I know. And I'm not even interested in him. You know … sexually. But for some reason I was kind of curious. I mean he's forty-two! But he was really charming and I thought it would be a laugh to go to the opening together. It's not like I planned on dating the guy. Especially considering he might be going to prison."

"So you went on a date? What's the big deal?"

"Look at your texts. What's wrong with you, by the way? I've been trying to reach you all morning." She paused, and let out a little gasp. "He's not in your room, is he?"

"Is *who* in my room?" I asked, putting Kareena on speaker so I could read through my messages.

"Uh, Pierce? Who else? Every time I call you mention him at least a dozen times."

My mouth almost dropped to the duvet. "No, Pierce is one hundred percent not in my room, thank you very much."

Thirty-eight new emails, five texts, and getting accused of sleeping with my boss. That's what I got for relaxing in bed for once.

I opened the most recent text from Kareena, containing a screenshot of the gossip story.

Rod Pump might be under fire for his business activities, but now it seems like he's looking for some heat outside the boardroom. Pump was spotted wining and dining Good Morning New York star Kareena Khan, daughter of Bollywood legends Santosh and Rekha Khan, at the opening of organic restaurant Clean last night. Our spies said what he was doing in the bathroom with the Channel Three beauty wasn't quite washing up, if you get our drift. With his trial on the horizon, we say enjoy it while you can, Mr. Pump ....

I set my phone down. "Wow. I think I'm actually at a loss for words."

"I know! Imagine what my parents thought when they read that."

Picturing her tech-aversed parents even using a computer made me want to laugh, but I resisted. "Be honest: did you ... you know? *Pump it up*?"

She gasped and sputtered a few "Well I never" type sounds before responding. "No! Of course I didn't have sex with him in a restaurant bathroom. What kind of woman do you think I am?"

"Sorry! I had to ask. But if you didn't do anything, can't you just tell your parents? I'm sure when you explain what happened, they'll come round ...."

"Doubtful. I told them that we just had a kiss. That was it. But they didn't want to hear it. Being seen with him was bad enough. They cut off the credit card and everything."

I leaned back on the stack of pillows. "Well ... just give it time."

"I guess. Anyway, would you mind if I came to Pennsylvania? The fresh country air would probably do me some good."

She said "country air" as if we were on a farm in Middle America versus one of the most affluent suburban areas in the country, but I just let her ramble on for a bit. "Look," I said. "How about you stay at the hotel with me for the night? You're off tomorrow. Get on the next Amtrak and I'll pick you up at 30th Street."

"You're amazing! Okay, gotta pack. Kisses. I'll text you when I'm getting in."

I sighed and pulled a pair of jeans and a floral top out of the dresser. So much for my relaxation time. Kareena needed me though, and that was all that mattered.

A quick check of the train schedule told me the earliest she'd be in Philly would be 12:30, and I knew she'd take forever to pack and probably miss that train anyway. I rang the spa where I had a massage appointment and canceled, then sent Anne a text. *Can I come see you today? Could use your input on what to do re: Mum.* If I couldn't rest and enjoy a day to myself, might as well tackle some business, and Anne was taking a break from filming since Ruby had a bad cold.

Fine, but come at your own risk, she replied. I sent back a quick reply and made a mental note to use some of the germ-fighting nasal spray that I stocked up on when I visited England.

On the way to Anne's, I drove past Mum's house for a quick check. Bright lights illuminating her white floral curtains made the house stand out on the gray, drizzly morning. Pierce's ridiculous rental car sat in the driveway behind the crew's van, and a "WE TAKE JUNK" truck was parked at the curb.

I stopped in front of the neighbor's house. Maybe I should

go in, just for a few minutes to check on Mum, I thought. Pierce *had* asked me to let him know how I was doing. But then I remembered the harsh words I'd said, and the look of hurt on Mum's face. Why would she want me there? I put the car in drive before I could change my mind.

I was so engrossed in my thoughts that I tripped over Ruby's Disney princess bike when I got to Anne's house, just barely catching my footing as my body dipped toward the pink training wheels. Toys left out in the rain, no Valentine's Day decorations ... something was wrong. I rang the bell and braced myself for the worst.

Anne confirmed my suspicions when she came to the front door a few moments later with the baby. While her shiny hair, cable-knit turtleneck and dark jeans looked immaculate as usual, the foyer didn't. In fact, it appeared like someone had set a bomb full of toys off, then sent an army of small children to kick them all over the house afterward.

"Don't just stand there and let the cold in," she said. "And be quiet because Ruby's napping."

Well at least some things were normal.

I stepped in, kicking a block out of the way and hoisting Charlie onto my hip. "Sorry if I came at a bad time. I guess your cleaner is coming today?"

She slammed the door. "No, she's not. Or ever again, probably."

"Did she leave soap scum on the tub again?"

Anne shook her head. "Rob and I had another ... disagreement. He's spending a few days at a hotel to clear his head. And I thought maybe I should do more things on my own. In case I end up having to support myself."

Not many things shock me; I do live in New York, after all. And I knew Rob wasn't happy about *Stuff*. But Anne's magazine-worthy home and marriage were the last things I expected to crumble brick by perfect brick.

"I'm so sorry. What happened?" She just stood there, staring into space. "Here, take a seat." I pushed Anne over to the kitchen table, expecting her to confess everything. But she just folded her arms and plopped down in a chair.

"I told you all there really is to tell. Enough about me. What's going on with Mum?"

"And you think *I've* got an avoidance problem."

I took a seat with Charlie and patted his wispy brown hair as I waited for my sister's explanation, or lack thereof. Babies really did have the life. As long as they were fed and changed and loved, they were oblivious to every bad thing going on around them.

Finally, Anne took a deep breath. "I don't want you or Will to feel guilty about this, but Rob flipped out when I mentioned going to the yard sale. The filming is one thing, but what if I'm at the sale and anyone we know sees me working? He told me I was forbidden to go, so I basically told him to screw himself … and there you have it."

As much as my heart hurt for my sister, I understood where her husband was coming from in terms of the embarrassment; my initial reaction had been the same. I tapped my fingers on the table, planning my words in my head before I spoke.

"Well, Rob can join the club since everyone at GMNY was upset as well. Not that it's the same thing. But what I'm trying to say is that as long as you explain how the sale's helping Mum with her problem, he'll get used to the idea after a while, even if he doesn't like it."

She shrugged. "Maybe, maybe not. I told him I had to be there to support my mother, and my siblings for that matter. But he took off anyway. Such an A-S-S."

I hated situations like that. Agree with her, and I was saying that her husband was an asshole. Disagree, and she'd be upset with me and think I was taking his side.

I chose a tactful "I'm sure it will blow over eventually."

"I don't know. This was like the straw that broke the camel's back. He's always traveling for work, and when he's here, he's working late. All we do is argue about the kids, and his lack of spending time with the kids ... and I feel like I married Dad and F-U-C-K-E-D up my whole life. Just like Mum did."

She gestured at the mess around us. "Might as well complete the scene!"

This is even worse than I thought. I went to the hall closet without a word and threw cleaning supplies into a bucket. "Where's your vacuum?"

"Dunno. Ruby probably took it. Takes after her aunt."

"Clever girl." A few more opened doors and I found Anne's Dyson in the playroom. "Is there anything I can do to help with Rob? I could speak to him if you want ...."

She shook her head. "Thank you, but no. It would probably make it worse."

"But you're still coming to the sale this weekend?"

"I told you I'd be there." The muscles in her jaw clenched, and her determined, almost defiant expression reminded me of a kid who wanted to do something just because their parents said they couldn't.

"Well, I'm glad," I said, although I didn't truly know if I should've been. What if Anne wound up divorced and blamed it all on me and Will? Or if (more likely situation) Mum did?

"Mum will be excited to see Ruby and Charlie there. Maybe it'll help ease the stress over selling her stuff." I tossed toys in a pink fabric-covered bin that I'd found in the playroom as I chatted. "Or you could even have Ruby 'buy' a couple of little things ... you know, important stuff. So it doesn't seem like they're going off to strangers."

"And how is that helping? I don't need my house to turn into Mum's part two."

I cleared my throat.

"This is just temporary! It's not like it'll look like this forever," Anne said, settling Charlie into his play yard and grabbing a few dolls to throw into the toy bin.

A loud, hacking cough interrupted my train of thought. "Mommy! More juice please!" Ruby shouted in a voice that sounded like a 75-year-old male smoker.

"Be right there," Anne said, opening her fridge to pull out a plastic straw cup that looked like a Mason jar, pre-filled with green juice.

I took my phone out to make sure Kareena hadn't texted me. I had two messages. One from her: *Be there at 1:15!!! Philly are you ready?* and one from Pierce: *Saw you drive past earlier, Miss not-so-Secret Agent. Don't worry, your mom's fine* ☺ *See you tomorrow....*

I tapped back a reply. *And I thought I was being stealth! Glad all is well. See you in the morning x*

Anne came back down holding Ruby's hand. "What are you smiling about?"

"Nothing, just reading my texts." The fluttery feeling in my stomach felt too new —and confusing—to share with Anne.

Ruby ran over to me and I took a step back. "Air kisses when we're sick, remember?" She pouted and then blew me a kiss.

"So Ruby, I've got to leave to pick Kareena up in a half hour," I said. "Want me to read you a book?"

"No. My mommy said we were going to talk about grandma's yard sale and what I'm supposed to say. I'd rather do that."

I shot Anne a skeptical look. "I'm sure we can do this later if she's not feeling well."

"It's fine. And isn't that why you came here anyway?"

We retired to the sofa, where Ruby propped herself up with two heavily embroidered red velvet cushions. "Okay, now the most important thing to know is that it's okay for Grandma to be sad about giving things away." I said. "You know how we donated some of your old toys to the homeless children and you cried at first?"

Ruby nodded. "But then I thought about the other little girls who didn't have any dolls. And it made me sad."

"Exactly. That was so kind of you, Rubykins," Anne said, patting her arm. "But Grandma might not think that way. She could even get mad about having to sell her toys. So we mustn't get upset if she does, all right?"

Ruby seemed to ponder this for a moment and then nodded. "You can give her a hug and make her feel better. And I can give her air kisses."

We both laughed. "Lovely idea," I said. "And your mommy, she's going to help Grandma decide which items from her collection we should put out to sell. Maybe you can even put the price tags on them, Ruby."

"Like a store!" Ruby clapped her hands. Some things were definitely genetic.

We chatted for a bit longer until I looked at the clock. "Time for this cab service to head off to collect my passenger. I'll see you on Saturday, right?"

Anne nodded. "Whether or not I'm still M-A-R-R-I-E-D by then is TBD, but yes, we'll be there."

I grimaced, mouthing "no divorce talk." I didn't need my only niece to be scarred for life. Just then a text flashed on my phone.

See you then, agent Percy....

"Go ahead, I'm sure that's Kareena bugging you," Anne said.

I typed back a smile face. "Something like that."

As I drove to the station, the niggling feeling I'd had in my stomach all day got worse. Will and I thought being on *Stuff* was worth it; whether everyone else did was a different story. What I did know was that it was helping Mum, and that made me feel accomplished. But would it come at the expense of our relationships?

❦ Debbie ❧

"COME ON, QUEEN DEBBIE. Surely you can leave the house for a lunch break. And please don't worry about making me ill. I've probably caught your cold after last night, anyway."

Rich's warm voice on the line sounded like a tempting escape from the chilly weather, and from a long day of filming. But even though I wanted to see Rich's friendly face—and I admit it, share another kiss—how could I explain my lack of renewed cold symptoms, and need to rush back to the house to carry on with *Stuff*?

I coughed a few times. "I don't know if I should be infecting the world with my germs or attitude right now. But I do miss you. Should we try and meet for coffee on Friday?"

"That would be nice. Is everything okay though? Other than feeling sick again, I mean." There was a long pause on the line.

"Fine, fine. But I probably should go now. Let's touch base about Friday when it gets closer."

I set my phone down on the table and frowned.

"Gentleman caller?" Pierce asked with a twinkle in his eye, sidling up to the table.

"How'd you know?"

He shrugged. "Men's intuition. So is it serious? You hadn't mentioned anyone special on your application."

And that was for a reason.

"I hadn't started seeing him until recently."

"Ah, I see. Is he coming to the yard sale?" I knew this was Pierce's roundabout way of asking if Rich knew about my house.

"No. I haven't exactly told him about the show. Or my collecting ... although he owns a shop and should probably have an idea, since I buy a lot."

Molly peered her head around a stack of bins and shook her head. "Of *course* he owns a shop."

"Exactly," Pierce said, his eyes lighting up in that way when someone reads your mind.

"And what's that supposed to mean?"

"Well, you go shopping to find things that provide a sort of companionship," Molly said. "It makes sense to build a relationship with someone who works in a store, and probably has an interest in collecting. Or who can give you access to the stuff you want, for that matter."

I opened my mouth, but all that came out was an odd tutting noise, which gave her free reign to keep on blabbering away.

"And don't you think that's just slightly problematic, that you haven't told him, considering this is going to be on national television in a few months' time?"

Pierce nodded vigorously. "Debbie, I don't want you to get hurt. This is going to blow up in your face if you don't tell him soon."

"I'd appreciate it if you left this problem to me and stayed out of it. Both of you."

I left the room, and the conversation. Why did everyone have to bug me about telling Rich? It was my life, and my relationship. I'd tell Rich when I was good and ready.

I found Will sitting on a folding chair talking to some of the cleaning crew. "Now go easy if you can on Mum, okay? She had a rough go of it this morning with the magazines and all ...."

I shuddered at the memory. Sorting through years of my news collection had taken all morning, and that was just the early 1980s. After all was said and done, I'd recycled a stack of about 50 papers, only because they were duplicates, and only because Molly made me do it as an exercise to see how anxious it got me. Ten out of ten.

I really didn't want to dig back into the bins; we were only up to the Prince Harry birth announcement media. That task alone would take hours, and we only had a few days left of filming before the sale.

Pierce joined us, with Molly trailing behind. "We ready to get back to it?"

"I suppose," I said, biting my lip. Maybe I should have told Rich I'd come to lunch after all.

"You still upset about Sarah?" Will asked.

Pierce patted my shoulder. "Debbie's worried about her boyfriend. Don't you think she should tell him about the show?"

What happened to minding your own business?

"Mum, the sale is this Saturday. What if someone else sees the advertisements and mentions it to him?"

"I'm happy you're all so concerned about me, but really, I'm a big girl and can handle my own affairs, thank you very much."

Of course as soon as I said that, Molly decided to chime in. "It's perfectly valid to have these feelings. But can we address the reasons that you aren't telling Rich?"

The cameras started rolling, and my gut twisted.

"Would you want a man you might be dating to find out that you're a hoarder?" I said.

Molly raised her eyebrows. "Well, no. But how could you carry on a relationship hiding something of these proportions? Surely you don't agree that lies should form a solid foundation for the start of what could be a loving partnership? You have to give and take, but how can you move forward without opening yourself up to all of the giving?"

I'm sure I would've been annoyed at whatever Molly said, but I literally had no idea what she was talking about.

"Look, I made friends with people in stores since I felt alone. And Rich was one of them. I never felt the need to tell someone who was a friendly acquaintance that I had a collecting problem. It was only recently we began to see each other on an, um, romantic basis."

I don't know why I kept talking, but maybe I was trying to out-talk the professional talker. Or tell Rich through the TV that I was sorry. "Unless you have a problem like me, you can't understand what it's like to keep this secret from everyone you know. I'm just not ready to let a man in like that, as much as it's absolutely painful to hide it. I can't risk ruining another relationship because of my hoarding."

"And may I ask, is your relationship with Rich sexual in nature?" Molly asked.

I grabbed one of the magazine and book bins and looked down so all of America didn't have to see my face flaming. "Can we just get started on these?"

Molly threw her hands up, but discontinued her line of questioning to sit on the floor and talk about how I felt about going through the objects, while Pierce unloaded the bins and handed books to me.

"How 'bout this one?" he asked, handing me a "Prince Henry commemorative photo album."

"I'm remembering when the twins were small, because Harry was born around the same time as Will and his sister."

Molly nodded. "And that was a happy time?"

I thumbed through the book, smiling at the pictures of the rosy-cheeked baby prince and his young family. "Mostly. It wasn't until the twins were around ten that things started to really go downhill. Before that, Alan and I managed. And having little ones around the house was fun ... most of the time."

"And your ex-husband? If you got rid of this book, would that make you feel likc your marriage had been more of a failure?"

Talking about Alan was the last thing I wanted to do, but it seemed to be the only thing everyone else wanted to touch upon (unless you counted talking about Rich).

I sighed. "Not precisely. But it would take away some of the happy feelings I had over those years. And I like looking at the pictures. Harry was a lovely little boy. Still is, although he's grown up of course."

Molly put it to the side in a box labeled TO KEEP. "Like I said, you're in charge here. But let's be clear here: we can't decide to hold onto every single thing like this."

And here I thought maybe she was getting soft.

"So, that being said ... what percentage of things do you think we need to get rid of?" Molly asked.

"I dunno. I suppose if I was being honest ... none of it. But let's go with half. I think I could eventually deal with that."

Molly nodded, seeming appeased by this answer; probably the first time she looked pleased since I'd met her. We sorted through some more magazines, and I agreed to let quite a few (twelve) go; I knew I had backups of those issues in my filing cabinet. I even let them take a bunch of old Christmas ornaments for the yard sale merchandise, since I never had room to put a tree up, and who was here to enjoy it, anyway?

As we combed through bins, the path to the kitchen opened up more and more, and by four o'clock I didn't have to walk sideways or climb over anything to get to the BOA. But my positive afternoon, and my stomach, took a nosedive when I looked at my phone. One missed call, and a text.

Call me as soon as you can. It's urgent. -R

I felt all of the color drain out of my face. "Excuse me, I'm just going to step out for a phone call," I said to no one in particular, throwing my parka on and rushing as best as I could through the now wider path to the front door. Trey followed behind me, and I heard him mutter "sorry" under his breath.

I didn't even care about the camera for once. All I could think about was how angry Rich would be with me if he'd found out, and what a first-class wanker I was for ignoring everyone's advice. *Please be about something else. Please, please, please.*

My heart pounded so loudly I could barely hear myself say "Rich? Is everything all right?"

"Not exactly."

I braced myself for the cold outside, and for the worst.

"Actually, I'd like to go ahead and buy back all of the items that you've bought from my shop. Because I'd rather see them go to a collector who will appreciate them than have them tossed into a rummage sale by someone who obviously thinks nothing of accumulating for the sake of it."

Stunned silence was my only response, so he kept going.

"I was just talking to one of my customers. She mentioned going to a yard sale this weekend, and that it was for *Stuff*. When I looked into it, I realized the sale was at your house. Is there something you want to tell me?"

My hands shook and panic set in. I looked at Trey for reassurance, and then realized as much as he was sorry, and a nice person, this was his job. To capture the whole shitshow on film. I racked my brain, trying to think of an excuse. But the jig was up.

"I ... I'm sorry. I was going to tell you, but it never felt like the right time. Please try and understand."

"I understand," Rich said, and I let out a deep breath, until I heard the rest of the sentence. "I understand you've been hiding so many things from me that I feel like I don't know you at all. And I'm taking it you aren't even sick, are you?"

My silence probably told him all he needed to know, because he just let out a bitter laugh.

"Wow. Although I guess this explains all the shopping. And why you always insisted on driving yourself and not inviting me over. God, I watched you buy a pile of royalty books and thought nothing of it."

My lips trembled as I tried to think of something, anything, to talk him off the ledge. "I realize you're probably hurt and angry, but please try and see it from my point of view. My kids strong-armed me into doing the show. Before this month, I'd never told a single person outside of the family about my house."

"So you didn't trust me enough to let me in?" It sounded more like a statement than a question, and a hurtful one at that.

"Rich, that's not it." I paced back and forth in the grass, pretending that the entire country wasn't witnessing my breakup.

He sighed deeply. "I can't ... I'm just not capable of getting into this kind of complicated relationship. I'm sorry."

The most painful pause ensued, and it stung like the cold wind on my face. I managed to squeak out one last plea. "If you don't want to speak to me anymore, I can't blame you. But I hope we can overcome this. You're important to me."

"But not important enough. Am I right?"

Why was everything so black and white with him? Hadn't he ever made a mistake, but for a good reason? "I never said that. But since you don't seem like you're going to change your mind, maybe I should get back to the film crew in my house. Obviously finding this out disgusts you."

"Disgusted isn't the word. I feel like I've been collected, too. You've strung me along, and then tossed me aside with all of these excuses and avoidances, and it's … hell, it's just unbelievable that you've been dealing with this and I had no idea. I just saw you last night!"

"It's my burden, always has been. I should go."

I tapped the *end call* icon before he could do it to me.

An angry teardrop slid down my cheek. I turned my back to the camera and brushed the tear away with a quick flick. Trey, bless him, didn't walk around to capture my emotion. I just stood there covering my face with my hands until I heard his footsteps and the creak of the door.

I don't know why I thought I could get away without telling Rich. What did I expect to do? Meet at bookstores and restaurants forever? Elope at an antiques festival in upstate New York and conveniently never return to my house? Once again, my collection had ruined everything.

I sat outside, staring into space until my ears and hands started to lose feeling and I realized I wasn't wearing gloves or a hat. Frozen, disgusted and disheartened, I opened the door and walked back into the house in slow motion. What was the point of all this anyway, for me to sit alone in a hollow, empty house without all the things that I thought made me happy?

Trey sat at the kitchen table, slugging back a cup of coffee with a dead look in his eyes. "I had to," was all he said. I nodded at him and kept on going.

I stopped at the end of the path to find Pierce engrossed in texting, a silly grin on his face. Will and one of the production assistants sat on the floor, packing things inside two small boxes marked "YARD SALE," while members of the cleaning crew swept and stacked empty bins inside one another. But my attention was drawn to Molly, who sat on the sofa filming a confessional.

"Debbie's not like a lot of the other patients I've seen. When you step inside, you see labeled containers everywhere. Everything is organized. It's not just stuff piled up like most hoarders' houses."

She paused, which I assumed was for dramatic effect. Either that or she saw me walk in. "But that doesn't mean we aren't in a crisis situation. She can't sleep in her own bedroom, and trying to navigate these pathways is a fall risk, not to mention she's got arthritis. I don't know how I'm going to get her to where she needs to be. This is my BIGGEST. CHALLENGE. YET."

"Perfect," Pierce said, looking up from his phone. He gestured to Jon that they got the shot. "Is Debbie back?" He whirled around and smiled when he spotted me. "Ah, okay. Let's get back to the magazines then. I'd like to get this corner over here cleaned out by the end of the day so we can move on to the china and other stuff."

I stared at him blankly. "Why?"

"Because we've got a whole house to tackle and only a few days to do it, so we better get crackin."

I tossed my coat on top of one of the bins. "I mean, why bother? Everyone thinks I'm just going to collect more crap anyway. So why are you wasting your time? Might as well just leave." My tone sounded as hollow as I felt inside.

Pierce shot Molly a pleading look, and as I turned to look at her, Jon started shooting again. Will stood on the sidelines in silence, and I realized he'd probably been the one to tell the cameraman to switch on. My own son wasn't going to stand up for me. Not if it made good TV.

"Debbie, did that phone call you just took outside have any bearing on what you're saying right now?" Molly said.

I took a few steps backward and held my hands up. "I don't want to talk about my private business. Why can't anyone understand that?"

Molly stepped closer. "Your past has caused a lot of hurt. But that doesn't mean you need to shut everyone else out. What is any of this accomplishing?" She gestured at the stack of bins I was leaning against.

"I don't want to give away any more of my things. Just leave me alone."

"You know what? You're right," Pierce said, throwing his hands in the air. "Why *are* we wasting our time here? I have a list a mile long of people who need and want help. This is time you're taking away from them. So either you're in, or you're out."

I knew he was just trying to push my buttons and scare me into thinking they'd leave. They'd certainly invested too much at this point to quit, so I pointed at the door. "Right now, I'm out."

"Mum, you don't mean this," Will said, rushing forward, his eyes wide with panic. He wasn't supposed to be on camera, but I guess he thought it was time to break the rules.

"If you'd let me finish, I was trying to say I'm out ... until tomorrow. I just need some space. Please humor your sad old mother for a moment."

He turned to Pierce, who shrugged and shook his head. "Fine. We'll leave and come back bright and early. Do what you need to do tonight. Take some deep breaths and recharge."

"I think that's for the best," Molly said. "And if we try to—" Just then I leaned back, and it all happened in slow motion. Will pulled my arm toward the hallway while Pierce dove in front of me, knocking me to the ground as the stack of boxes fell with a massive thud. The three of us laid there in a pile on the floor for a moment ... until Will started laughing, then Pierce, and to my surprise ... me. If the boxes had held china, it would've been a different ballgame, but they were only filled with more books, papers and magazines. Heavy ones at that, from the sound of the fall.

"You're wonderful and everything, but I can't actually breathe right now," I finally said with an "oof." Trying to shove six feet of strapping Southern hunk off your person is easier said than done. In the same situation, I don't think Sarah would've been in any sort of hurry.

"Sorry 'bout that. Are you all right?" Pierce sat up, brushing dust off his flannel shirt, and held his hand out to me. But then I spotted Trey's camera above us ... and the pieces of Princess Diana's cracked face on the shards of porcelain to the right of Will's arm.

"Don't move!" My shrill yelp could have shattered china itself, and I jumped to my feet in an instant, arthritis be damned. *Maybe it wasn't as bad as it looked.*

Will, bless his heart, stayed lying in the same spot on the ground as I crouched next to the broken crockery. The largest pieces confirmed that they were two of my favorite Diana mugs from the late '80s. Will put his hand on my leg. "Mum, I'm sorry. I know you loved those."

I swallowed back tears. "I'd bought them both at Portobello Market when I was out with your grandmother in London Christmas shopping, and Grandpa insisted on staying at the hotel because he didn't want to deal with crowds."

Will laughed. "Sounds about right."

"Come now, Will. Get up," Molly said. "And Debbie, there's no need to worry. There's only the two broken cups, he won't get cut."

"I'm staying here because she's afraid I'll break something else. Not because of any concern over my safety."

My heart sunk, and shame washed over me that this was my son's instant conclusion. But I still couldn't get the image of the smashed china out of my brain. "I just don't understand how these got in the book boxes. I'm so careful about sorting everything."

"See what I mean?" Will said, finally sitting up. Pierce reached out and helped him off the ground.

"It's best not to rile her up in this situation, man. I've seen it before when things are suddenly broken. Believe me, it's really traumatizing."

"No shit," Will said, picking a tiny shard of porcelain out of his finger.

"Can someone on the cleaning crew grab us a broom and dust pan?" Molly called out. "And let's try and get Debbie out of here before this gets worse."

They continued like that, talking about me like I wasn't in the room for another few minutes while I stared down at the broken pieces of my life.

"Debbie, I'm sorry you lost your mugs. But at the end of the day, they're just things to drink out of, and frankly you weren't even using them for that. Your relationship with your children is much more precious." Molly took my arm and guided me into the kitchen.

"I don't know why everyone thinks I'm such a crap mother just because I like to hold on to things that have meaning to me." I slumped down in one of the kitchen chairs and put my head on the table.

"That's it," Pierce said. He marched over to the table, grabbed an iPad, and started tapping at the screen. "We're leaving."

I didn't bother lifting my head, but mumbled, "I think that would be best."

"That's not what I meant. Hey, Will, could you please get someone to book us four tickets for tomorrow?" I looked up to see him hand the tablet to Will, who stared at whatever was on the screen with an open mouth and raised eyebrows.

"What about the yard sale?" Will asked.

"Don't worry about that part just now," Pierce said. "And Debbie, I mean we're leaving as in all of us are going to England. I'll pay. You need to meet up with your ex and settle this once and for all. Off camera. If you don't face your past, you're never movin' forward, and all of this will be pointless. Trust me, I've been there."

"I … I don't think I can do that."

The idea of calling Alan on the phone like Rich had suggested was scary enough; how would I actually face him in person? My palms started to sweat and I felt the kitchen close in on me. But if going to my former home helped me escape this mind prison, maybe Pierce was right.

"Is your passport expired?"

"No. I renewed it last year to go to Bermuda with Anne and the kids."

"Then we don't have a problem." Pierce threw some things into a backpack and grabbed his keys. "I'll see y'all at the airport tomorrow evening."

After the pieces were picked up, and everyone cleared out (and I'd assured Will and Molly that I'd be fine on my own for the evening), I sifted through the BOA. The fact I might actually be on my way to England the next day, in the same place where these things originated, seemed like a crazy dream. Perhaps I was looking for some sort of sign to keep going … or to quit. To stay, or to go. What I found was a ticket stub from Heathrow to Philadelphia from 1992.

I grabbed my phone and brought up the "last minute deals" section on the British Airways website.

Pierce was right; this had gone on long enough. It was time for some closure, and I couldn't wait another day.

∿

Brentwood, December 1992

Alan kicked the overflowing box of magazines out of his way. "The house has gone to shit, Debs. How many times can I ask you to move these?"

It was our typical row, but Alan was particularly heated that afternoon. Sarah had tripped over one of the bins that I accidentally left in the living room and twisted her ankle. After a long wait in A&E to confirm it wasn't broken or sprained, she was convalescing in her grandmother's plush bedroom, being waited on hand and foot whilst the twins played with their cousins at Uncle Mark's house. One thing my mother-in-law was gifted at was knowing when we needed time alone.

I tossed the errant magazines on top of the box of books I'd been packing up and carried it out of the room, bumping the office door open with my hip. "I'm sorry, but if I just had a day to myself to get everything organized, we wouldn't have this problem. How am I supposed to get anything done with three kids?"

"Who are in school," Alan added, trailing behind me. "I don't even know what you do all day. And whenever we argue, you go shopping."

He was right about the shopping bit, but to be fair, I shopped when we weren't arguing, too. What else was I supposed to do in Brentwood? When I got bored, I took the Tube into London for some entertainment, or to visit Carol. And usually that meant popping into a shop or two ... or three. Honestly, who could resist Selfridges at Christmas? Or the beautiful architecture in Liberty? The thrill of finding the perfect scarf, or tea set, or brooch that you'd been looking for and finally bringing it home. It was unbeatable.

"Fine, I won't go shopping ever again. I'll sit in the house and stare at the walls all day whilst the kids are at school."

I knelt down on the shiny new hardwood floor, unpacking magazines and arranging them by date. "And that's the rudest thing you could ask a stay-at-home mum. What am I *doing* all day? Do you think I'm just sitting here eating bon bons and watching Corrie?"

He folded his arms and his nostrils flared. "Maybe. How would I know? We've got a nanny, and a housekeeper, so really, humor me and tell me exactly what it is that happens around here. Because if you're not shopping, then I'm absolutely fucking baffled as to why the house looks the way it does."

"No need to be baffled. I won't let anyone touch my things, so they have to be cleaned around. I'll straighten everything up soon, okay. What's the big deal?"

"The big deal is our daughter got hurt. Again. Whilst she was trying to clean up your mess, might I add."

It was bad enough when my collection was just an inconvenience or a mess to Alan. But when my own child got injured, it stung. Still ... that didn't mean I should get rid of it all.

"Don't you think I'm upset? The poor girl was crying her eyes out. I held her the entire time she got examined. But accidents happen. Kids are always falling down and getting hurt, aren't they?" I pulled out an issue I hadn't seen in a while and let out a small "ooh."

Alan rubbed his temples. "You're unbelievable."

I continued thumbing through the old *Hello!* as if he wasn't there. It was one of my favorites, with Diana running a race at William's school in a casual white outfit, arms outstretched and laughing in victory as she crossed the finish line. What a moment of normalcy she must've felt. I tried to absorb her cheerful expression and adopt it as my own, but managed only a half-hearted smile ... which was wiped from my face when I saw Alan's hand reach for the magazine and the ones under it.

"Will you please snap out of it?" For a second all I saw was Fergie's face fly across the room before the sound of pages folding and bending turned my stomach. I watched as the copy with Diana's race picture slid across the newly polished floor and hit the door with a soft thwack.

"Get. Out. Now." I leapt to my feet and grabbed the magazine, then pointed to the door.

"It's my house, and I'm not going anywhere." Alan's cheeks had turned about five shades redder, the same way they looked after a late night and one too many pints at Beats.

"Fine. Then I will." I stomped out of the office, tossing random objects, like Alan's hideous hunting dog bookends, on the floor as I went. "And by the way, it's OUR house!"

"And who paid for it?" He shouted after me.

"Your parents!"

Once upstairs, I realized Alan hadn't followed me. It shouldn't have come as a shock, but every time I threw a shirt or pair of jeans into my overnight bag, I listened for the squeak of the stairs. Silence.

I'd show him. I would pick up the kids, head to the airport and get on the first flight home to Philadelphia. See if he complained about my magazines and tea towels when his children were all the way across an ocean. The worst part was, in the back of my mind I wondered if he'd even care. It might've even been a relief for him to be rid of us. He could go out all he wanted, and have the cleanest bachelor pad in Essex. Living the dream, all thanks to me.

It took less than five minutes to throw the essentials together for myself and all the kids, versus two days of stressing like the last holiday we had taken. I decided the speed of one's packing must depend on how pissed off the person is at one's husband.

I grabbed the kids' Mickey Mouse suitcase, my tote and purse, and lugged it all down the stairs, not caring if I scratched the wood with the wheels. I made it to the front door ... but then I remembered my collection.

What if he sold everything while I was gone? Or worse, threw it out or broke it all out of spite? My bag slipped out of my hand and hit the floor with a thud.

"Didn't think you'd actually do it." I spun around and saw Alan, shaking his head. "Come here, will you? I'm sorry."

I remained rooted in my spot. I didn't know why he'd suddenly decided to apologize, but I hadn't cooled down yet. In fact, I felt like I had a 102-degree fever.

"Why? I'd ask if you were afraid you'd lose the kids, but honestly I don't think you'd miss them that much."

"Are you actually bloody serious? I'm afraid I'm going to lose everything. I'm afraid our relationship is going to be ruined by all of this ... stuff. And I want the old Debbie back."

Hell, *I* wanted the old Debbie back. But she was in that pub in the cheap white shoes, happy and clueless. This Debbie, defeated and cashmere-clad, felt like a stranger.

I sighed. "I wish things could be like the old days. But they're not, and I don't know what to do."

Since I showed no signs of moving, Alan finally stepped forward. "Look, why don't you go home to see your parents. Take some time to recharge. I'll call Mum's travel agent and book you a ticket for the weekend."

He held his arms out to me, but I still couldn't find it in me to touch him, so I nodded instead. "We can talk when I get back from the States. I guess we both need to do some thinking."

For the first time I noticed the lines around his eyes. We were only in our thirties; when did those show up? And how hadn't I noticed before? When we'd first met, I could have drawn a detailed map of his body, down to every last freckle and mole. Three kids could have been an easy excuse, but I knew it was something more serious, and potentially fatal.

That afternoon we called a temporary truce, and carried on like usual chasing the kids and watching TV. But that glimmer in Alan's eye was gone, and I wondered how long it had been since it left.

The next morning, breaking news flashed on the telly as I was feeding the kids their breakfast. John Major was reading a statement with a most serious look on his face, but with the twins arguing so loudly over a cup of milk ("THE BLUE ONE IS MINE!" Anne yelled) the only words I heard were "they will both continue to participate fully in the upbringing of their children." I shushed the kids and rushed over to the TV, still grasping my favorite royal wedding tea towel.

Charles and Diana had separated.

Sarah Says
Just Don't Ignore

We've all been there. The phone's ring-
ing, and you're cooking dinner/out
shopping/watching a movie. You don't
want to be bothered, so you tap the
"ignore" button. Now your friend (or
worse, your mum) knows you don't have
the time to speak to them. Either let
it ring through to voicemail, or answer
and quickly explain why you need to
call them back. The ignore button is a
Sarah Says DON'T.

"THERE'S NO POINT in arguing, so let's just get on with it." I yanked the ponytail holder out of Kareena's matted braid and fluffed her black strands with my fingers, eyeing up her crazy mane in the hotel bathroom mirror. "Brush?"

She sighed and handed it to me, but not without an eye roll. "I don't see the need for an intervention."

Anyone who knew Kareena would've done a double-take when she got off the train. All of us at GMNY kept it a bit more casual on days off, but unbrushed hair, an old Disney sweatshirt and sweatpants? What if a viewer had spotted her on the street? More negative social media attention was the last thing my friend needed.

After detangling her hair and applying a detoxifying face mask, I went through her things to find a suitable outfit. "Right, so just put these on with the leggings," I said, gesturing to the Alexander McQueen skull-print scarf and black tunic sweater I'd pulled out of her overnight bag, "and then we'll grab a bite and go into a few shops. Maybe a glass of wine, too?" I almost regretted adding the wine part once I carried over the only other pair of shoes she'd brought—skinny heeled, NSFW (not safe for walking) boots.

She grabbed them and shooed me out so she could change. "Wonderful. And you don't need to convince me to do a bit of day drinking."

Half an hour later we were sitting by a roaring fire in the bar at Cecily, an upscale, old-school fancy restaurant Will, Anne and I always took Mum to for her birthday. It felt weird being there without them.

"I'm guessing you spoke to your parents' publicist?" I said, taking a healthy sip of Pinot Grigio.

"Of course. We had a conference call about two seconds after my parents stopped shouting at me. I'm supposed to be lying low."

"Well that explains the sweatshirt," I said with a grin.

"I'm going to ignore that remark. But anyway, all of this fuss over a stupid drink with a *possible* convict! And then I have to hear how I'm thirty years of age, why don't I have a husband, yada yada."

Will's name flashed on my phone. "Sorry, one second," I said to Kareena. I'd never been a fan of taking calls at a restaurant (*Sarah Says* don't), but who knew what was going on at Mum's on my day off?

"So, we have a bit of a problem." I could tell Will was keeping his voice purposely casual to hide his panic. "Mum knocked over a bunch of boxes and practically killed herself, and a few of her mugs broke."

My leg started twitching under the table. "But she's okay? Did anyone get hurt?"

"She's fine. And other than a sore back, I'm okay. The problem is I'm afraid she's going to back out of the show... because Pierce wants us to go to Essex."

My mouth dropped open. Was Pierce naïve or just crazy to think Mum would willingly step foot in the same place as Dad? "What? When? Now?"

"Tomorrow. And I can't imagine how we're going to get Mum to actually show up at the airport."

"All right, let's not get ourselves worked up. I'm sure we can sort this all out." I realized I was doing the same thing as my brother when Kareena called "TV voice!" from across the table.

"Is that Kareena? Where are you? Oh my God, please tell me you didn't go back to the city."

"Calm down," I said, stepping away from the table to take the call outside. "No, we're at Cecily for a late lunch. Kareena's having some personal issues of her own so she came down for the night."

Will let out a loud "whew." "Anyway," he continued, "can you try calling Mum? I just want to make sure she's in a better state than when we left. I said I'd spend the night on the sofa but then she was all 'where on earth would I sleep,' and you know how that goes."

"Preaching to the choir, dear. And I'll call her straight away. Let me know the second you hear anything."

I ended the call with a groan. A fun, girly afternoon just wasn't in the cards, exactly like my day of relaxation wasn't, either. And now I had a flight to pack for, too. Who thought I'd be making two trips across the pond in the matter of a few weeks, let alone with my family? It didn't even occur to me to ask Will if he was okay with the trip.

Mum's phone rang once, twice. And then stopped. *Oh no she didn't.* Why you should never ignore a call was one of my most hotly debated *Sarah Says* posts ever, and Mum knew it. Way to send a message.

Back at the table, Kareena had already finished her first glass of Moscato and was making an impressive dent on a second.

"If I wasn't driving I'd be joining you," I said. "My mother went mad when they broke some of her Princess Diana mugs. Will's afraid she's going to back out of the show full stop, Pierce said we were going to Essex to confront the past, and she's still not answering my calls."

"Whoa," Kareena said, gritting her teeth. "What are you going to do? Should we go to her house now?"

The thought of showing up at Mum's house uninvited, and with someone who'd never seen a hoarder in action, hadn't crossed my mind, but I figured that was par for the course for someone with a parent who collected. Plus, surprise pop-ins weren't her thing, considering some days she couldn't even get to the door.

I shook my head. "I don't know if that's the best idea. She's already angry with me, and Pierce, and now she's got anxiety over going to England. I think she needs to cool down."

"I'll totally fly over with you to London, by the way. I need to get out of New York until this blows over and Andrew told me to take a week off. I think he doesn't want any bad press."

"But who's going to fill the segments?" I paused. "Oh. Katie, I'm sure."

Kareena nodded. "It is what it is. Let's just try and forget our troubles for an hour or two, okay?" Kareena clinked her glass against mine. Unfortunately, my Pinot now tasted like vinegar.

By the time we walked out of Cecily, Kareena's spirits had lifted considerably, but I couldn't shake the feeling something had gone terribly wrong with Mum. My second call had been ignored as well.

Just give her some space, Will texted me. *But if we don't hear from her by the morning, we need to go over. Also, she did sign a contract....*

He was right, so I tried to enjoy the afternoon with my friend. We went into a few boutiques, and Kareena purchased far too many bracelets and tops for someone who'd been crying about being cut off from her trust fund two hours prior. "Oh, this place looks cute," Kareena said, pushing open the heavy blue door to a store called Something Old.

"Afternoon," a friendly voice called out from the back. "Cold enough out there for you?"

A sixtyish-year-old man appeared around the corner in a chambray shirt and flashed us a warm smile. It faded when he saw me. "You're Debbie's daughter."

I'd never met the man in my life, and stared at him blankly. Then it dawned on me.

"Are you Rich?" I asked, extending a hand. He gave it a firm shake and nodded. "Sorry, I didn't know the name of your shop. My friend and I just happened to pop in here. But how did you know who I was?"

"Your mother showed me photos of you and your siblings." He stared at me for a minute, and awkward silence ensued. Of course, that was when I always started rambling.

"So … this is a lovely store. These candleholders would make a great gift. I might actually— "

"She didn't tell you?" Rich interrupted.

"I'm going to go with 'no,' since she hasn't a clue what you're talking about," Kareena said, examining a tiny music box with a bird on top. Thankfully the wine had (mostly) worn off by then, or she could've been a victim of the "you break it, it's yours" sign.

I just shook my head at Kareena. "Sorry, ignore my friend here. And no, my mum hasn't told me anything about you, other than you owned a shop. She's frustratingly private, in case you haven't guessed by now."

"Oh yes, I've learned a thing or two about that. Actually, I only just found out about the yard sale. And your show."

I winced. *Oh no.* I could've bet a million dollars that he hadn't found out from the source. "Let me guess … you heard about it around town."

He nodded. "It came as quite a shock. I've never even seen a hair out of place, let alone … that." He paused to straighten the display of music boxes that Kareena had made a mess of, while she gave him an apologetic shrug. "I'm just curious, but how long has this been going on?"

"If you mean the hoarding, since I was a kid. As for the show? Just the past few weeks. I'm sorry she didn't tell you, on both counts." I didn't want Rich to think I pitied him, but I did. *How could Mum do this?*

Rich shoved his hands in his pockets and shifted his weight from one foot to the other. "It's not your fault, Sarah, so I hope I don't seem rude. But I don't know that I can get over her lying to me. Every time I asked her to come out and meet me, she had an excuse. Here she was filming the whole time."

His cheeks were flushed, and he loosened his collar. I might've been an etiquette guru, but even I felt at a loss for words. Now I was the one who had to clean up Mum's mess with Rich, as if the house wasn't enough.

"As you can guess, my mother will do anything to hide the condition of her house. The only reason she's on *Stuff* is because Will, Anne, and I talked her into it. So really, it *is* my fault, in the end."

"She didn't have to hide it, though. I would've helped her. Sure, it would've taken some time to process, but I would've shown up with a garbage bag … or a hundred. She just shut me out instead."

I saw the hurt in his eyes, and even though it was the first time we met, I could tell there was more to this than being pissed off about the hoarding. He had feelings for her. Real ones. My heart ached for Mum right then, and for poor Rich as well.

"She can be quite stubborn. And if she thinks you're not on her side, it's hard to get back on it. Not that you've done anything wrong, obviously," I said. "But maybe you could meet for a coffee, straighten things out?"

Rich sighed. "I don't know what to do. And I don't think she wants to see me anyway. I wasn't exactly kind to your mother on the phone. The idea of her buying things I'd worked so hard to find for the shop, then letting them get thrown around her house kind of put me on edge."

Ouch. I realized maybe Rich wasn't so different from Mum in the end, although he kept his collection in a controlled environment, for other people to bring home. If his things weren't giving joy to their new owners, it must've felt like a slap in the face.

I lifted the bird music box and wound it up, letting "Wind

Beneath My Wings" soar through the little blue shop.

"Well here's my advice: don't give up on her. She could use a friend like you, romantic or otherwise."

Rich seemed to ponder this and then disappeared to the back of the store. A moment later he strode over to me, holding out a small, wrapped red box with a silver bow. "Doubt I'll get to give this to her now, but it was a lot of work, so I'd like Debbie to have it, regardless."

I took the box and slipped it into my purse. "Thanks. I'll see that she gets it. It was nice to meet you, although I wish it was under better circumstances." I waved Kareena over, eager to get out of the shop to try and talk some sense into my mother.

Rich held the door open for us and the merry jingle of it seemed ridiculous, given the somber mood inside. "Maybe we'll meet again," he said. I knew from his tone he didn't believe that.

I dialed Mum's number as soon as we stepped out into the cold, and this time it went straight to voicemail. My throat tightened.

"You know what? Maybe we should swing by and see what's going on at the house. If you don't mind, that is." I linked arms with Kareena, since she was in the process of proving why her boots were indeed NSFW and went flying over a crack in the sidewalk.

"You're the driver," she said. "And by the way, I feel bad for him. It has to be horrible to find that out about someone you're dating. At least I already knew Rod was a snake charmer."

I barely heard the rest of what Kareena was jabbering about during the drive to Mum's. What if Mum had lost her one shot at a relationship because Will, Anne and I forced her into this show? Not to mention I'd risked my job for her to potentially bail on us. My stomach was in such a state I nearly pulled over to throw up.

"Do you want me to wait here?" Kareena asked as we parked along the curb. Mum's car sat in the driveway, but the house was completely dark. I wondered if she was taking a nap, or had gone out for a walk.

"Yeah, if you don't mind," I said. "If she's okay, I'll come out for you."

I appreciated Kareena's sensitivity to the situation; curiosity surely would've compelled me to want to come inside if the roles had been switched.

I walked to the side door and was about to knock, but instead, I found a note taped to it on "London Olympics 2012" paper.

Sarah, Will, Anne, Pierce, Molly & the rest: I desperately need to take care of some business on my own so I've headed to London early. Grabbed a deal on the BA website, don't worry about me. I hope you understand. See you soon. xxx Mum/Debbie

My mouth dropped open and my voice echoed off the empty carport. "She's gone."

৵৹ৎ Debbie ৹ৡ৹

"FANCY LENDING US A HAND HERE?"

I put my copy of "Princess in Love" on the sofa, shaking my head. Everyone had been talking about the tell-all, but I didn't want to believe that Diana really could have carried on an affair for so many years. Once I picked the book up, obviously I couldn't put it down, and Alan was cross with me over not tidying up again.

I strolled into the kitchen, where Sarah and her father were stacking some books and magazines on the table. *My* books and magazines. "What are you two up to?"

"I'm organizing some of this rubbish you throw all over the house, and Sarah's helping me," Alan said, slinging a coffee table book about Buckingham Palace across the table. I caught it before it flew onto the floor and shot Alan a dirty look, but he didn't even notice.

"Just bought a new floor-to-ceiling bookshelf from Mr. Dwyer down the road, and he'll be over to install it at the weekend," Alan said. "It'll take up the whole wall in the office."

I could've been happy that he'd bought me new shelving, but I wrinkled my nose. "Thanks for asking. I would've liked to choose the finish, or have some sort of input considering they're for my things."

"Don't be cross, Mum. We thought you'd be pleased." Sarah handed me a crinkled newspaper. "I'm taking it you don't need this one, or else it wouldn't look so tatty." I flipped it over, checked the photo on the front of Diana and Charles on tour in India, and shook my head. *Duplicate. Had two, in fact.*

"No, go ahead and bin it."

She smiled at her father, as if to say, "see, she's not *that* unreasonable," and tossed the paper into the bin. "So how's that new book you got about Diana? I'm dying to know what it said."

I took a seat at the table, glad at least *someone* showed a shred of interest in royal watching. "It's fairly sensational, but I expected that. They definitely portray her as the aggressor in the relationship and him as a bit of a victim, but it's his story he sold, so that goes with the territory. The problem was, when I looked at the photo of Captain Hewitt and Prince Harry, they do look awfully alike ...."

"Here we go again with the conspiracy theories," Alan said, his voice tight and clipped.

Sarah pushed up the sleeves of the oversized pink shirt she wore over a daisy-print dress and reached deep into a box. "Well, if he's not really the son of Prince Charles, then that means he's not a real heir. Right? Or spare, I guess."

"Let's not worry about that now," Alan said. "We've got our own mess to deal with, like this kitchen."

"The girl's allowed to ask questions, Alan. An inquisitive nature is important for a woman to have these days."

"Fine. Ask whatever questions you want, my dear. I'm going out for a smoke." He deposited a stack of novels on the table in front of me with a thud.

"What crawled up his arse?" I said, and Sarah giggled. Just then the phone rang, and Sarah rushed over to answer it. "It might be Kirk," she said, her voice low and breathless. *Ah, Kirk. The teenage crush of the moment.*

"No, he's not here," she said into the receiver instead, frowning. "Yeah, sure. I'll give him the message." Her hand wobbled as she placed the fancy cordless phone Alan had insisted on buying back on its cradle.

"Who was that?" I casually flipped through the book in front of me, but my heart was beating so fast I had to turn my head and take a deep breath, covered by a well-timed cough.

"Oh, no one. Business for Dad. Boring as usual." Her eyes drifted to the door and she twirled her hair a few times, then abruptly left the kitchen. "I'd better tell him."

I knew it was her.

Alan and Mark had been meeting regularly with their PR rep, a twenty-something bimbette named Holly, since the launch of their new club in Brentwood, Studio B. But word around town was that Alan "met" with her in the Biblical sense. He denied it when I asked, and what else could I do? She called every so often if there was something major going on with the media, and Studio B was hosting some big music industry party that weekend. It made sense for her to call. So why bother stirring the pot again? I'd just look like another jealous COW (Club Owner's Wife).

I heard the door close and Sarah's chunky platforms clomp across the hardwood and up the stairs. I couldn't blame her for avoiding me, or for fibbing; she wanted to keep the peace, and her parents together.

Alan bounded in a minute later and picked up the phone, then carried it into the office, closing the door behind him. I grabbed three books off the table and clutched them against my crocheted vest. If I got caught snooping, I'd pretend I was on the way to put them back in the office.

I pressed my ear to the door. "Course it does. No one will think twice. And tomorrow at noon's great." I could hear the smile in his voice. He never sounded like that when he spoke to me. Not anymore.

"Me too, babes. Gonna be the party of the year. Can't wait. Bye then."

I took a few quick steps away from the door and exhaled. What would Diana do? She'd managed it for so long with Charles and Camilla; surely I could hang in until the kids were away at university. A few more years ... but then what? I couldn't imagine leaving England, and I'd have to get a proper job to support all of us. But with a university degree and no work experience, what was I even qualified to do?

The door creaked open and Alan jumped back. "Ah, it's just you."

"Who on earth would you think it was?" I kept my tone light, brushing past him. "Just going to put these away."

"Cheers. I'll be at Mark's if anyone needs me."

I shelved the books and stepped out of the office to watch him throw his Barbour jacket on. "What?" he asked, cocking his head to the side.

"Nothing, nothing at all. Just ... are we okay?"

"Debs, do we have to speak about this now?" He avoided my gaze, thumbing through his wallet and counting the notes in it. "Gonna need to get some cash," he mumbled to himself.

"You know what? Don't worry about it. Have fun." He waved and headed toward the door.

"Oh, I almost forgot."

He turned.

"Tell your girlfriend I said hello."

I was glad I could see his mouth drop.

Sarah Says
Pack Light, Pack Right

Last-minute air travel can stress out
even the most seasoned of travelers.
Whether you're flying for work, pleasure
or something in between, just worry
about the essentials and leave your
heavy baggage behind. Basic separates
that coordinate (black, white and a
jewel tone always work well), a pair of
casual shoes, a dressier pair, and
undergarments will get you through an
entire trip. Look at all the space—and
time—you've saved!

WHEN THE GOING GETS TOUGH, it's nice to have a boss who won't take no for an answer. The flight we wanted to take appeared to be sold out, but after Pierce made a few calls, suddenly we had four business class tickets and a driver on the way to the Marriott. Being on TV had its perks, but even I couldn't have pulled that one off.

While getting our tickets was a massive relief, I had one more unpleasant task to deal with: breaking the news about the trip to Andrew.

"Everything ready for your return Monday?" he said. I had him on speaker phone whilst I updated my "pack light, pack right" blog.

"About that ... well, I'm actually leaving the country tonight."

"Excuse me, say that again?"

"My Mum had a bit of a breakdown, and she took off to London. Will and I are flying over with Pierce, and Kareena, actually. Hopefully we can convince her to let go of the past and not go completely apeshit on my father, and also get back in time for this yard sale on Sunday."

"Wow. Sorry to hear that. I hope she's okay." An awkward pause ensued, with plenty of throat clearing on his end and the background noise of Will and Kareena laughing at a makeover show on mine.

"Thanks. I'll let you know how it goes."

"Oh, and when you get back Monday, there's a few things Leslie wants to discuss about your future at the station," Andrew added, as if my career was some sort of afterthought.

I was so annoyed it took me a moment to realize he still thought I was coming back to GMNY on Monday.

"You do realize that it's an overnight flight, and today is Wednesday? I don't know that we'll be able to sort everything with the family in three days' time."

"Well you're going to have to be back for that sale, anyway, right?" Andrew said.

"There won't be a sale if we can't get my mother to get past her issues."

"Sarah, I don't mean to sound like a jerk, but this is hardly my problem. We need you back."

I chewed my lower lip. *Seriously*? This was a family emergency, but all he cared about was work, as usual. Maybe I'd mistaken his mentorship over the years as actual friendship when he only wanted me to succeed at the station, and not in life.

"One second." I took the phone into the bathroom and turned on the faucet so I'd at least have a modicum of privacy. No need to air my dirty laundry in front of Will and Kareena.

"I'm sorry, but I can't guarantee we'll be home Monday. We're going to try, but I won't rush my mother's recovery. And it all depends on what flights will be available at the last minute since we've only booked one-way tickets." I sat down on the toilet lid, then thought better of it and perched on the side of the tub. It was bad enough to be having the conversation in the bathroom.

No need to do it on a toilet.

"Calm down, Sarah," he said. "Am I out of line for expecting one of my employees to be at work on the day they've promised?"

"I'm not just your employee. We've worked together for years. I've always looked up to you. You've never let me down, and I don't think I have either. Until recently."

"Then why would I go out of my way to defend you to Leslie? And can't you just book a ticket for Sunday and let the rest of them deal with it?"

I let out a deep breath and shook my head. "No, I can't. My family has to be my first priority right now. I've let work come first for long enough. And you defending me to Leslie looked a lot like recommending Katie for my job. Why was it so easy for you to threaten to sack me if I started working on *Stuff*? And what were we going to discuss about my 'future at the station' then? You were probably planning on canceling my segment all along, as soon as you knew Katie would work out."

"Does that even matter now?" he said.

"You know what? It doesn't. This isn't working out. And I can't actually believe I'm saying this ... but I quit."

"So that's it then?" His tone was laced with anger, and a heavy dose of annoyance, but also something else. Impatience. Like he was trying to rush me off the phone in the middle of my resignation speech.

The tears started to slide down my cheeks, but I held my fingers under my lashes to catch them and stop the mascara from smearing. One of my most popular beauty tips, and I couldn't believe I actually had to use it in the bathroom of a suburban chain hotel because I was quitting my job.

"Look, Pierce mentioned the possibility of a permanent job on *Stuff*, and I just shrugged off the idea, because I didn't want to give up everything I have at GMNY, but now ... well, the offer is looking a lot more attractive. I haven't been truly happy for a long time, but it took a while for me to actually realize it."

"Unbelievable. Well, if this is what you want ... good luck. I'll have a courier service send your things when you're back in New York."

"So I guess this *is* it then," I said.

"I guess it is. Listen, if you need anything, let me know. But I need to get back to work, so ...."

"Of course." I ended the call.

My head dropped to my knees. How did I end up sitting on a hotel bathtub, suddenly jobless? There was no one to blame but myself. It was like staying in a bad relationship for too long, and for what? Because GMNY looked good on paper? Because I looked up to Andrew as a father figure because my own was mostly MIA?

I was still gripping my phone, listening to the sound of the running sink, when I heard a knock.

"You all right?" Will called out. I turned the faucet off and opened the door.

I shook my head and pushed past him. "I don't want to talk about it right now."

Kareena was still giggling away at the TV when I stepped into the room. "Sarah, you missed it! This woman looks like she hacked her hair off with a pair of kid's scissors and then went out in the rain and shook it like a dog."

A few beats later, her features softened. "Wait, are you crying? What's wrong? Did Andrew get all weird about you favoring *Stuff* over GMNY again?"

"Something like that." I wasn't going to burden them with another drama, at least not yet.

Will twisted a feather from the duvet between his thumb and forefinger with a hesitant half-smile. "On another note, I meant to ask you this before but ... is there something going on between you and Pierce?"

"No, I am most definitely not sleeping with Pierce." I gave my hair a huffy little toss behind my ear as I bent down to roll up the last of my socks and underwear in a lingerie bag and place it in the corner of my suitcase. *Not yet, at least.* I almost jumped back in surprise at how automatic the thought came.

"I didn't ask if you were sleeping together. I asked if something was *going on*. I see the way you two interact. There's chemistry, sis. I mean, it took all of two seconds for him to make the decision to fly to England. He's generous to a fault, but he's never gone out of his way to help someone on the show like that. Plus, you smile like an idiot whenever you're speaking to him."

"No, I don't. And I'm sure he's just jumping on a plane to save his show and help Mum. It has nothing to do with me."

Kareena sat up. "Ah, the workplace romance. Can you imagine what Andrew would do if we dated someone at the station?"

"That would never happen, even if I *hadn't* just quit GMNY." I zipped my suitcase closed with a bit more vigor than needed.

Their collective response could've knocked the "Do Not Disturb" sign off our doorknob.

"It was Andrew's reaction to me possibly not coming back to work on Monday that set me off. I hate to be clichéd, but it was like the straw that broke the camel's back. I could've told him Mum had died and he probably would've asked if I was planning to be on air the next day. I know we're in a cutthroat business, and ratings matter, and everything else that goes into making a show work. But is it too much to look out for someone you considered to be a friend?"

I was too angry, and hopped up on adrenaline, to cry at that point, and I think Will and Kareena mistook my matter-of-fact attitude for indifference. They both stared at me in stunned silence, and a second later Will let out a small whoop, turning to high-five Kareena.

"Cheers, thanks for the support, guys," I said.

"I'm sorry, truly I am. But does this mean you're going to stay with us on *Stuff* permanently?"

I took a seat in the hideous gold toile chair (why do hotels pick the worst fabrics?) and sighed. "Maybe? I wasn't even thinking about *Stuff* when I quit. GMNY hasn't been the right fit for a while, but it's a bit soon to be making another huge decision."

"Well this sucks, and I'm going to miss you. But I think it's probably for the best," Kareena said. "Although I promise I won't become BFF with Katie." In my rush to show Andrew I didn't need him, I didn't actually think about the fact I wouldn't be working with my best friend anymore, and my tears threatened to come back.

"I'm sorry, I don't want to leave you and the rest of the team, or put the show in a bad position. But I can't work with him."

"Well, no kidding. And you already have a job offer. But, the bigger question: now that you're going to be spending a lot more time together, are you going to 'pump it up' with Pierce?"

I couldn't help but laugh, even if she was being completely inappropriate. "I don't know. Let's just say, it's not out of the realm of possibility."

"On to more serious topics, have you called ...?" Will scrunched up his nose.

I looked at him in confusion. "Uh, who?"

"You know. He who shall not be named."

"Dad? You know you actually *can* say his name. What is this? Harry Potter?"

Will did his version of the huffy hair toss, which involved folding his arms and sniffing loudly while turning his head to the right. "Whatever. Did you?"

"Yeah, I let him know Mum was coming and not to be surprised if she showed up at the house. I just said she needed a break and thought it would be a good time for them to talk, and we'd be there soon."

Kareena reached across me to touch Will's knee. "I'm the last person who should be talking about mending bonds with their parents, but maybe you can start to sort things out with your father whilst we're over there, too. Kill two birds with one stone? Or three, if you count me fleeing the country."

"Yeah, dunno about that," Will said, looking up at the ceiling. I almost thought he was tearing up, but then his phone rang.

"Brilliant, thanks. We'll be right down."

His eyes shone. "I hate to break up this little self-help session, but we've got a town car waiting and a flight to catch."

Essex or bust.

ᴥ Debbie ᴥ

THE GATES OF PERCY HALL opened like magic as the car approached. February meant the towering trees were bare of the lush, full leaves that shaded the gravel drive like a massive canopy, but it felt just as impressive—and more representative of my mood—driving up to the house with the grounds in their stark winter glory.

I don't know what possessed me to do it. Maybe it was the boxes crashing around me, or Rich finding out about *Stuff*. Maybe I was too old and tired of it all. Or maybe a mere six hundred dollars for a round-trip flight and the idea of escaping my clutter and latest mistakes without Pierce and the rest of them to influence me, even for a few days, was too good of a deal to pass up. Somehow my feet took me out the door, into a taxi, and across the walkway to the international terminal at PHL.

Those feet hadn't touched English soil in nearly two decades, and I'd be lying if I said my nerves hadn't almost gotten the best of me. It would've been easy enough to turn around, cut my losses, and apologize to everyone. But I'd put this off long enough.

The lake wasn't frozen over like the times Alan and I had taken the kids skating, and a new, yet rustic-looking bridge stretched across the water, but Percy Hall looked exactly the same as the first time I saw it. And when Alan's mother opened the door, I'm pretty sure her outfit might've been the same as our first meeting as well. The white hair and wrinkles: those were new.

"It's lovely to see you," I said. Even after all we'd been through, it *was* nice to see my former mother-in-law. She'd clearly adopted a bit of the new Essex girl mindset, since her teeth were at least three shades whiter (not to mention a heck of a lot straighter), and her skin a few shades tanner. She must've caught me staring because she smiled and said "Veneers, my dear. Lovely invention."

"Oh ... ah, that's great. Always meant to get some myself." I stepped into the house, half expecting Alan to pop out from behind an Edwardian settee and yell "Boo!"

"I'm afraid Alan won't be back for a few hours, and Gemma's doing the school run. But I think a proper catch-up is in order," Mrs. Percy said. "I hope you're still Earl Grey, black?"

I nodded, touched that she'd remembered how I took my tea after all that time, and followed her wordlessly to the drawing room. Tea was already waiting for us in the space where Alan and I had butted heads with my late father-in-law. Same fire crackling, same over-the-top antiques. I felt just as many butterflies in my stomach then as I did back at that meeting in the eighties, but for a much different reason.

"So, tell me what really made you come all the way to England. Other than the hoarding show. Because after 20 years, I can't imagine you suddenly found yourself dying to visit your ex-husband and mother-in-law."

"Oh, I didn't realize Sarah had shared the news. I don't grill her about her conversations with Alan."

Mrs. Percy gave me a tiny, steely-faced nod. I made a note to look in the mirror one day and practice that move, because the overall effect was absolutely intimidating. "Sarah told us at Christmas. And then she saw the note on your door and was absolutely gutted. Rang us straight away, poor thing."

Her eyes glistened at the mention of her namesake. I knew my daughter's pain was Mrs. Percy's, and this time I was the cause of it all. "She was making plans to fly out here with Will, and their boss, but it didn't seem like they could get on a flight until tonight. Anne has to stay home with the kids, of course."

"Of course," I said. As if she actually knew anything about Anne's life.

We sipped our tea in silence for a moment, and it seemed like neither of us wanted to be the one to make the first move. Perhaps it wasn't the best idea to air all of our issues within the first five minutes of my visit. Luckily, Mrs. Percy chose a more neutral topic.

"How *are* the twins, by the way? I don't hear much from them."

"Busy as usual. You know Anne and Will," I said. The truth was, she didn't. Other than her sporadic visits to the States over the years, Mrs. Percy had barely seen either of them since we moved. The occasional phone call or Christmas card filled with cash didn't exactly count for much. Sarah had always been the glue that held the family together.

She gave me a tight smile. "Will was always a smart child. And Anne's children, they're doing well?"

"Ruby and Charlie are lovely. Spirited, for sure, but I think that comes with the territory."

My head ached from the forced small talk, but the truth was a tricky thing. Either she'd sympathize with me, and therefore pity me, or think I was even crazier and more useless than the family thought I was in the nineties.

"I know you're probably wondering about Alan," she said, after what felt like the entire length of my overseas flight. "He was a bit surprised when you said were coming, as you can imagine. And Gemma ... well, I thought it was best I spoke to you first."

What if Gemma threw a fit and kept Alan from speaking with me? I hadn't flown across an ocean just to have tea with his mother. "I'm not sure I'm in the best state to see him after a long day of traveling, anyway. But there are a lot of things I'd like to say, and probably should have said years ago. It was Pierce who talked me into coming here in the first place, because he felt like I needed to get some closure in order to move on and get my house in a better state."

"He sounds like a smart fellow," she said. "It would be healthy for you to clear the air. And I'm sure Alan has some apologizing to do on his end as well."

Some apologizing? That was putting it extremely mildly, but I didn't want to start an argument when Sarah senior had taken me into her home without question. How did one even apologize for giving up on their family, anyway? *"Right, very sorry about that, hope the past few decades have been good!"*

"I don't mean to place blame on anyone, because we all know my collection started well before I left England," I said. "But as soon as I went back to America with the kids, it was like reverse culture shock. So I started picking up anything I could that reminded me of England. Good thing I didn't know about eBay back then, ha ha."

She pursed her lips and said nothing, but Mrs. Percy had never been big on jokes. "Anyway, I guess the pain of my marriage ending was too much for me to deal with. So instead of becoming an alcoholic like most people, I went shopping."

"With my family's money," she added.

I slinked back in my chair as if Mrs. Percy had slapped me across the face. "That's not exactly fair. I always worked once we moved to America, so it was my money spent as well. And it's not like I didn't use the money you and Alan gave me to support the kids. Your grandkids, might I add."

"Debbie, it's an impossible situation. You can't see what this did to our family. We wanted *so badly* for it to work with you and Alan. Even my late husband, rest his soul."

It might've looked like I was bowing my head in remembrance, but really I was looking down at the table in order to prevent her from seeing how *badly* I'd rolled my eyes. The man never approved of me, no matter how hard I tried. Why pretend he was devastated when Alan and I broke up?

"I'm sorry you're hurting. And how things got out of control. I wouldn't have met with you if I didn't care. But you can't pretend you're blameless in this situation, Debbie."

I was tired of defending myself, and my collection, but what did I expect? A red carpet rolled out?

"I'm sorry I blew so much money on collector plates and international magazine subscriptions. I'm sorry I ruined my marriage with your son. And that he didn't think it was worth saving. I'm sorry his kids barely have a relationship with him, and his grandkids a nonexistent one. But not everything is my fault."

"Debbie ..." there was a warning in her tone. Like, talk smack on my son, and you're out of here.

I sighed. "I'm here asking for help, and forgiveness. And to get some closure that will help me move on. That's all I can say."

"That's good enough for me. But for Alan, I don't know."

"I just hope that we can smooth things out," I said. "Maybe you can put in a good word."

Mrs. Percy sipped her tea for what seemed like eternity. "I'll speak to him," she said. "But I can't make any promises."

After we finished our drinks, we said our goodnights and parted ways for the evening. I was thankful I didn't have to sip nightcaps in the drawing room or sit in awkward silence watching *The Great British Bake Off*. Everything about the house held memories of Alan, from the front door to the garden where we held Sarah's first birthday party. Precisely why I booked a room, even though Mrs. Percy made a half-hearted attempt at insisting I stay with them.

Back at the hotel, I unzipped my suitcase and set a framed photo of Ruby and Charlie on top of the dresser, then opened one of the creaky wood drawers. *Sarah Says: Make it Homey.*

I reached inside the suitcase to grab pajamas when my hand touched the cover of a worn leather brag book. It must have ended up in the case when I grabbed a pile of clothes and tossed them in, but I wouldn't have been surprised if Mrs. Percy had somehow transported herself across an ocean and planted it. I flipped through to find a mish-mosh of the kids' school photos, dance recital pictures, and sullen teenage snapshots. At the back was one that felt like a punch in the gut.

The three of them stood in front of the Egerton Crescent

street sign, where I'd made them pose in the spirit of new beginnings. Sarah smiled a bright, if not forced, grin at the camera, wearing a Lilly Pulitzer shift my mother had sent over; Anne hadn't bothered to hide her scowl (or take off her headphones), and a twelve-year-old Will stood nearly a head above his sisters, resting a skinny arm next to the words "The Royal Borough of Kensington and Chelsea" and flashing an expression somewhere between the ones worn by his sisters. None of them bought our new beginning, and I didn't blame them.

I set the album down and put a finger to my lip. Maybe a trip into London was in order. Head back to the scene of the crime ... and figure out how to solve it.

❧

London, September 1996

The white stucco houses arched along the crescent, perfect as icing on a cake, lined up in a neat little swooping row. The epitome of order, precision, and posh address. Their wrought iron balconies boasted manicured potted shrubs and the occasional flower, with no one daring to deviate from the norm and say, put a garden chair out there.

It was like they were mocking me.

I wondered if the residents were keeping secrets and those houses were just beautiful façades hiding a mess inside. No one could be that perfect.

"Well this is a far cry from the dump in Soho where your father and I lived with Carol," I said when we stepped inside. Three stories, a roof terrace and a private garden across the street, plus a high-class postcode (who ever thought I'd wind up in SW3?) were nothing to shake a stick at. But living in Chelsea wasn't so exciting when you'd practically been dumped.

Moving back to London was the last thing I thought I'd do, but a trial separation and twice-a-week counseling back in Essex seemed like the only hope for our marriage. Or so it seemed ... before we actually started the sessions.

Listening to Alan talk about how staying home with the kids was boring, and how I never wanted to go anywhere, and with his job it was essential to flirt with beautiful women so it wasn't *really* all his fault ... well, I didn't know anymore. And butting heads every day in the house wasn't going to make anything better. Absence makes the heart grow fonder, as they say ... so I left.

I'd drawn the line at the Percys paying for a moving company; I had *some* pride, at least. And God forbid Alan offer to do something useful. So that's how the kids and I wound up unpacking the contents of a moving van into the Percy's London house. Alan's mum was good enough to offer it for as long as I needed, and a large part of me wondered, *What if that was forever?*

Sarah pushed three boxes into a corner and wiped her brow with a white handkerchief embroidered with an *S*. "Please tell me this is the last of them."

"Sorry. Just a few more in the lorry. I'll take everyone to the chip shop before your Dad comes and picks you up."

"Ooh, chippy!" Will yelled, always easily appeased. Anne shook her head and narrowed her eyes as if to say, "commoners."

We'd agreed that the kids should have as little disruption to their lives as possible, which meant that they'd stay in their schools back home in Essex. Where my real home would end up being was yet to be determined.

Once the last of the boxes were in the flat, we set to work on unpacking the important bits: my display pieces. Luckily there were already at least five empty shelves on the wall, although I had an extreme suspicion Mrs. Percy had them hung before our arrival. Sarah helped me arrange my favorite Diana plates and dolls on them, and I turned to see Anne gazing up at the display.

"Looks *great*. So glad we had to ruin our family for all of this."

Will put a stack of books down and rushed over, touching her shoulder. "Sis, leave it. It's not our business. And you shouldn't—"

"I can. And I will. What concerns them, concerns us."

Sarah's head turned to Anne and then me, her eyes flashing panic, and a question of allegiance. But she said nothing.

"Kids, what's going on between me and your father is complicated. But I need you to trust that we're trying to do the best for everyone involved."

"I know, Mum," Will said. "We all understand. Right?" He shot his twin a dirty look.

"Whatever," Anne said. "And we're not *kids*. We're teenagers."

"Actually, you're only twelve-and-a-half," Sarah said. "But nice try."

Anne shot her sister a look that could've smashed the Queen Victoria vase in her hand. I wondered how on earth my poor mother ever put up with a teenage me. *This must be cosmic payback.* Then again, I guess my parents had the last laugh, because my English adventure turned out just like they expected: a failure.

Sarah finished arranging some trinket boxes. "Don't you think it's funny—well, not ha ha funny, but ironic—that you and Dad got together right around the royal wedding, and now you're both basically divorced?"

"Princess Diana isn't *basically* divorced, Sarah. They *are* divorced, as of last week. And I'm sure Mum and Dad are next." Anne plopped down on the floor, leaning up against the blue toile wallpaper and tapping her platform T-strap sandals against the hardwood. She pulled a Discman out of her mini backpack and was lost to us, no doubt in the glittery world of those Spice Chicks or whatever they were called.

Since it seemed apparent she didn't want to help, I gave Will a box of clothes to put away in the bedroom, and tasked Sarah with organizing some mugs in the cupboards. For a while the only sound in the flat was the clinking of china and glass as I took teacups and music boxes and plates out of their boxes. But then I went to unpack a new box, and my shoulders slumped as reality dawned on me. *Where was I going to put all of this?*

I'd been spoiled by living in a massive house, but even then most of the royal collection stayed in boxes. With at least five more containers left (of just the stuff I'd taken from the house; the rest was in storage) I threw my hands in the air. I wanted to tell myself it was temporary, but that was definitely questionable.

Alan might've admitted he'd been unfaithful during our therapy sessions, and said he was sorry, but he didn't seem like he necessarily felt … well, responsible. It seemed like he was apologizing for actions that happened to someone else. Or because he knew he'd screwed up and gotten caught, he'd better apologize and throw some money at someone to fix the problem. And me? I didn't know if I was even capable of forgiving him for the years of loneliness and broken promises, although I wanted to think it could be a possibility.

"This stuff will have to stay in storage for now," I said to Sarah. She frowned and looked at the boxes, then around the room, no doubt trying to devise some sort of organizing solution. The rise in her anxiety level was palpable as she paced in front of the window; I could blame Alan's family for drilling that whole Percy perfection mantra into her.

I glanced at my watch, then out the white lace curtains to see Alan pull up in his new Ferrari. He looked every bit the bachelor with his slicked back hair, tanned skin and leather jacket, taking the steps up to the house two at a time. He was actually whistling. *The man doesn't have a care in the world.*

"Dad's here early," I said, masking my annoyance as best as I could with a cheerful tone and tight-lipped smile. "Guess we'll be skipping the chip shop. Come now, get your things."

Will opened the door before his father could knock. "Oh, hey there," Alan said, taking a startled step back. He looked at me, but I couldn't read his expression … indifference would've been my best guess. "You all right?"

"Oh sure. *Brilliant.* You?" I said, flicking my wrist behind me to wave him inside.

"No need to be sarcastic," he said, rooted outside the door.

I hugged Sarah and Anne, and patted Will on the head. "Well, since your father doesn't want to come in, I'll say my goodbyes. Be good. I'll see you in a few days."

Sarah and Will shuffled out the door to join Alan, but Anne remained in her spot on the floor, arms crossed, headphones on.

"I don't see why any of this has to happen. Why can't you just make up and move home?"

"I know this will be hard on all of us at first, but you'll see," I said. "It's going to be fine, my dear."

"But what if it's not?"

I avoided Alan's gaze, which I could feel boring into the side of my head as I watched Anne fighting back tears. *What kind of crap father stood there and said nothing?*

Will pushed past his father, grabbed Anne's hand, and pulled her up to standing. "Come now. We've got homework to do and *Fun House* is on later."

"Fine," she said, but her eyes told me otherwise. Will tugged on her hand again, and she put one sullen foot in front of the other, following her brother out into the late afternoon sun.

Alan shifted his weight and shoved his hands into his pockets. "So, I'll bring them back here Saturday."

I can't believe we're actually having this conversation. I kept my gaze steady as I said, "If you can come around nine, that would be fantastic."

There's no way I would let him see me cry.

Alan stared at the ground. "Yeah, no ... yeah. That's fine. Cheers. Right then, I'm off."

I slammed the door behind him and my heart sunk to the floor, along with the rest of my body.

The kids were really gone. Alan was gone (thank God). It was just me, alone with my stuff. Maybe for good.

I wiped my eyes, brushed my hair, and headed out to find the nearest shop.

Sarah Says
BYO Travel Gear

With airlines cutting back these days, you can't rely on them to provide you with the essentials on an overseas flight (and even when they do, they're not always up to snuff). Nothing says luxury like your own blanket, pillow, eye mask and favorite snacks. A bit of comfort on a long-haul flight goes a long way, doesn't it?

"SO CAN WE FINALLY talk about this?" Pierce's face came into view as he lowered the divider that separated our little business-class cubicles. "Your mother took off without any explanation, you've barely said a word since we got to the airport, and then you literally put up your guard."

As usual, Pierce had my number, but I didn't even know where to start. Add in a healthy dose of exhaustion and stress, and I suppose I'd just shut down.

I closed my magazine with a sigh. "I thought you were sleeping. Why *aren't* you asleep, by the way?"

"I could say the same for you." Due to the overnight flight, it was sleeper service, and most of the people around us had already folded out their seats into little beds (like across the aisle, where Kareena had pulled her bedazzled "Princess" mask over her eyes). But I knew getting some shut-eye was an unrealistic wish, and had been staring at the same page of *Vogue* for a good fifteen minutes.

"Where do I even begin?" I pulled my fluffy pink blanket up to my chin and inhaled the calming lavender scent I'd sprayed on it.

"You do know they give you a free one on the plane," Pierce said, eyeing my blanket.

"Yes, but I'm not going to cover myself in a piece of polyester other people used a hundred times before me. And that's a bit off topic, isn't it?"

His eyes crinkled. "True, but you don't seem in the mood to talk about your mother, so I've got to get you to open up somehow, darlin'."

I tilted my head up and laughed for the first time since I'd heard about Mum leaving. "You've been hanging out too much with Molly. And I don't know much other than what I already told you. I spoke to Dad, and my Nanny. She tried to calm Mum down before she goes off saying God knows what to my father."

Pierce rested his arms on the divider. "I didn't think Debbie kept in touch with your grandmother, right?"

"No, but maybe she's decided to forgive and forget. Who knows? Nanny was very matter of fact about the whole thing on the phone, but that's her way."

His gaze turned thoughtful. "What else is she like, your nana?"

An image of us, heads together with a recipe book in her kitchen, crossed my mind, and I felt suddenly nostalgic for the old days. "I'm named after her, for a start. But Nanny was the only one who accepted my mother when she got pregnant, and Mum never forgot that ... until the divorce. My grandfather, on the other hand, wasn't quite the warm and fuzzy type."

"What about the rest of your family?"

I shrugged, although who knows if he could tell under the blanket. "They're very work-oriented. My dad and uncle are always doing something with their nightclub business. Uncle Mark never married, and we're all in America, so there's just the two of them and Nanny. And Gemma, of course, and Richie. My mum's parents died years ago, but I guess you know that."

I clammed up, hoping he'd decide my family was too boring and go to sleep.

He waved his hand in a "get on with it" sort of way. "And?"

"And … they're lovely. But it's a different world there." Suddenly the words started spilling out, and I couldn't stop myself. "Like, my grandmother's house has a *name*. Percy Hall. Did I ever tell you that? There's a lake, and a guest house, and every stereotypical rich person feature you can imagine. My dad's ancestors were big into courtly intrigue and you know, trying to usurp the throne and such. And so there's all these *expectations*. To carry on the family name. To not just be good, or great, but perfect. And then there was my mum, an embarrassing American who ruined everything. At least in my grandfather's words."

My mouth went dry. It felt good to let it all out, but I also felt exposed, like I'd showed up to class in my knickers. I'd also just word vomited all over business class more than I'd ever told my last boyfriend in our entire relationship.

"Wow," Pierce finally said. "I had no idea … that anyone used the word 'usurp' in everyday conversation." He almost succeeded in keeping a straight face, but his mouth showed the tiniest twitch at the corner.

Despite myself, I burst out laughing. "Oh shut *up*, will you?" We weren't even halfway across the Atlantic but I could already hear the Essex in my accent.

"Sorry, kidding. Seriously though, Debbie mentioned a bit about her life in England, and how your dad's family had money. But I didn't realize it was to that extent."

I shrugged. "It wasn't abnormal since I never knew anything else."

"And I'm the guy in jeans at the dinner party, messin' up which fork to use."

"I doubt that, Mr. *People* magazine." He looked down, shifting in his seat, and I instantly wanted to take the comment back. When I'd first met Pierce, part of me wondered if the whole down-to-earth Southern everyman thing was part of his TV personality. But after spending more than five minutes in his company, it became apparent he really was just a normal, middle-class guy who happened to luck out and hit it big with his show.

"I'm just teasing," I added. "I know you're not the type to go running around with Hollywood types at fancy parties."

He finally looked up and cracked a grin. "I'm too busy sortin' through trash while you're up there in the big city."

"So about that ... I quit GMNY today." I looked him straight in the eyes when I said it, partially to show him I was fine, and not some kind of woman who needed to be pitied, but also so I wouldn't miss his reaction. What I didn't expect was the brief flash of what seemed like excitement in his eyes, and the almost smile, quickly replaced with a concerned frown.

"Shit, Sarah. I don't know whether to say I'm sorry, or congratulations."

"Both? I think they were going to sack me anyway, so it's for the best. It's just awkward because my producer and I used to be close; he was more like my mentor. I looked up to him more than anyone. But lately he's just so ... robotic. It's like everything is moving along on train tracks with him and you can't veer off the rails. Don't we all want to change routes once in a while?"

Pierce propped his chin on his fist and his gaze turned contemplative. "You did the right thing. It's like being in a bad relationship, even if you're not dating. And this is coming from someone who knows all too well what a crappy marriage is like."

The camera guys told me never to bring her up, but I took a leap and asked anyway. "What made you decide it wasn't worth it anymore?"

He tapped his finger on his nose a few times before responding. "I was traveling around so much with the show. The more I started living out of a suitcase, the more she got used to the 'single' lifestyle of doing whatever she wanted. When I'd come home, we'd fight all the time. I thought relocating to LA would be a new start for us, but then ... well, you probably know the rest."

I grimaced. "I've read about it, yeah."

"She ran off with that baseball player, and it was in all the magazines ... I've never been so humiliated in my life."

I didn't respond, but felt a sense of relief the tabloid drama that popped up when I first Googled him wasn't Pierce's fault. You'd think it would be weird to chat about such intimate topics at however many thousand feet in the air, but lounging in our cozy pods across from each other felt completely natural.

"And you probably think I'm some kind of playboy running around sleeping with model after model, and I can't even say I've never done that. But mostly it was to get back at her. And to ... forget. I was numb for a long time. On the bright side, I guess I learned a lesson about long-distance relationships never working, so there's that."

My heart dropped. *Guess that takes us off the table.* Not that I'd mapped out how a potential relationship could work, considering we'd never even kissed, but if something did happen between us, it would probably be a fling. Pierce must've met hundreds of women out on the road filming, like a rocker on tour. Was I prepared to be another notch on his bedpost?

Before I could respond, he let out a deep breath. "Whew. And now I've gone all Oprah's couch on you. Anyway, I'm sorry about your job. Not the best time to be dealing with a blow like this."

"Thanks. I guess I don't have an excuse not to finish writing a book now, considering I'm unemployed."

"Not if you don't want to be. I was serious when I said you could be part of our team."

I don't know why I didn't jump at his offer; I'd fully intended on asking for the job, after all. Maybe I didn't want to seem too eager, or maybe I was afraid he'd think *Stuff* was the default choice instead of the best one. Either way, I stalled.

"Thank you. I appreciate it. All of this is just ... a lot to think about. But I'm taking your offer very seriously."

I regretted it as soon as I said it.

Pierce's face fell, and his tone turned noticeably cooler. "Well, you know where I live."

I could have pointed out that I actually *didn't* know, but nodded instead. Pierce said nothing, and just sat there staring at me for a moment, so of course I started babbling.

"Will and I really appreciate you arranging this trip, by the way. It says a lot."

"Course," Pierce said, as if it was ridiculous to even question it. "Debbie's never going to be able to get to the place she needs to be if she doesn't address all of this stuff with your dad, and hopefully we can talk her into coming back and finishing out the episode. She'll listen to me, I think."

"Yes, of course," I said, clearing my throat and flipping through *Vogue* to the same "spring fashion preview" article I'd been staring at before.

I was right. He just wanted to cover his arse and save the show. He wasn't giving Mum any sort of special treatment because he had feelings for me. I'd been an idiot to think otherwise.

"Well, I'll leave you to your reading," he said. "I'm going to try and get some sleep after all."

I didn't look up, in case he saw the hurt in my eyes. "Night-night."

He pressed the button to make the frosted privacy screen raise up between us, and suddenly I was alone again. Whomever invented the phrase *out of sight, out of mind* had no idea what they were talking about. All I could see when I closed my eyes were images of Pierce.

After abandoning the magazine ten or so minutes later, I touched the little monitor in front of me until I saw the flight map. *Argh. At least five hours left*. I spritzed myself with some Evian facial spray, slathered some Rosebud Salve on my cuticles, and flipped through every option for movies and TV, but nothing could hold my attention.

It felt like everything had come crashing down at once, and

jumping into a new show hours after resigning from my last one felt strange. Then again, I probably would've been ready to jump into dating Pierce if he'd offered ... which he hadn't.

Pull yourself together, Sarah. We were friends-slash-colleagues. Nothing more. I'd have to keep it professional until the show was over, and then we'd go our separate ways.

The problem was, I couldn't imagine never seeing Pierce again.

I tried to force myself to relax, but stretching out in my little makeshift bed and closing my eyes lasted for all of thirty seconds. I drummed my fingers on my leg. *Why was this plane so bloody quiet?* I couldn't even eavesdrop on any good conversations. And Pierce's presence on the other side of the divider felt like a humming, radiating ... disappointment.

Finally, I reached across the aisle and tapped Kareena's leg.

"I'm good, thanks. No drink for me," she mumbled, clearly still half asleep. Will, who was on the other side of Kareena, had the shade pulled up between them and I couldn't see the glow of his TV, so I figured he was asleep, too.

Every voice in my brain told me not to do it, but I ignored them, and pressed the button. "Pierce!" I said in a loud whisper, leaning over into his space and poking his leg as the divider lowered.

He blinked a few times in a confused, adorably sleepy way. "Can I help you, my lady?"

"Sorry," I said. "I can't sleep and I might actually die of boredom over the next however many hours with the Internet being down."

He shook his head and yawned. "I have no idea why I like you so much, considering you're the most high-strung person I think I've ever met."

Wait, he likes me? Or LIKES me?

Naturally, the obvious thing to do was to give him a little "humph" and roll my eyes.

"What do you normally do on long flights?" he asked, leaning forward and draping his arms across the divider. Our faces were inches away from each other, and I instantly slunk back into my space.

"Read. Work on this book that I should have finished ages ago. Write blog posts."

"And why aren't you doing any of those?"

"Because I'm worried about my mother, and I no longer have a job to write blogs for, obviously." I rolled my copy of Vogue up and gave him a little swat.

"Oww!"

A loud "SHHHHH" came from behind us, and suddenly Pierce and I were giggling like kids caught doing something naughty in school.

"Sorry!" I called out between laughs.

"Honestly, will you two go join the mile-high club and get it over with already?" Kareena said, lifting her eye mask to give me The Look and then snapping it back down with a huff.

Pierce's cheeks colored and he coughed a few times, then fell back into his seat. "Really, I do need to sleep a bit now, okay?"

The wall went back up.

At some point between obsessing over Pierce, and Mum, and GMNY, I must've fallen asleep, because the next thing I heard was, "Miss Percy, we're about to serve breakfast before we begin our descent. Could you please make sure your seat is back in its upright position?"

I blinked a few times and nodded, gathering my blanket and stretching. The partition was down, and Pierce was tapping away at his laptop. "What are you up to?" I asked.

"Working on a book of my own, actually. About hoarding."

"Really? That's brilliant. I had no idea." If anyone was qualified to a write a book on the subject, it was Pierce. And, well ... me, for that matter.

"That's because I hadn't told anyone." He kept his eyes on the computer, but I could tell he was proud, and also a little bit embarrassed, to be talking about his project.

"I won't tell anyone if you don't want it to be public knowledge," I said, placing a hand over my heart. "Scout's honor."

"You were a Girl Scout?" His eyes widened and I could tell he was trying not to laugh. "I can't imagine you camping or making rope knots. Well, actually I can, but you'd be making really fancy ones."

"God no. It's just a figure of speech. And I'd make a damn good knot, you're right."

"I don't doubt it for a second." He moved his computer to the side as the breakfast tray arrived, and we dug into our meals in companionable silence, other than the satisfying clinking sound of real silverware against our plates. My mind was all over the place. He claimed he was only flying to the UK to save the episode, but I could've guessed otherwise after all the flirtatious banter.

After the plates had been cleared and tray tables stowed, it dawned on me we were actually going to England. I wondered what was going through Will's mind. Nanny Percy and I kept up with our monthly phone calls and a regular letter-writing correspondence, and I loved Dad for what he was, and didn't expect anything more. But the twins were a bit more complicated. If Will didn't want to stay in touch, Anne didn't either.

Regardless of whether we were ready, soon enough we were in Terminal 5.

"I can't wait to get out of these clothes and take a hot shower," Kareena said after we'd waited in what seemed like the world's longest immigration line. We still had to trudge through the rest of the airport, and meet Nanny's driver. Then what? Hope Mum hadn't already told Dad off and blamed him for the hoarding?

I'd been trying to put on a brave face, but my mood must've colored my expression. "Come on now, Sarah. Cheer up," Will said. "*Love Actually*?"

He broke out into "God Only Knows" as we walked through arrivals, and Kareena joined in, belting out the chorus. She even ran up and jumped on Will, wrapping her legs around his waist for good measure like the ending of the movie. No matter what, international arrivals at Heathrow always made me smile.

"You're a little younger than Hugh Grant, but A for effort," I said, as a laughing Pierce stopped and snapped a picture of the pair.

And that's when I saw him behind the barrier, holding up a small sign that said "The Percy Kids."

Will stopped singing.

"Dad?"

✿ Debbie ✿

I KNEW IT WAS HIM as soon as the phone rang in my hotel room, but even though I was expecting it, my heart still threatened to thud out of my chest as Alan's deep voice rang out over the line. "Debbie. You all right? It's been a while, eh?"

"It has." I fiddled with the buttons on my sweater, hands shaking. What on earth was I supposed to say?

"Look, my mum said she saw you yesterday. Maybe you can come round later for dinner later, since the kids will be here?"

I don't know why, but I hesitated. This was the whole reason I'd come to England, but the reality of actually sitting down and talking to Alan? That was another story. "How about I call when I'm heading back from London later today? Going to do the tourist stuff, and I'm sure the city has changed quite a bit since the nineties."

Alan cleared his throat. "Right then. Well ... I'm sorry to hear you're going through a hard time."

"Thank you."

"And I guess, speak later?"

I nodded as if he could see me, then squeaked out a good-bye.

That didn't go exactly as I expected. Not like the conversation went terribly, but I imagined it being much more dramatic to hear his voice on the line. It almost felt like I'd just heard his voice yesterday, in the way it does when you talk to an old friend you haven't heard from in years.

I didn't want to ruin my plan of sightseeing and reminiscing, so I pushed the confusing feelings down and focused on the day ahead. First a trip to Regent's Park, and my school, then Big Ben,

Westminster Abbey, Buckingham Palace, and Harrods, of course.

Even though I had access to the car whenever I wanted, I asked the Percys' driver to drop me off at the Tube station instead. I wanted to travel like a normal person, like the old days.

Obviously, it'd been a while since I took the Underground. Some things, like figuring out what an Oyster card was, were new, but others remained the same, like the kitschy Sherlock Holmes tiles on the wall at Baker Street and the buskers playing guitar as oblivious commuters rushed past.

As I walked out of the station, past the little newsagent where Alan had bought the Diana and Charles postcard, I didn't even stop. It was like the whole story had happened to a different person. But after three decades, it would be impossible not to feel like the exact opposite version of my carefree uni self.

My feet took me to the park, across the footbridge and over to the college, all ivy-covered bricks just as I remembered. Except it wasn't called Bedford anymore, which made me feel old as dirt, and as I pulled on the wrought iron gate to Regents University, I realized you needed a special fob to open it.

"Good for you, being all security-minded," I mumbled. There weren't even any students in sight to bribe into letting me in. Instead I headed along the path toward the Boating Lake, plopping down on a bench and remembering rowing with Carol, studying on the grass, and dreaming of where our weekends would take us. How could I have ever imagined that a trip to the pub would change everything so dramatically?

Moping on a park bench wasn't how I'd planned on spending my trip to London, so I walked back to the station, pausing outside The Volunteer. The chilly wind blew in sharp contrast to the sun-drenched day when I'd met Alan, and I pulled my scarf tighter around me. Although I wasn't overcome with dread or wanting to retch on the pavement like I expected, I still thought it was best not to step inside. Instead, I snapped a photo of the pub's gold-lettered sign with my phone.

Pierce had asked me one day if I ever wished I could change

my past, but when I really thought about it, the answer was no. I didn't want to forget that night at the pub; in fact, I didn't want to forget any of it. Well, maybe some of the fights ....

The point was, just because I had some traumatizing things happen to me didn't mean I wanted a do-over. As I walked past the queue at the Sherlock Holmes museum (unfortunately devoid of a Cumberbatch), and window-shopped at the cheesy Beatles store, I felt the whisper of a smile cross my face. Perhaps the old Debbie wasn't so far gone.

Those feelings of excitement and energy the city had injected into me so long ago flooded back, and I realized that although England was a part of me I never wanted to erase, maybe giving a few things away wouldn't take those memories from me.

"And there's your revelation," as Molly would've said. I hated to admit it, but she knew what she was talking about, at least some of the time. I almost picked up my phone to call her, but what would've been the point? I hopped on the Tube instead. I had a list to tackle, after all.

My knees and feet ached by the time I plopped down on another bench with two Harrods bags. Before my very restrained shopping trip, I'd taken my first-ever selfie outside Buckingham Palace, and before that, toured Westminster Abbey and rode the London Eye. Even though I wanted to try hard not to look the tourist, I ended up being *that* lady, wearing the audio tour head-set, snapping photos left and right, reading every plaque and grabbing every brochure. But Molly's voice echoed in my head, and I binned them all after reading them. The sad part was I had no one there to share the accomplishment.

I considered texting some of my photos to Sarah, if I could figure out how to do it, at least; surely she could've used them for some travel tip blogs, especially the ones I snuck of Elizabeth I's tomb when that chap wasn't looking in the Abbey. But I thought twice before sending. She didn't want to hear from me.

As I flipped through my snapshots from the day and admired the Harrods teddy bears I'd chosen for Ruby and Charlie and two new tea towels, a mug, and magnet for myself, a teenage couple strolled past the bench arm in arm, wearing matching backpacks and smiles. They almost reminded me of a younger version of Alan and Debbie.

"Can we go to Kensington Palace next? Maybe we'll see Will and Kate," the girl said, twirling her braid. Her boyfriend just laughed. "Doubt it, but whatever you want, babes."

The missing piece of the puzzle.

I grabbed my purse and hoofed it to the Tube. *High Street Kensington it is.*

⁓⁓

London, September 1997

I stood outside the gates of Kensington Palace, staring at the sea of flowers, piled so high you could no longer see the ground. One after the next, people laid their tributes down, tears streaming down their faces. A Queen of Hearts balloon fluttered in the breeze.

This isn't happening. This can't be happening.

But it was. The princess was dead ... and I was divorced.

It almost made sense, in a screwed-up sort of way. She'd been there through it all with Alan. That tenuous connection we had couldn't survive.

A few fat tears finally slid down my cheek, but I just stood there and let them roll down until they dripped off my chin, then splashed onto my royal wedding t-shirt. Between Diana's tragedy and the end of my marriage, I could've filled a moat with the crying I'd done that month.

And what was the point? Sobbing wasn't going to bring her back. And it surely wasn't going to change Alan's mind. But sob I did. Every night, every morning, and a whole bloody load of hours in between.

"Here, Mum," Sarah said, handing me a tissue. Ever prepared, my daughter had brought two new purse packs of Kleenex, although both of them were reserved for me. She'd never been fond of public displays of emotion ... a true Brit.

Our flight to Philadelphia was scheduled for the day after the funeral. *Funeral.* Even thinking the word felt like a kick to the gut.

At least the kids (except Anne) were excited about a new start in America. Carol said to think of it as a clean slate, but to me, I was nothing but a failure. Therapy, and me living at Egerton Crescent, was supposed to be a fresh start. Our counseling sessions were supposed to make everything better, but all it did was give Alan more reasons to be pissed off. I never wanted to go anywhere, so he went out with other people (read: women). All I wanted to do was read about other people's lives, so he lived his own.

It felt like each session pushed us back further, until he just stopped showing up. The papers were served with no warning. And then he was gone.

We stood there for a few minutes, just looking at the ever-growing memorial. It felt like a living organism, expanding by the minute.

Anne bent down, placing her offering of daisies in the lap of a massive teddy bear. "Well, at least the floral sellers are seeing an increase in business, I'm sure."

"Anne, honestly!" Sarah turned and elbowed her sister. "Have a heart, will you?"

"I've got one. And it's broken," she said, her expression never changing from the numb, detached look that had been in her eyes for weeks. She turned and left to sit far back in the grass with her brother, who didn't want to deal with the crowds.

"She'll calm down ... eventually," Sarah said. I just nodded and we went back to glum, side-by-side staring.

An older woman wearing a red, white and blue sequined top and matching baseball cap approached the palace gates and stood next to us, clutching a crown-shaped balloon tied to a pink bouquet. She took in our expressions, and then patted Sarah's arm.

"She meant so much to everyone, didn't she? Never saw a more kind or beautiful woman."

"You're American!" Sarah said, although I don't know why she was surprised. We'd heard at least five languages in the short time we'd been outside the palace, and it seemed like every tourist in London had convened there all at once. Maybe she was excited to have found a tie to her soon-to-be home country.

A warm smile lit up the woman's face. "Yup, Texas. Here visiting for the first time ever, and this happens. What are the odds? I was so excited to see the palace, been saving up for years. Now my poor husband has to listen to me crying the whole vacation. It's a darn shame."

"I know. This is the biggest loss our country has faced in years," I said.

After it came out of my mouth, I realized I could no longer claim England as my own. *Our country* was now across an ocean, and my heart sunk a little further.

"You're American, too?" she said, sounding slightly confused. I didn't blame her; my children were English, and spoke with English accents. And whilst I might've adopted a slight hint of Britishness in my voice (and definitely my vocabulary) there wasn't a doubt that I was American-born.

"Married a Brit, relocated here ... and now we're divorced and I'm moving back to Pennsylvania." It's funny the things you'll confess to a stranger, but I figured I'd never see this woman again, so might as well lay it out there.

"Life takes you in funny directions, doesn't it? My Bobby and I have been married for twenty years, but I had another husband before that. Dropped dead of a heart attack in the middle of Easter dinner! Can you imagine?"

"I'm so sorry," I said. "That's terrible."

"It was so long ago, and everything's better now. But the point is, you'll get through this. It might seem like you won't, or you can't. But you can. Trust me on that one, dear."

The woman crouched down and laid her bouquet on top of

the pile, muttering a prayer under her breath. "Well, it was real nice meeting you. I hope everything works out."

I waved goodbye, thankful for the kindness, even if I couldn't believe her words quite yet.

"Wow. Americans will tell you their life story within two minutes of meeting them," Sarah said. "Is that normal?"

I started to laugh, and then cursed myself for not taking her overseas more often growing up. Her experiences with America were limited to Disney World and a couple of trips to see her grandparents. Hardly enough exposure to her mother's birthplace. "Not everyone, but people are more apt to talk to strangers than they are here. You'll see."

A young couple took Mrs. Texas's place, speaking in rapid-fire German and snapping pictures left and right, then leaving just as quickly as they came. I wondered how many were like them, and had just come to gawk. It was surely a moment in history. But the whole scene felt like traffic slowing to a standstill to look at an accident on the highway.

How many would do the same when I flew back home? Stopping by the house under the pretense of saying hello, just to see how bad things had actually become? I'd be the laughing stock of the Main Line. At least Alan was decent enough to buy us a place to live, although it was Mrs. Percy's idea (and frankly, money) in the end. I think she felt like she owed me one for her son's atrocious behavior, and I secretly agreed.

I'd flown over for a few days to house hunt and get things in order for our arrival, and had fallen in love with a sunny, one-story brick house on a quiet, tree-lined street. I refused to go flashy, even if the word "budget" had never been mentioned. This house had the perfect amount of room for us, plus it was close to all of the restaurants and shopping on Lancaster Avenue, Wayne's answer to a British high street. To be honest, I was grateful for any solution that didn't involve moving in with my parents.

"I'm so sorry about all of this," I said. "But I think you'll like your new school. And you know your grandmother will fly you over whenever you want to come back to England."

"You did your best. It's not like you and Dad didn't try." Sarah squeezed my arm.

I didn't want to bash their father, but the wound was still too raw. "Well, you're right about one of us at least."

"Let's go look at the rest of the lovely flowers," Sarah said, tugging on my hand. I knew it was a distraction, and a subject changer, but I was happy for it. We walked in slow motion along the edges of the pile, taking in the hand-written signs, framed photos and stuffed toys of every size and color.

"Do you think she knows?" Sarah asked.

"Knows what?"

She paused and looked down at the bright pink glittery heart in front of her. "About all of this. That people are crying for her, and everyone's so mournful."

"I don't ... I hope so."

Sarah nodded and smiled up at the sky. "I think this is as good a spot as any." She put her own pink card, which she'd painstakingly worked on for days, next to the giant heart. It was covered with pictures of the princess; I'd even let her use some of my duplicate copies of *Hello*. This was a special occasion, after all.

"You know what?" I said. "I changed my mind. She knows. She's looking over all of this and telling us not to be sad. If we don't believe that, how can anyone get through the day?"

With that I placed my bouquet of pink roses next to Sarah's card, blew a kiss toward the palace gates, and walked away.

I might live in heels, but I can't live without my trusty wellies. From rain to muddy fields to snow, a sturdy pair from Hunter, Joules or Le Chameau are an absolute essential in my book. Dress them up for an outdoor date, or down for gardening, but this is one purchase you won't regret!

"WELCOME TO BRENTWOOD," Dad said, gesturing toward the busy high street as we drove toward Percy Hall. A pair of blonde, furry-coat-wearing girls teetering in black knee-high boots stopped at the corner, and Dad waved them across.

"Alan! You all right?" The taller of the pair waved and giggled, clutching her friend's arm. I looked closer and realized it was Lolly from *Essex Girls*. I resisted the urge to yell out, "Are you and James back together again, or what?" and watched Dad's reaction instead.

"Yeah, yeah. You? Coming to the club Friday?" Dad was totally in his element, but witnessing him in smooth-talker mode was just as cringey in person as it was on TV.

"We'll be there!" they shouted in unison as they attempted to run through the crosswalk in their heels.

"Wow. Essex Girls in the wild," Pierce said, pressing his face to the glass. "Should we make an appearance at the club, too?"

"I don't think we need to end up on any more reality shows. And stop drooling." Annoyance flowed through my veins, but then I felt annoyed at myself for being annoyed in the first place. I had zero claim.

Dad just laughed. "Lovely girls. Proper down-to-earth as well."

"Not as pretty as our Sarah, though," Pierce said.

I felt my face flush. *Nice save.*

"Of course they aren't," Dad said. "Right, Will?"

"I wouldn't notice. I'm gay, remember?"

My head whipped around and I shot Will an oh-no-you-didn't look, but he remained staring at his laptop as his fingers flew across the keyboard. It was the first word he'd uttered since Dad's surprise ambush at the airport, other than "wasn't expecting you here."

Dad coughed a few times. "Will, I'm hoping we can have a pint whilst you're here, just us. Clear the air a bit, eh?"

Will still didn't look up, and started tapping his right foot incessantly. "All right, fine. Wouldn't want to make anything uncomfortable, now would we?"

I sighed, but none of my usual Sarah'isms seemed to apply there, and I turned back around. Pierce whispered something to Will, and it must've worked because I heard nothing more than an "okay" from the backseat the rest of the trip.

Dad explained to Pierce how the insane popularity *of Essex Girls* had brought in a ton of business to the area, and his clubs, and Pierce asked plenty of interested questions, even though I had to translate a few times because neither of them could understand each other's accent.

Kareena had left us at Heathrow to head to her aunt and uncle's house, and I suddenly wished she'd have come to Nanny's with us. At least Pierce was there as a buffer, but there's nothing like your best friend when it comes to diffusing awkward family situations. My stomach was already in knots thinking about Mum and Dad's first run-in since the nineties.

A few minutes later we pulled up to Percy Hall's long, winding driveway. "Bring back memories, Will?" Dad asked.

I wondered how it felt for my brother to hear the gravel crunching under the car's tires again, and to see the big red front door where we used to love banging the lion head knocker. But he wasn't sharing, and we rode the rest of the way up the drive in uncomfortable silence.

"Wow," Pierce said under his breath, giving the house a once over as we got out of the car. "We're definitely not in Kansas anymore."

The door opened, and Nanny's smiling face appeared. "William! Sarah!" She opened her arms, and I ran up to give her a hug. "So good to see you, little ones."

"We're in our thirties," Will said, his voice muffled in Nanny's shoulder. "But it's nice to see you, too."

"You'll always be little to me, my dear." She stepped forward. "And you must be Pierce."

He extended a hand. "It's so nice to meet another member of Will and Sarah's family."

"Lovely to meet you, too." She turned to look at me.

"Now I'm afraid Agnes had a family emergency, so you'll have to see to your own bags. Gemma's in the kitchen, and your mother went into London for the day. We should expect her back later this evening."

I felt the tension in my shoulders escape, but a new worry set in. What if Mum got back too late, and decided not to come over? I'd mentally prepared myself to rip this off like a Band-Aid (or a plaster, since we were in England after all) but now we were just delaying the inevitable.

Dad set my things down in the entryway and we all stepped inside. "I'm just going to have a quick word with Gem in the kitchen. Why don't you get settled and we'll have a nice dinner later." He strolled away in that same casual gait he'd always had, arm around my grandmother.

"You're in your old rooms, kids, and Pierce is set up in the green room," she called behind.

Will wrinkled his nose. "I'm sure they don't want us around so they can talk shit about Mum with *Gem*," Will said, clutching his beloved MacBook against his chest like a suit of armor.

"This is going to be a long visit if you're going to constantly be on the defensive. Let's just try and relax until Mum gets here, okay?"

He turned and headed upstairs without answering, and Pierce just shrugged. "Leave him be. It's a lot to confront at once."

"And it's not hard for me?" I turned to grab my suitcase, but Pierce already had it in his hand.

"I never said that. But you ... well, you're Sarah."

I stomped up the staircase past him, and then paused at the landing. "Just because I pretend to have it all together doesn't mean I never get nervous, or worried, or stressed out. And frankly, I'm sick of everyone expecting me to carry the world on my shoulders."

Pierce kept walking and placed my bags at the top. "A) You need a nap. B) I'm happy to take anything off your shoulders, and C) Try asking for help sometimes."

I looked away so he couldn't see the shame on my face. "Thank you for carrying my things. Our rooms are just here to the right."

I picked my bags up without further comment and escaped into the bedroom. What was my problem? Pierce was only trying to help. I took a few calming breaths and set my things on the floor.

My bedroom looked just the way I'd left it; pink floral curtains, white lace duvet, pale oak furniture. My little toy broom and dust pan were even sitting in the corner. Suddenly I felt like a child playing dress-up in her mum's clothing. No matter how hard I tried, or how much I wanted everyone to think I was perfect, I had no idea what I was doing in the end.

After an hour of unsuccessfully trying to sleep, I changed into jeans and wellies, then slipped down to the empty kitchen before coming back upstairs and knocking on Pierce's door.

"Come in, Sarah."

I opened the door to find him under the duvet, disheveled and way too sexy for having just recently stepped off a seven-hour flight. My pulse quickened. "How'd you know it was me?"

He shrugged. "Just did."

"I want to apologize for my rudeness. I was just tired, and

stressed out. And it wasn't right of me to take it out on you. So, here." I held out the bottle of Nutella I'd been holding behind my back, and a spoon.

Pierce's face lit up like he'd just won the lottery. "Apology accepted." He just laid there, staring at me. I didn't know if he was going to invite me in, or if he was even wearing clothes for that matter. I gripped the door frame, and the spoon, tighter.

"If you don't come over here soon, I'm going to be forced to tackle you in the name of Nutella."

"You're not allowed to eat in bed here, but I suppose I can look the other way." I set the container and spoon on the night-stand and perched so far on the edge of the bed that I had to consciously try and keep myself from falling off.

"Cheers," Pierce said. "And come here, will you?" He pulled me next to him in one swift motion, and the next thing I knew I was practically on top of a shirtless, and possibly trouserless Pierce.

Every voice in my head told me it was a bad idea, but for once, I told them all to piss off. If I wanted to indulge in a heated snog fest with my potential new boss in my grandmother's guest room whilst still wearing my Hunters, then so be it. His hands twisted in my hair. "I've wanted to do this for a long time."

Suddenly his lips were on mine, my sweater was being tugged over my head, and my brain turned to mush. God, when was the last time someone kissed me like that? Had I *ever* been kissed like that? When it became apparent this make-out session was going to head in another direction, I sat up, wondering if I'd made the biggest—or best—mistake of my life.

"Pierce, I—"

He brushed my hair aside. "You don't have to say anything. Let's not overthink it."

"Oh. Yes, of course."

It felt like a rejection, even though I didn't think he meant it that way. Even more so when he said, "Okay, let's pretend I didn't do that. Casual conversation from now on."

My chest felt empty and my arms weak. What had I expected to accomplish by jumping in bed with him?

"Sorry. I … I'm just going to get some air." I pulled my sweater back on as fast as humanly possible and stood up just as Pierce dipped his spoon into the jar of Nutella. His arm hung in the air limply, and I realized he was holding it out for me to have a taste.

"Sarah, wait …" But I didn't hear the rest, because my feet were already flying down the stairs.

I put my hand on my chest to try and calm my racing heart. In less than twenty-four hours I'd quit my job and jumped in bed with a colleague. If I didn't slow down, who knew what else I'd do.

I slammed the front door, not even bothering to stop and grab my coat. The crisp late February air hit me in the face, but I just wrapped my arms around myself and headed toward the lake. It was always the place we went to clear our heads growing up, and mine was full of cobwebs.

Of course, I'd barely made it halfway down the hill when a huffing, puffing, pink-pea-coat-carrying Pierce fell into step with me. "Good Lord, Sarah. What just happened there?"

He held my coat out, and I stared at him in disbelief as I put my arms in the sleeves. "I figured you'd need this."

"Thanks. You didn't have to do that." I should've been pleased, but his actions just confused me even more.

Neither of us said anything as we walked down the sloping lawn, the grass rustling under our feet. "You mind if I ask where you were headed?"

"Things started moving too fast. And I know you're here to convince Mum to smooth things out with my father so she won't ruin the show, and maybe you thought this would be a bit of fun, but I can't be a one-night stand. Not with you."

"Wait, is that what you think?" He stopped in his tracks and I saw the hurt in his eyes. "That I would drop fifteen grand on plane tickets just because of the show? Not that I don't care about Debbie, of course. But there's someone else I came here to support, too ..." He reached out and squeezed my hand.

So I was wrong after all.

"I like you, Sarah. I hope you realize that. But we barely know each other, and I'm not going to push you into anything you're not ready for."

His palm felt warm and comforting in mine, and I squeezed it back. But that was about all I was capable of saying.

The silence eventually grew too awkward, and Sarah-babble came flying out of my mouth. "How about I show you more of the property? It's about a twenty-minute walk to the high street, give or take. But we could walk around the grounds or through the park, too. It's actually a quite—"

"This is your show, darlin'," Pierce said, zipping his coat. "I'm just here for the ride."

I tried to forget that he'd just mentioned the word "ride." Crude thoughts equal *Sarah Says* don't. What had gotten into me?

"This must've been a fun place to come as a kid."

I looked out at the old stone wall lining the drive, where Will and I used to climb, the manicured shrubs we played hide and seek behind, and the little footbridge crossing the lake where Mum and I would take walks. "When my parents weren't fighting, it definitely was."

"So ... when did your Dad move back in?" Pierce asked.

"He used to live in a bachelor flat inside a converted stately home, but once he married Gem, Nanny invited them to live here. It's a lot of house for one person."

"You English and your stately homes," he said, making air quotes around the last two words.

"You know that's a *Sarah Says* don't, right?"

"Huh?"

I wagged my fingers. "Air quotes."

"Everything's a don't with you." He swung his arms and continued looking around the grounds, but I could tell he was hiding annoyance. If he was annoyed that I ran off from his bedroom,

I couldn't blame him, but at the same time ... why did he care what I did anyway?

"Well *someone's* got to teach people about these things. Otherwise we'd live in a completely uncivilized world." Little did he know, my little tips and rules were the only things that made sense to me sometimes. What else did I have to cling to?

"Come on, Sarah. Lighten up a little!"

"If I had a pound for every time someone had said that to me, I probably wouldn't have to work." I said, leaning against the carved end post of the bridge.

Pierce raised his eyebrows.

"Okay. Well, I could at the *least* buy a very nice handbag."

We walked across the bridge, but Pierce stopped me in the middle. "There any fish in here?" he said, resting his arms on the railing and staring into the murky water.

"Yeah. Dad tried to get all of us to go fishing with him once." I wrinkled my nose at the memory.

"Well considering your brother is a card-carrying member of PETA ... I can imagine that went well."

I grimaced. "Exactly. Poor Will was only five or six and I think he's still scarred for life. He tried to act like he was okay with it, but just couldn't go through with hooking the worm. Ran off in tears and Anne went after him, of course. Meanwhile, I think I was sitting on a blanket with Mum reading gossip magazines."

"Color me shocked. Well, I'd be happy to go fishin' here sometime."

I kept walking, wondering what that comment was supposed to mean, and climbed up on the wall. Holding my arms out for balance, I walked with one foot in front of the other, imagining circus music in my head like the old days. Pierce kept pace next to me, and I wondered if he thought I was going to fall.

"So, what's your favorite movie?" he asked.

"What is this? An online dating application?"

Pierce laughed. "I'm trying to start some casual conversation. Remember?"

"Fine. But promise you won't mock me?"

The look on his face told me he'd have a hard time keeping his word, but he nodded.

"*Royal Wedding.*"

As I suspected, he burst out laughing. "Ah, so the apple doesn't fall far from the tree, as much as you try to hide it."

"It's a classic musical," I said, stepping over an uneven bit in the wall, then doing a little ballet leap. "Fred Astaire dances on the ceiling! Who wouldn't like that? Plus, I've always secretly wanted to tap dance."

Pierce reached out and grabbed my hand. "You're making me nervous. And re: the film, you're in luck, because I happen to love musicals."

"You? A musical aficionado?" I chose to play dumb and not rat Trey and Jon out to their boss.

"Shh. It's my dirty little secret. I've even got one of those binders to keep your Playbills inside."

"Now that," I said, "is the strangest thing I've heard all day. And that's saying a lot considering the circumstances."

"Stranger than a salon that does vajazzling?" he said, referencing one of the shops we'd passed on the high street earlier advertising rhinestones for your lady bits.

"A thousand percent." We continued traversing the entire length of the wall until Percy Hall disappeared from view. I couldn't imagine how many times I'd pretend-tightrope walked next to that driveway, but never with a boy. It only took three decades.

"I never thought I'd leave here," I said. "Do you know how weird it is to move to an entirely different country as a kid?"

"No, but moving out of the South is practically the same thing."

"I thought the money looked fake when I first came to the States. It still makes no sense to me how all the notes are the same size."

"What about the food? I reckon that was kind of a culture shock?"

"Don't get me started on the excess. The massive portion sizes, and the junk food ... my parents only let us have sweets on special occasions. The first time I went to a grocery store in Wayne, I'd never seen so many varieties of candy in my life."

Pierce laughed. "When I first moved to LA, I had to repeat myself about five times whenever I opened my mouth. And my neighbors looked at me like I was about to steal their wallet when I said 'good morning' to them."

It felt nice to confide in someone who knew what it was like to be the outsider with a funny accent. The wall came to its end, and I turned to Pierce, who grabbed my waist and lifted me down. Except he didn't let go. This time I was the one who initiated the snog fest, and I felt the world spin.

This kiss wasn't what I expected. Not like our prior, rip your clothes off and roll in the hay interlude. It was better ... like a proper romantic comedy, "I can't believe this is happening to me" moment.

"So much for casual conversation," Pierce said, pressing his lips to my forehead.

My heart was racing almost too fast to speak, but I managed to pull myself together. This was important. "About earlier, I just panicked a bit after we kissed, and we don't even live on the same coast ...."

"No need for apologies. I shouldn't have pounced on you like that. You're going through a lot of stress. Whatever you want to do is more than okay with me."

What I wanted —or what Pierce did, for that matter—certainly could've been debated. But right then, I was just happy to forget about my troubles. I leaned in and closed my eyes ....

And then a black town car pulled up.

৵ Debbie ৵

"COME NOW, LET ME SEE YOU." I rolled the window down, pretending I hadn't just seen Sarah and Pierce sucking each other's faces off. The memories at Kensington Palace had been a bit much for me to handle, and I decided to head back to Percy Hall early ... but never had I expected to witness a teenage make-out fest in front of a Grade II estate.

"Mum! Sorry, we weren't expecting you for hours," she said, approaching the car with a sheepish grin. A red-faced Pierce waved and followed behind.

Good for you. If I thought it wouldn't embarrass her, I would've given my daughter a high-five.

"You all right?" Sarah said, gripping my hand through the window. "We were worried sick. Why didn't you just tell us you were leaving?"

I covered my face with my hands. All of the confusion and mixed emotions of the weeks leading up to that moment seemed to hit me at once, like a slap in the face. "I don't expect you to understand, my dear."

The glow had disappeared, and Sarah stood there looking utterly defeated. Pierce put a hand on her shoulder. "Why don't we just ride back up to the house with your mom, okay?" He guided her around to the other side of the car and they climbed into the backseat.

"Hello there," I said, giving Sarah a squeeze. "And, Pierce, I'm glad you're here, too. Why don't you fill me in on your day?"

Sarah sighed and leaned her head back against the leather seat. "I don't even know where to begin."

"Luckily, we've got at least an hour-long ride up this driveway," Pierce said.

"Har har har," Sarah replied, but she said it with a smile.

I could feel a pleasant buzz between the two of them, and despite everything else, it made my heart dance. At least one Percy woman deserved to be happy, since the status of Anne's relationship seemed precarious, and let's face it, I'd given up on Rich, and love, for good. But one thing I hadn't given up on was my family.

"Sarah, let me speak first. I'm sorry for what I put everyone through the past few days ... hell, years. I've made a lot of mistakes, and done things I'm not proud of. But I hope you'll forgive me."

"Of course I do, but Mum, are you really sure you're ready—"

"Why don't we just have a proper catch-up when we get inside?" I said as the house came into view. The car stopped and the Percys' driver opened the door, or at least I thought he did. The man who opened the door was a stranger to me.

The leather jacket was still there, and the slicked back hairdo. A few more lines graced his face and grays scattered his hair on this older version of the man I left behind. Seeing Alan for the first time felt surreal, strange, unsettling. But like our phone call, not the complete disaster I'd imagined. Maybe the years had dulled the pain more than I thought, after all.

"Hi there, Debs," he said with a hesitant smile. He seemed to feel just as awkward as I did, at least. He reached to grab my arm and help me out of the car, but I waved him off.

"I'm all right," I said. "And hi."

I wanted to ask Sarah what the etiquette should've been in this situation. Hug? Shake hands? Stand there awkwardly and stare at each other? We chose the latter.

"Dad, maybe this isn't the best time ..." Sarah said, sliding across the seat and taking her father's hand as she climbed out of the car. "What I mean is, perhaps we should all go inside and freshen up first?"

"Course. I shouldn't have ambushed you like this, Debs. I'm sorry."

What was this? An apology? I looked at Sarah but she shrugged and motioned for me to go in the house.

"So ... how've you been?" Alan asked, the gravel crunching under his shiny, pointy black dress shoes.

I could've gone tactful, but my gut said to just lay it all out there.

"Ah, just the usual, filling my house up to the brim so I need to end up on a hoarding show. You?"

Alan let out a sort of half laugh. "Well, I can't say I'm totally surprised, but I'm sorry to hear it. Honestly. And I'm fine, thanks. Club business is going strong, and I'm sure you know about *Essex Girls*."

"I've seen an episode or two." *Or all of them.*

Pierce held the door open as we stepped into the house. "After you."

"Well, I guess chivalry isn't dead," Alan said, patting Pierce on the shoulder. He winked at Sarah. "Keep this one around."

And now he had an opinion on one of his kids' love lives? Maybe this was a new Alan, although the jury was still out on whether he was improved.

The sound of heels clacking on the hardwood echoed through the entryway, and soon a woman in a tight black skirt and a fuzzy cardigan came into view. "Ah, you're home," Gemma said, acting as if it were perfectly normal for her husband, his ex-wife, their daughter, and a TV star to walk through the door together. "We've got a nice meal set up in the dining room, hope you're all hungry."

Sarah looked from me to Alan to Pierce with panic in her eyes, although her lips were curved in a smile. "Well, let's tuck in then. Sounds delicious." I could see her chest moving in and out and guessed she was counting cleansing breaths in her head.

"Hi, I'm Gemma. It's lovely to meet you after all these years."

She extended a red-manicured hand. "You all right?"

"Good, you?" was all I could think to say to this woman. If Sarah or Alan expected anything else, well it would be asking too much.

"Where's Will?" I asked to no one in particular.

"Upstairs," Gemma said, her tone sounding almost like a sigh. "Hopefully he'll be down soon."

I widened my eyes, looking at Sarah, then toward the steps, but Sarah just mouthed "what?" So much for nonverbal communication.

"So, when do you think you'll plan on coming back to the States?" Pierce asked as we walked through a high archway toward the dining room.

Already with the 20 questions?

Before I could answer, he stopped in his tracks and let out a low whistle. "Whoa."

I watched him spin around in slow motion, taking in the elaborately carved ceiling, the dining table that comfortably sat twenty, and the eight-foot-or-so-tall painting of Alan's great-great-great grandfather in a gilded frame. I'd almost forgotten how imposing it felt to enter that room as a newcomer; I had been shaking in my boots when Alan brought me there for our first Christmas.

Sarah grabbed Pierce's arm, clearly sensing his discomfort. "It's not that scary, once you get over the paintings. And the gold. And well, all of it. It's just a dining room. Moral of the story: be yourself."

He laughed. "Got it."

I'd never seen her act like that with a man; secrets and sugarcoating seemed to be the basis of every relationship. Maybe Sarah had turned over a new leaf, too.

I took a seat next to her and across from Mrs. Percy, who was already sitting at the table; Alan sat to his mother's right and Gemma took the place next to him. I found myself suddenly wistful for the days of the family's huge dinner parties, when you could not see someone for the entire night yet be sitting at the same table.

Finally Will sulked into the room, eyeing up the empty chair next to Gemma, then crossing to the other side and sitting to my left.

Us against them.

Alan raised the glass of red wine in front of him. "Here's to family together again, no matter the circumstances."

It was an odd reason for a toast, and an odd toast at that. But I raised my glass. "To family," Mrs. Percy added, clinking glasses with each of us.

Salads came out, and we busied ourselves with the meal.

"Where's Richie?" Sarah asked. I'd been wondering the same thing, but wasn't about to ask Alan where his new son was.

"Having a sleepover with my parents. Thought it was best given the circumstances, ya know?" Gemma said.

Now I was a *circumstance*, it appeared. Lovely.

"So, Pierce," Alan said. "Tell me more about your show. I'm interested to hear how you found Will, and Debbie, and all of that."

Pierce cleared his throat and looked at Will. I could tell from the look in Pierce's eyes that he was confused as to why Alan would ask, but he didn't know the extent of what a crap father Will had.

"We haven't talked in years, so he doesn't know anything about my job," Will said, staring at his plate. "You can go ahead and tell him."

I bit my lip. *Stay out of it, Debbie.*

If Pierce felt embarrassed for Will, he didn't show it. "Will applied for an associate producer gig we had open, and I hired him on the spot. He mentioned his mum needed some help with her house, and the rest is history. You've got a talented son here. You should be proud." I could tell he wasn't using his TV voice like Sarah did when she was under pressure. He didn't have to. A wave of affection rushed over me.

"That's brilliant," Alan said, lifting his glass in the air once again. "Us Percys, taking over the TV world, eh?" I saw him look down, frowning for a split second. A crack in the easygoing façade.

"Hanging all over 22-year-olds in nightclubs must be such hard work. Meanwhile, Pierce has been nominated for how many Emmys?" Will didn't look at his food this time, and met his father's eye with a challenge.

"William!" Mrs. Percy said, standing up and tossing her napkin on the table. That was practically the equivalent of throwing a chair in her world.

Alan stood next to his mother and put a hand on her shoulder. "It's fine, Mummy, have a seat. I'll deal with my son." Gemma bit her lip and opened her mouth, but no sound came out.

I imagined the massive gold chandelier crashing down a la Phantom of the Opera, and landing straight on Alan's head.

"Alan, may I have a word?" It was my turn to do some napkin tossing.

"Uh, sure. Now?" He looked at Mrs. Percy, his eyes seeming to plead for her to intervene. She just shooed him off with a quick flick of her hand.

"Yes. Now."

I marched out of the dining room and didn't stop until I reached the foyer.

"What is this all about? And I don't just mean interrupting dinner. Why have you *really* come after all this time?"

I folded my arms. "First of all, you're acting like a jerk to our son. You've got no relationship with him, or Anne, and a poor excuse for one with Sarah. The only reason you even know about *Stuff* is because of Sarah."

"And part of the reason he doesn't want to speak to me is because *you* poisoned the kids' minds against me. What am I supposed to do?"

"Fly out to visit? Have you ever seen your own grandkids, other than the times Sarah sneaks them on Skype when she's babysitting? Oh wait, no." I felt the blood rushing through my veins. I wasn't going to let Alan get away with it this time.

He sat on the bottom stair and ran his hands through his hair. "Christ. Everything's always been my fault."

"That's just it. I need to know that it wasn't all *my* fault. That our marriage was doomed, collection or no collection."

"Why? So you've got an excuse to keep doing it?" he asked. "Then you can say 'well he was just a cheating bastard, and it wasn't me after all. Sod this intervention, back to shopping as usual.'"

You've got to be joking me. While his words weren't that far off the mark, why was he always the victim?

I shook my head. "You are absolutely *unbelievable!*"

"Am I? Or are you just pissed off that I've got your number?" He paced in front of the stairs, waving his arms. "And frankly, it's not a bloody shock that you've ended up on a hoarding show, now is it? I can't imagine how bad your house looks without someone there to keep you in check."

"You ... you're acting like a tosser!" I said, almost spitting with anger. The nerve, the absolute *nerve.* Like I needed a man to keep me in line.

"A Tosser? Seriously?" Alan raised his eyebrows. "We're in our sixties, for God's sake."

Will came rushing into the foyer. "You all right, Mum?" I nodded, and he turned to his father. "What's going on here? I heard raised voices."

"Your mother and I are just having a chat. Nothing to concern yourself about," Alan said, putting his hand on Will's shoulder. He shrugged it off, and moved close enough to Alan that he was inches from his father's face.

"Actually, it's every bit my concern, since I'm the one who has to look after her. And there's no need to shout at her. Don't you think she's emotional enough if she's had to fly across an ocean to confront you?" The veins in Will's neck throbbed, and the color of his face rivaled the bright red silk wallpaper in the entryway.

"There's no need to shout? Then why are you *shouting* at me?" Alan said, matching Will's tone—and volume.

"Because you're a first-class wanker," Will said. "You always have been, and always will. Nothing's changed, so why bother trying?"

I covered my mouth. "Will, darling, let's not—"

"No, Debs, he's right." Alan took a deep breath. "I deserve it. I've been a crap father, and he's got a right to call me every name in the book."

Will bit his lip, and looked at the ground. "Frankly, you can stick the apology up your arse, because I don't want it."

"Everyone stop, NOW."

The room turned silent as we all looked to see Mrs. Percy standing there, hands on hips, with Gemma, Sarah, and Pierce standing behind. "Alan, Debbie, get into the drawing room. The rest of you, please enjoy the rest of your meal."

Pierce opened his mouth, but Sarah shook her head no and ran over to grab Will's hand. She knew well enough that her grandmother's request was an order, not a suggestion. Miraculously, Will listened and headed back through the archway, while Alan and I, heads down, trudged to the drawing room like scolded children.

She pointed at the chairs where we'd had our "so, we're pregnant," talk years ago. "Sit."

We obeyed.

"I don't know how to get through to either of you how much both of your lifestyles have impacted your children. But I'm closing these doors and I don't want you to leave until you've sorted things out." We both turned to watch her close the French doors with a thud, then stared at each other.

"So ...."

"So ...."

I shook my head. "This is ridiculous. We're both adults. And I flew all the way here to speak to you, so let's make this civilized. To start off, I wish you'd face responsibility for your actions. It's taken me a long time to get over our divorce, and well, maybe I never did get over it. All I want is an apology. For you to admit at least *some* of the destruction of our marriage was because of your wandering eye."

Alan gripped the chair's arm. "Right then. I apologize, Debbie. I'm sorry for the hurt I've caused you. I didn't know how to be a dad. Or a husband. We were so young. It wasn't supposed to be like that ... but it was, and I can't change the past."

It was the first time I'd heard him admit any sort of wrong-doing. It only took a few decades.

"Why couldn't you just tell me you needed help before letting everything go tits up?" I said. "Running out with your friends and God only knows how many women didn't solve the problem."

Alan sighed. "Because I was too immature? Because I liked to go out? Like I said before, I've acted like an arse. And my kids have had to suffer for it. And you, too. I don't know what else to say, Debbie ... other than I'm very sorry."

The next part took a lot of pride swallowing. "I'm sorry, too. I could have tried harder with you, instead of compensating for my loneliness by shopping."

"Cheers," Alan said. "Appreciate that. But I do need to say some things about the kids. Why do you think Sarah and Anne are so obsessed with appearances? With being perfect? It's because they lived their teenage years in a house of sodding cards. They're terrified to let anyone in for fear of them finding out what their lives are really like."

His words sunk in, and I jolted back as if I'd just sipped a too-hot cup of tea.

"Don't even get me started on Will. He's terrified of commitment, just like I used to be. The second he finds a decent partner, he finds an excuse and bolts. I hear it all from Sarah. And how many jobs has he been through since college? I love the boy, but he hops from opportunity to opportunity, always thinking the grass is greener."

I stared at Alan, open-mouthed. I was expecting name-calling or placing of blame, not astute observations about our kids' behavior. I couldn't even argue with him, because he'd hit the nail on the head.

"I guess we're both to blame for the kids. And you're right. About it all. Can't believe I'm actually saying that, by the way."

He chuckled. "Me either."

"Well, I know you have another little one now, and it's a lot of work raising a family. And running a business. But maybe you could try harder to get back in the twins' good graces. It would mean a lot to Sarah, too."

"I know. I will. Really. Gem has been talking to me about that a bit lately, too. I don't mean to sound like a typical bloke, but I don't talk about my feelings. That doesn't mean I'm not gutted Anne and Will don't speak to me, though. No one wants to live life with regrets, yeah?"

I stood up. "Agree. I hope you can sort things out with them. And I'm glad we could speak about this. Not saying I'm going to start calling you to shoot the breeze, but we can be civil, okay?"

He reached out and squeezed my hand. "Sure thing."

Did he still piss me off? Of course. But the years of hate and regret seemed unimportant when I thought about my kids—our kids—and the grandchildren. We had to do better for all of them.

Alan headed upstairs, probably to look for his mother, and I pushed the heavy old doors open and peeked my head into the dining room. Will was picking at his food while Sarah and Pierce, who sat on either side of him, seemed to be giving Will some sort of pep talk. The three of them seemed so small alone in such a grand room, thirties or not.

"It'll be fine," Sarah said, tapping her nails on a wine glass. "I'm sure Mum can hold her own in there."

Pierce nodded vigorously. "Absolutely. I'd hate to get on her bad side. Well, actually I have."

Sarah snickered. "Sorry, but it *is* kind of funny." She looked up and met my eye. "Mum! Everything all right?"

"Alan and I are fine, I guess. It actually felt good to get everything out in the open."

Will and Sarah exchanged skeptical glances. "You made up with Dad?" he asked. "Did hell freeze over?"

"You'd think. But it's been years ... and you were right, Sarah. It's time to move on. Clearly, your father has. I want this year to be a new start for me, and this is a step forward."

"*Sarah Says*: forgiveness is always classy." She looked at Pierce and mouthed something I couldn't decipher, then rushed out of the room.

"What the ...?" I said, but Pierce and Will just shrugged.

She returned a few minutes later clutching a small gift box. "I think you should open this."

I had no idea why she was giving me a gift, but pulled the silky ribbon and red wrapping off to reveal a wooden trinket box with a note card taped to the top.

> *Thought this would make you smile, Queen Debbie.*
> *-Rich*

I pulled the card off to reveal the box's lid, engraved with a swirly five-pointed crown and my initials. I ran my finger over the design, and my heart broke just a little more. He carved it himself; I was sure of it.

"How did you get this?"

"Long story," Sarah said. "But I don't think he's given up on you, Mum."

"I don't know about that." I crumbled up the wrapping and closed my eyes. "I probably don't deserve to be forgiven, anyway."

Will put his arm around me. "It's never too late. If you can forgive Dad, then pretty much anything is possible, eh?"

His logic made sense, but I couldn't imagine Rich wanting anything to do with me again. I let out a deep sigh, then took my phone out of my pocket. "How do you get the Internet to work in this place?" I asked Sarah, tapping away on the screen with a frown.

"Emailing Rich?" Pierce asked, then winced as Sarah elbowed him.

"No, I need to book a flight home."

Sarah Says

Decide With Your Heart

THE WOOD CREAKED beneath my boots as I walked across the bridge, pausing to take a deep breath of the chilly morning air. It still felt like home, there at Percy Hall, but at the same time utterly foreign. My apartment in New York wasn't steeped in generations of family history, nor did it contain any priceless works of art (unless you counted Ruby's drawings). But it was mine, and it was home. And I felt ready to go back.

I'd resigned myself to being neither totally English or totally American long ago, but suddenly I realized what I was: an English American. And what was wrong with that?

I heard footsteps behind me and turned to find Will walking down the hill, hands in the pockets of an oversized quilted jacket that looked like he'd pulled it out of my grandfather's wardrobe.

"Fancy finding you out here so early. Thought I'd clear my head, get some fresh air before we've got to head to the airport."

"Same," I said, gesturing to the bench at the end of the bridge. "Have a seat."

We plopped down, letting the sound of the water lapping against the shore be our only soundtrack for a few moments. "Oh, Kareena called me," I said. "I think she's going to stay out here for a while longer and lay low, although it sounds like her aunt must've talked to Mr. and Mrs. Khan. I think they've cooled down considerably, so that bodes well for Kareena."

"Whew," Will said. "What *would* she do without an endless supply of McQueen?"

I laughed. "And you? Feeling any better after last night?"

"Had a chat with Dad this morning." He didn't elaborate, and I didn't want to push it, so I decided to act casual, managing only a minor raise of my eyebrows.

"Did you? How'd that go?"

He scuffed his shoe against the dirt. "I can't imagine us ever being best pals or anything. He's got his new family to worry about. He did say he was sorry for being a rubbish dad, and was all 'I don't want to fall out with ya!' blah blah blah."

I couldn't help but laugh at his exaggerated impersonation of Dad's accent. "Well, that's a start. Maybe you could talk over email or texts once in a while. See how things go." I still felt like I was toeing a line; I didn't want to act too pleased that they'd spoken, or he'd think I was taking Dad's side.

"Doubtful. I let him get things off his chest … he can make the first move."

It was silly of me to expect some kind of instant reconciliation, but my heart sunk all the same. "So what made you approach him if you're still pissed off?"

"Anne made me do it."

This time I couldn't prevent my eyebrows from raising to almost touch the gray sky. "Really? When was the last time she even spoke to Dad?"

"This morning. I put her on the phone, then I came out here."

I couldn't have been more surprised if he'd told me that the Queen herself had rang our father that morning.

"I called her after the row last night, and we had a long chat," he continued. "She's been upset about being stuck at home while we're over here, and about Rob obviously … anyway, we started talking about Nanny, and being kids. And she got pretty emotional. She encouraged me to talk to Dad before we left, even if he *is* a wanker. If Mum could do it, so could we."

"Wow." Maybe our family would never be perfect, but everyone on (sort of) speaking terms was good enough for me. There was only one thing left to resolve until I felt totally whole.

"I'm going to accept Pierce's offer."

Will broke into a wide grin. "I was waiting for you to say that."

"It's not just because I quit GMNY and I don't have other options. I like helping people. I know this is only one episode, but *Stuff* feels right to me. And I love everyone on the team. Well, Molly can be ... Molly. But she's starting to grow on me."

We both laughed.

"So ... you and Pierce?"

"He's lovely, and it's been fun here. We'll see when we get home." It felt too new to say anything more.

Will turned toward the house. "Speak of the devil ...."

I could just make out Pierce's figure at the top of the lawn, but my heart fluttered all the same. Will stood up. "I'll leave you guys to it. Don't do anything I wouldn't do." He winked and headed down the path toward the back of the property, waving at Pierce as he went.

"Thought I'd find you out here," Pierce said when he finally reached me, bending down and pressing warm lips against my cold cheek. "Everything all right?"

"Yeah, actually. It is now." I grabbed his hand and pulled him down to sit on the bench next to me. "I've made a decision about the show."

He rubbed his hands together. "And?"

"I'm in."

"Wahoo! You sure?" He let out a deep breath. "Sorry, I was bracing myself for the worst."

"Did you really think I was going to turn you down?"

He shrugged. "Dunno. You've just seemed so unsure the past few days, and I can't say I blame you. I was ready to give you all the time you needed."

I turned to face Pierce and took both of his hands in mine, my voice thick with emotion. "Molly told me that the brain doesn't recognize future reward as much as it does the fear of losing something. And I totally get that now. I mean, Mum's afraid of what will happen if she gives things away, but I was afraid, too. Of what would happen if I gave up what I was used to, and took a shot at something special."

"Geez, this guy must be pretty good looking, convincing you to leave your job and whatnot," Pierce said. "What's his name? Should I have a word with him?"

"You love windin' me up, don't you?" I said with a giggle, then wrinkled my nose. "Funny how I'm here for two days and the accent comes straight back."

Pierce pulled me into his lap. "For the record, I think your *real* voice is pretty sexy."

I binned *Get Rid of Your Accent* as soon as we got home.

❧ Debbie ☙

I PULLED A LACE CURTAIN BACK and peered out the window, then quickly shut it again, as if it would make the crowd outside my house disappear. People had lined up starting at seven-thirty for the yard sale, and the line snaked around the corner like it was Buckingham Palace at the height of tourist season. "Remind me why I thought it was a great idea to come home again?"

"Don't panic. This is a good thing," Sarah said, steering me away from the window just as Pierce strolled into the living room, dressed in an immaculate white button-up. I wondered if Sarah had shared her ironing tips ... or maybe she'd ironed it herself, considering the amount of time the two had been spending together since we got back from England.

"Just saw Anne outside, she'll be in shortly," he said. "She spotted some neighbors and they wanted to see the kids. Cute little buggers."

My spirits lifted a notch at the thought of Ruby and Charlie; at least they'd make the day bearable. My new motto was family first, and I vowed to try to never put my things before any of them again. The actual process of letting my things go, however, would likely be easier said than done.

"Hellooo?" A little voice called out from the kitchen, and I rushed in to meet Ruby, with Jon and his camera following behind. To be able to hurry into my own kitchen felt like such a novelty that I wanted to do it always, even when no rushing was required.

"Darling, how are you?" I said, sitting at the kitchen table and patting my lap. "Sorry, grandma's knees mean I can't lift you up."

She climbed onto my lap, pulling off her ruffly pink coat. "Everyone else is still outside. Are all of those people really going to come and buy your princess things?"

"Sorry we're late," Anne said, with a sheepish looking Rob in tow.

"Oh. We weren't ..." I stopped and forced myself not to look surprised; he seemed uncomfortable enough. We didn't need all of America witnessing my shock at him showing up. "Rob, thanks for coming. It's nice to see you."

He bent down and kissed my cheek. "It's nothing at all. But you should thank your daughter." He took Charlie from Anne's arms and went off to say hello to Will and Sarah. Luckily the camera followed behind, leaving me looking at Anne in confusion.

"Let's just say someone had a come to Jesus moment. And ... I may or may not have threatened D-I-V-O-R-C-E."

I winced, but none of it came as a shock. "Well, is everything all right now then?"

She gave a noncommittal sort of half shrug. "We shall see. Therapy works wonders."

"Don't I know it." I glanced around the house, devoid of at least a hundred of my bins. We had a ways to go, or at least Sarah and the team did. They had two more days to pull it all together, and I was being forced into a hotel after the yard sale to "relax and reflect" while they created the transformation. But already my house felt like a brand new one, and I couldn't imagine what it'd look like after it was all over.

Pierce clapped his hands. "It's nearly go time! Is everyone excited?"

"If by excited, you mean sick to my stomach, then sure."

Molly took a seat next to me. "It's perfectly normal to feel this way. And I'm going to help you through it every step. Just remember what we talked about."

"My memories won't disappear without these things. My past won't change."

She nodded vigorously. "Yes! Exactly. Hold on to that attitude today, especially when things get rough."

"How many people do you think just wanted to be on TV, versus actually have an interest in royal memorabilia?" I whispered to Anne.

"Does it matter? As long as they're buying stuff, I'm happy to see them."

Molly narrowed her eyes. "Wrong answer. If your mum thinks people will buy items and not take care of them, she won't want to let anything go."

I gave her credit; that would've been true a few weeks before. But right now I had to focus on people, and not things. At least that's what I kept telling myself. No one can take your memories ... but they can take your stuff. I had to reprogram myself to realize they weren't one and the same, and that wasn't going to happen overnight. The idea of even one little teapot being sold had already sent me running to the bathroom on more than one occasion that morning.

"Debbie, can we do a quick interview before we let people in?" Pierce asked, guiding me outside to the front step where we sat down. I was more than happy to escape Molly.

Trey came over and started rolling. "So we're about to start the sale," Pierce said. "Tell me what's going through your mind right now."

No one could know what this felt like, but I could try to make them understand, at least a bit. "It's kind of like getting a surgery that you know you desperately need. It'll save you, but you're still scared and don't really want to do it, even though deep down, you know it has to be done. Does that make sense?"

Pierce rested a hand on my knee. "It absolutely does. And you explained it beautifully."

Sarah, who stood off to the side, looked on the verge of happy tears. Pierce's head turned slightly and I caught a barely perceptible change in his eyes as they met hers. Whether or not this fling, or whatever it was, became serious, I knew right then he'd changed her for the better.

"We've spent some time getting ready for today, and I know it was a struggle for you. How have you overcome those anxious feelings about letting things go?"

A flashback to the day before, when I told Molly to hand me the stack of Diana and Charles Christmas cards or die, came to mind. "It wasn't easy, of course. But I think giving me choices helped. For example, Molly said I could keep as many mugs as would fit on two shelves in the cupboard; that made sense to me and it was a little easier to let go of the others knowing they didn't fit."

By a little easier, I meant I'd only vomited once, and hid four of the mugs in my car for safekeeping. But America didn't need to hear that bit.

Pierce cocked his head at Sarah. "And I heard a little birdie taught you about something called Pinterest?"

I whipped my phone out of my pocket and showed Pierce the new app on my home screen. "Ah, yes. We took pictures of a lot of the things I was putting in the sale, and then organized them into boards. Now I can look at them whenever I like, and think about the memories associated with them, even if they're not with me anymore. Saves a lot of room, I suppose."

"Good for you," Pierce said. "And what do you think the biggest thing you've learned about yourself so far has been?"

"I bought all of this to make me happier. But the more I bought, the unhappier I actually became. All of you showed me that what I needed to make me happy, and to move on from the past, was to focus on my relationships with the people around me."

Pierce's face lit up. "Darlin', this sounds like a breakthrough."

After that we manned the tables, and the first-ever *Stuff* sale was in business.

Ruby, it turned out, was a fierce negotiator, wise beyond her five years. "Can we have thirty?" she asked, after a teenage girl wearing a Beatles hoodie tried to buy one of my Emma Bridgewater teapots for a tenner. "My mom told me these are 'spensive."

"A natural businesswoman, this one," Sarah said, taking the cash and beaming with pride. "Thanks for your purchase!"

I wandered from table to table, taking in the tea towels, collector spoons, books, dolls ... decades of memories. We'd already sold $700 of merchandise on eBay, and expected more of that to go soon. Pierce brought all the eBay items to a local company who sold your stuff online, so there was no temptation for me to keep any of it. There was no way I'd have been able to ship my things off to strangers, so I was thankful to outsource.

A few teacher friends walked out with armfuls of floral teacups ("We're going to use them as planters in our kitchens and you can admire them!") and another teacher stopped by to pick up quite a few of the magazines for a class history lesson.

"Debbie, I had no idea. You know all of us at school would've done something to help." She looked around at the lawn crowded with tables and shoppers, either embarrassed for not knowing, or embarrassed for me in general, but I reached out and grabbed her hand.

"It's fine. I needed a kick in the pants and I got one." Similar encounters ensued with coworkers, neighbors, random friends of friends ... Molly had prepared me for it, and I'd thought I knew what to expect; but the reality of the constant questioning was exhausting, embarrassing, and humbling. It took everything in me not to storm off or throw a fit after nearly every purchase, but somehow I made it through the first hour.

Will and I were talking to the woman across the street about some Royal Collection china plates (and how long I'd been collecting them) when I heard a deep voice.

"Excuse me, are these still for sale?"

Rich stood there, holding three mugs in each hand and a look of absolute fear of rejection on his face. Jon was already filming, so there was no hope of carrying out the interaction in private. And at this point, our whole relationship was the nation's business, anyhow.

"Depends on what you're offering," I finally said.

"Mrs. Reynolds, how about I show you some more of these …
over there?" Will asked, waggling his eyebrows and all but dragging my neighbor away from the table. *Way to be subtle, dear.*

"What I'm offering … that's a tough one. Friendship? Love?
Whatever you're ready to accept?" He paused. "Oh, and an apology. A heartfelt one at that."

I took the mugs from his hands and hoped he didn't see mine
shaking. "All of those would be great," I said, taking a deep breath.
"But I owe you a bigger apology for hiding all of this from you. I
wasn't ready to let you into my house, but that didn't mean I had
to shut you out completely."

He gave me a short nod. "I think both of us messed up in one
way or another. And don't worry about the things from my store.
It's okay if you've sold them."

"I haven't." I said, locking eyes with him. I hoped he could
see how serious I was. "All of them are special to me, and I made
sure the team knew they were off-limits."

"Well you certainly know how to flatter an old fart like me."

I laughed. "Now, about these …" I gestured to the Union Jack
mugs on the table. "They're going for five a piece."

"Ah. How could I forget?" He reached into his pocket and
pulled out a fifty-dollar bill. "Keep the change. My contribution
to the 'Clean Debbie's House Fund.' As long as I'm invited over
to see the results, of course."

My heart soared. "I think that can be arranged."

"Perfect," he said, then shuffled his feet. "Just to elaborate …
I really am sorry. Yes, it was a huge shock, but I could've taken
more time to listen to you. I didn't even consider what you were
going through. I feel like an absolute jerk-slash-bugger-slash-
tosser-slash any other insult you can come up with."

"Well, there's no need to think of any others. Fresh start,
remember?"

Molly came over, holding up a stack of London bus Christmas
ornament boxes. "How much for these? Ten?" She looked at
Rich, then back at me. "Oh! Sorry to interrupt."

"Ten is fine," I said, and she slinked back to the table with a glint in her eye.

Rich laughed. "I've seen her on TV before. Scary."

"I'll tell you all about it sometime. Soon."

Rich smiled. "Well, I should let you get back to business. I'll call you later, okay?"

Before he was even out of sight, Anne came rushing over, looking like a kid at Christmas. "Was that Rich? I hope it was at least."

"Yes, it was. I think everything's going to be okay."

Anne reached in for a hug. "I'm glad, Mum. Truly."

The rest of the morning passed in a flash, and $1,980.50 later, our sale was closed.

"Now like we agreed, the rest of this is going to the eBay lady. And whatever isn't sold, will be donated," Sarah said. "I don't want to see you throwing yourself on the back of the truck or anything now."

"I know, I know," I said, catching a glimpse of a few collector plates and wondering if I could talk Anne into bringing them home. I turned my body away from the table piled with the rest of the remnants. It was best not to look at it.

Will handed a fat wad of cash to Pierce. "That's all of it. I think this should be more than enough to buy what we need, between the sponsorships and what the show matches."

Pierce grabbed Sarah's hand. "Now you just have to work your magic."

"Actually, before you do that ... I've got something to give you," I said. It had taken a lot for me to come to that decision, but there was no going back at that point. I stepped inside and pulled the BOA out from the corner of the kitchen, carrying it outside.

"There's some things in here I want you kids to have," I said. "Memories of when I first met your father, of our time in England. It's time for me to stop brooding and move forward, and I think these would bring you more joy than they do for me now."

273

Sarah knelt down and pulled her baby blanket out of the basket, rubbing it against her cheek, and flipped through the magazine with Diana running the race. "Are you sure?"

"I've never been so sure about anything, my dear."

~~

While anticipating the yard sale felt like preparing for surgery, pulling up to my house before the reveal felt more like the good kind of jitters you get before your wedding day. Okay, maybe not to Alan, but you get my drift.

Will put an arm around my shoulders as we walked up the lawn. "Everyone's inside. Are you ready for your brand-new house?"

I leaned my head against his, then gave him a quick kiss. "Ready as I'll ever be."

The door opened, and I could almost hear the cheesy music that *Stuff* plays during the reveal, during which you'd expect to see cartoon birds flying around with ribbon like you were in the middle of a Disney film.

Tears welled up and I placed a hand over my racing heart. *This is my house*?

Beautiful white wood shelves covered the wall in the kitchen, with my best plates and teacups on display, along with a framed photo of my Buckingham Palace selfie moment. Underneath, about ten tea towels hung from tiny clothespins attached to a long white wood board. I didn't have to duck, sidle or climb to get into the living room, where a new, soft-looking gray sofa and floral-patterned ottoman sat, topped off with my favorite Union Jack pillows and a matching throw blanket. My old curio cabinets had been replaced with one massive white display piece that took up the entire back wall. Overhead lighting in the cabinet high-lighted five shelves of dolls, trinket boxes, salt and pepper shakers and the like. And, of course, the Prince William bear.

The animated creatures wouldn't have been out of place,

because it felt like a fairy tale cottage. But also foreign, like I'd stepped into someone else's house.

And empty. Very empty.

It was going to take a while to adjust.

"I don't know what to say," I said, turning in slow motion like Pierce had at Percy Hall. "How did you do all of this in two days?"

Sarah gazed at Pierce, then Will. "I had a little help from my friends. But, this isn't all of it."

"There's more?"

Sarah took my hand and guided me down the hall, with the rest of the team following behind. "Ta-da!"

My bedroom door was open to show off a sparkling clean, lavender-hued Laura Ashley dream of a room. A cube-shaped storage unit held wicker baskets that reminded me of the BOA, and I pulled one out to find some of my royal books. The duvet cover even had tiny flowers in a Union Jack pattern, and a single battery-operated candle sat on the shelf above the bed, next to my favorite photo of Diana wearing her tiara.

"Sarah, this is lovely. I don't know how to thank you." I felt the tears coming, not just because it looked gorgeous (and it did), but because I felt a sense of loss, too. I didn't want to admit to the kids I missed seeing all of my things, even if they had been boxed up and unusable.

"Well, we're still not done," Pierce said. They led me through to the guest bedrooms, which had matching floral duvets, and the office, where bookshelves were filled with my favorite titles, and archival binders with the magazines I'd chosen to keep. The shelves did look bare, but it would take no time to find a few trinkets to make everything more homey. Maybe I'd even look that chap up on eBay and try to track down my favorite teapot.

"Mum, it's time for your last interview," Will said. "Your throne awaits."

Pierce pulled out one of the new pink upholstered chairs for me in the kitchen, and then one for Sarah and Molly. "So, how does this feel? I can hardly believe the transformation myself, and I was here for it."

I stared at the tea towel display, noticing the framed photos of Ruby and Charlie sitting above it. "Well, it feels strange. And empty. In a good way, I suppose. All of this wore on me mentally but also physically. I can see already how much easier it will be to get around."

Molly flashed an actual smile that showed her teeth. "That was my biggest concern, and I'm so relieved to see that we've been able to do that for you." Despite everything, I appreciated that she was always looking out for me in the end.

"I do like having more of my collection on view, so people can appreciate it rather than it being shoved into boxes."

"And what do you think surprised you the most about cleaning up?" Pierce asked.

I paused for a moment. "That I've taken up country music. After you playing all that Brad Paisley and Big & Rich all the time I actually quite like it."

Pierce roared with laughter and gave me a high-five. "My work is officially done here. But we do provide a year of follow-up treatment. For the house, I mean. Not the country music addiction."

"I was so overwhelmed by everything today, I'd almost forgotten about that part," I said. Hopefully they wouldn't be inspecting to make sure I hadn't snuck in a bag of tea towels or something, but it sounded more like phone counseling and visiting an in-person group once in a while. That I could handle, as long as they didn't hassle me about updating my collection with the important bits, like royal babies and weddings.

"My last question for you is a big one. Are you worried about maintaining all of this?

I knew it would be a massive challenge, but it felt like the most important one I'd had in a long time. "Honestly? Of course I am. I'm terrified to let everyone down, and of letting myself down. But let's just enjoy the moment."

Sarah Says
Embrace the New

Sometimes we resist change. It's not always a good thing, and sometimes it's sad. But think of all the new possibilities when you're moving on to a new chapter. Pack your old things up and don't look back—it's a sparkly, improved you!

"I CAN'T BELIEVE IT'S ALL OVER," I said, tucking my legs under me. The crew was gone, the house was empty (of messes at least) and Mum, Will, Anne, Pierce and I had settled down with a picnic of pizza and champagne.

"Well *I* can't believe Sarah Percy is eating pizza on the floor," Will said with a smirk.

"Hey, I'm not that uptight." I frowned and cut myself a tiny square of pizza, stabbing it with my fork and taking a bite.

Pierce patted my back. "Don't worry. It's kind of endearing. You can take the girl outta Percy Hall, but you can't take Percy Hall outta the girl."

Despite everyone around us, I reached up and planted a kiss on his lips. I didn't even have the urge to take an Instagram poll on whether more people used a knife and fork or their hands to eat pizza. His approval felt like enough.

"Oh, get a room, you two." Anne shook her head, but in a good-natured, smiley kind of way.

"We have, in fact," Pierce said. "And later I intend to—"

"LA LA LA LA." Anne covered her ears. "Good thing the kids aren't here to listen to this. Just wait until you have to censor everything you say because little ears are soaking everything up like sponges."

Rob had opted to stay home with Ruby and Charlie during the reveal, and secretly I was glad that there was no awkward underlying tension. Well, I had been ... until my sister started talking about the future children Pierce and I were apparently popping out. I looked down at my pizza, hoping he didn't see me my cheeks flame.

"What?" Anne asked, oblivious as usual. "I didn't literally mean YOUR children, because that would be weird considering you aren't even—"

"Will, come show me and your sister how everything's set up in the office," Mum said, even though he'd already done it an hour before. I tried not to laugh at her obvious attempt at being sly, but gave her a thanks-for-trying smile as Anne and Will headed down the hall.

"What did I do?" Anne grumbled under her breath, just loud enough for us to hear, of course.

I could tell it still felt novel to be walking down a clear path by the way Mum nearly skipped. But part of me still wondered if she'd come back from the shops next week with a new pile of teacups and "Keep Calm and Carry On" posters to replace the old ones. I pushed my anxiety about the future down and tried to focus on the present.

"God, my sister really knows how to shove her foot in her mouth sometimes."

Pierce shrugged. "Eh, she means well. And I think I'd have to actually ask you on a real date before the topic of kids comes up."

"Agreed," I said, feeling my heart expand, even if we lived on opposite coasts and weren't technically even dating, as Anne helpfully pointed out.

"So that date. How about brunch tomorrow? I'll treat you somewhere real fancy, like that diner your mom likes."

I shook my head and laughed. "You do spoil me. And sure, I'm on board for anything, as long as you're there. As for the show, we should probably talk about that, too...."

"Ah, yeah," Pierce said, looking at the carpet. "I have something to tell you about that." He took a deep breath, and I felt my insides clench, preparing myself for a let-down. Had he changed his mind about me already?

"Can you start in two weeks? I know it's a lot to ask, but we're filming at this big house in Texas and it's going to be all hands on deck. Really would like you to jump straight in with this one."

"Wow. I don't know what to say." I was expecting some time to unwind, maybe do some research on hoarding or take a few psychology classes to get myself in the mindset. But maybe grabbing life by the horns was the best way to move on.

"We'll be staying in slightly less classy accommodations, but I've rented a little house for the week and it's an awful lot of room for one person ...."

"Say yes for God's sake!" Mum called out.

Pierce and I burst out laughing. "It's all right, come in," he said, and the three of them practically ran out of the office and into the living room.

"To answer your question, I'd love to come to Texas."

Pierce wrapped me up in a bear hug, and then followed it up with a blokey high five with my brother. "You guys ready for the next one?"

"Hell, yeah," Will said.

"Well I think this deserves a toast," Mum said, grabbing her crystal goblet. "To Sarah, Pierce, and Will. Good luck with your first shoot together, and I hope you continue making a difference in peoples' lives."

I held up my hand. "And cheers to Mum. None of us would be here without her."

"And Anne for being such a good sport!" Will added.

Pierce pulled me in closer. "To all of us, then."

"To new beginnings," I added, and we raised our glasses in the air.

The End

✎ Acknowledgements ✎

FIRST AND FOREMOST, thank you to Nancy Cleary at Wyatt-MacKenzie for giving *A House Full of Windsor* a home and for being such a cheerleader for Sarah and Debbie's story. For about five years I thought this book just wasn't going to happen, and thanks to Nancy, it's one good thing that came out of 2020!

I'm grateful for my longtime critique partners, Jessica Topper and Pat O'Dea Rosen, who helped to guide the early drafts of *A House Full of Windsor*, and Carly Watters, whose input and advice greatly shaped the final version of the story.

My publicist, Ann-Marie Nieves of Get Red PR, is a star. Thank you, thank you!

The writing community is so generous. Big thanks go out to all of you for your support, whether it was writing a blurb, hosting a giveaway, inviting me to your podcast/blog, or hosting an online event to help launch *A House Full of Windsor*. Cheers to: Emily Giffin, Teri Wilson, Olivia Hayfield, Kimmery Martin, Lisa Roe, Lindsay Emory, Amy Impellizzeri, Camille Di Maio, Jenni L. Walsh, Lainey Cameron, Jennifer Klepper, Jacquelyn Middleton, Clare McHugh, Adele Downs, Sarahlyn Bruck, Katharine McGee, Jessica Morgan, Heather Cocks, and all of my friends from Valley Forge Romance Writers, the Women's Fiction Writers Association, and the 2021 Debuts group on Facebook.

I'd also like to thank the reviewers, bloggers, and members of the Bookstagram community for spreading the word about this novel, with special thanks to Jessica Storoschuk of *An Historian About Town*, Courtney Marzilli of *Bliss, Beauty and Books*, Andrea Peskind Katz of *Great Thoughts, Great Readers*, and Hikari Loftus of *Folded Pages Distillery*.

A royal wave goes out to my colleagues at royalcentral.co.uk, the members of the Royally Good Reads book club, The Crown Squad, and the royal watching community for their encouragement and friendship.

I'm forever grateful for the support my family and friends have shown for my writing. Thanks to my mom and Mom Mom, whose love for the Royal Family (and reading!) helped to shape my interests and career, royal collector plates and all. Hugs to my sister, Diana, who—in very Debbie-esque fashion—is named after the princess, and to all of my other family and friends. Special thanks go out to my friend Nicole Lasorda, who was one of the first people I let read this book in its very rough state years ago.

And finally, much love to Tim and Alex for always cheering me on, waiting outside for ages to see The Queen, and going on the Kensington Palace tour more times than they'd probably like while I researched this novel (and future ones). Cheers to more adventures together!

CPSIA information can be obtained
at www.ICGtesting.com
Printed in the USA
LVHW110340271021
701667LV00001B/120